Alien Hunter's Captive

Sophia Sebell

This book is dedicated to you! That's right, you there, reading these words right now. I love telling stories and it's all because of you that I get to continue doing it. So, thank you! I love you. You're the best.

CONTENTS

CHAPTER ONE

RILEY

The blast shield rose in front of me and I let out a quiet gasp. All the surrounding scientists appear unphased by the sudden appearance of a swirling purple portal on the other side of the glass. Vibrant and lazy rotations from the wormhole mesmerize me, and I stare quietly.

"Prettier than you thought it'd be?" A voice says behind me. It's tinged with concern, something I don't want to feel right now.

"Yes," I whisper, never breaking my gaze from the wormhole. The purple glow reflects off the white floor and walls, giving the room an entirely otherworldly appearance.

"Are you excited or scared?"

"Both, I think." I'm really not sure what emotion I'm experiencing now. My hands grope behind me blindly, never tearing my sight from the wormhole, and locate a chair. It slides loudly across the floor as I pull it to myself and sit down.

"That's to be expected," the voice says,

tinged with concern. A hand clasps my shoulder and gives it a light squeeze. The sudden touch snaps me out of my trance and I turn around to find Carl standing over me, watching the wormhole as it spins slowly.

He switches his stare from the swirling purple mass towards me and a slight smile creeps up his face. The concern in his voice haunts his eyes. It doesn't do much to make me feel better about my decision, but there's no going back now.

"Tomorrow," Carl says before leaving the observation room.

Several other scientists murmur to each other behind me, each of them far more relaxed in their chairs than me. I take stock of the surrounding room, there's not much in it. A massive viewing window, several chairs facing the window, a small coffee bar, and a whiteboard with a podium in front of it. Lots of jargon I can't even understand covers the whiteboard in very sloppy handwriting.

Most of the people in the room are wearing the stereotypical white lab coats, complete with pocket protectors and glasses. They've all been friendly so far, and overly informative. I don't understand half the stuff they're talking about, but they sure love discussing how the wormhole generator functions. I just smile and nod politely.

I'm going into that thing tomorrow. They hired me a couple of weeks ago and I went through some rigorous training and exercises to survive once I go through. Seeing the wormhole in action was the final nail in my coffin of concern. This is real, and it's happening.

Traveling to another planet through a wormhole created by experimental technology? What was I thinking? Why on Earth did I decide this was a good idea?

Oh, right.

The money.

They're paying me an enormous amount of money to do this, more than I'll need for the rest of my life. It was hard to pass up. I've always loved adventures and seeing unknown places. I just never considered another planet as a possibility. Although, I secretly desired it. My love for sci-fi knows no bounds and I have dreamt of visiting another world. Dreams and reality are a lot different, though.

I pull a folded-up piece of paper out of my pocket and open it. The original ad that was delivered to my house. They headhunted me specifically for this. Well, me and a few others. Apparently, I was the best choice for this, or I'm sure they have the others as backups in case I die.

Stop. I can't think like that. This happens tomorrow. I don't need fear creeping up on me and keeping me from doing this.

Tomorrow I will enter the wormhole. Tomorrow I will go to another planet. Tomorrow I might die.

I shake my head and rub my face with my

hands. Breathe in, breathe out. I take several deep breaths to clear my thoughts. It works after a few seconds.

Okay. Everything will be okay.

"Riley?" A soothing voice says behind me.

Fay appears beside me. She looks concerned and asks, "Is everything okay?"

"Yes, I'm fine." I mean, I'm probably fine. We'll see as the day progresses.

The blast shield closes over the window, they're powering off the wormhole now. The test was a success, a minor relief at least.

"Come with me, let's discuss your final preparations," she says sweetly. I liked Fay. She was one of the people that interviewed me. I don't like that phrase 'final preparations' though; it feels ominous.

We leave the observation room and go down the brightly lit winding hallway towards her office. The inside is white like the rest of the facility and she has an enormous desk with various knickknacks on it and several framed pictures of her pets and family.

The urge to fiddle with some of the stress toys on her desk is almost overwhelming, but I keep my hands to myself as I sit down. I watch as she slides around the desk and takes her seat. Her bangs fall out of place and cascade across her face. It must happen frequently because she pushes them behind her ear without missing a beat.

"I know you're brimming with questions, Riley," she says, "ask away."

I am brimming with questions, but it would take weeks to answer all of them. I'm just ready to get this over with. Two hours on another planet, then I return. I have to put down some tech or other to anchor the portal and keep it open. Should be easy, right?

Fay watches me expectantly, and I just blurt out the first thing that pops into my head.

"Why me?" I ask. That's a dumb question, and I feel embarrassed instantly.

Fay smiles gently and says, "Because you were the most qualified, we searched you out specifically for this."

"Surely there were others better suited for this."

"You were a paramedic, you have survival experience, and you have a desire for adventure. Those are all well-suited for what you're about to do."

"Yes, but, there are a lot more people that have all of that and more."

"That may be true, but we have faith in your capabilities. Plus, the director likes you."

I talked myself up a little more than I should have in the interviews. Everything I said was true. I have experience with all of this stuff, but I may have stretched things a little. The allure of the money and the chance for adventure were a little too strong. Though, I had no idea I'd be entering a wormhole. That part they didn't tell me until I had agreed to the job.

They warned me repeatedly that this would be unlike anything else I'd ever experienced and might be dangerous. Carl, specifically, made sure I was well aware of that before I agreed.

"Wouldn't it make more sense to send a scientist in for this, or a couple of people?" I'm not sure why I'm offering counter ideas. I must be more nervous than I think. Think of the adventure Riley, think of the money!

"Yes, it would," Fay says with a quiet chuckle, "as you know, you're not the first person to go through."

"Yeah, two before me."

"Correct. They were two of the scientists that worked here."

"And they never returned..."

"Also correct, however, we've found they are safe and sound," Fay says with a smile, "and quite happy."

"On another planet?"

"Yes, ask Carl about that part. They told him."

A knock echoes from the door before it swings open.

"Speak of the devil," Fay says as she nods at Carl standing in the doorway. "Carl can answer more questions about the others if you like."

"Sure," Carl says, "I was just checking in to see how everything is going."

"So, what happened to the others?" I ask.

"Come with me," he says before abruptly leaving the room.

I glance at Fay, who just nods stoically, and I bolt out of the room behind Carl.

We go into his office just down the sterile hallway and surprise washes over me as we enter. Most of the facility feels barren and clean, with plain white hallways and floors, minimal decorations, zero colors. Carl's office is much more eclectic and colorful. He has several plants scattered around the room, with large lamps over them. I assume some kind of sun lamp, we're deep underground and there's no way they'd get natural lighting. The walls are warm, earthy browns and he has several knickknacks and artwork on display.

Carl sits behind his desk and motions for me to have a seat on the opposite side. His desk houses several pictures in frames. A Goldendoodle has its tongue hanging out in one, a small calico kitten is playing with a toy mouse in another, and the third has two women smiling widely in a field. The last picture causes me to pause. Something doesn't look right.

"That's them," Carl says, interrupting my thoughts, "Emily and Alyssa."

The blue-green grass behind them finally

clicks with me; they took the picture on another planet.

"That's amazing, they're really on another planet?" I ask.

Carl nods and picks up the picture. He carefully takes it out of the frame and hands it to me, revealing a note in flowing script on the back.

Don't worry Carl, we're safe and sound. Thank you for being there for us.

-Emily and Alyssa

"That's a little relieving," I say. It's nice to know they didn't die some horrible death.

"It relieved me to get it. I worked closely with both of them and went through a rough patch after losing them. This note lifted a tremendous weight off my shoulders."

I hand the picture back to Carl and sit quietly as he gingerly puts it back in the frame and sets it neatly on his desk.

"Why me?" I ask again after a few moments.

"You're qualified," Carl says simply.

"I mean, you sent two scientists through already. Why not another?"

"To be frank, we're worried we are going to run out of scientists to manage the wormhole," he replies with a hearty laugh.

I can't help but chuckle, "I suppose that makes sense."

"We've tested as much as we can at this point, but everything is safe for a human. The air is breathable, the water is drinkable, the flora and fauna have their dangers but it's no different from Earth."

"How so?"

"If it looks like a bear, wolf, lion, tiger, et cetera, stay away from it."

"Makes sense," I say, shifting in my seat with unease. I'm not one to shy away from adventure and action, but being teleported to an alien world makes me a little nervous. I've always loved sci-fi and consume it in all of its forms, so I'd be lying if I said the thought didn't excite me a little. It's different when you're about to actually go, not tucked safely on the couch enjoying a movie.

"Don't worry, we'll make sure you're well prepared. Tomorrow you're just placing the anchors. It will be a quick trip and an excellent exercise to see what you're in for with your own eyes. We have several others that will join you in a few days, but it'll be nice having you to tell them exactly what to expect."

A brief training exercise, I can work with that. I feel a little better viewing it this way. No pressure, just go in and out. The anchors are easy to install. I literally set them in the right spot and press a button. A smile crosses my face as I take a deep breath.

"It'll be fun," I say, and genuinely believe it. The nervousness has given way to excitement. I'm going to another planet!

"I think it will be. Once the anchors are in place, the wormhole will connect to the same spot and time. After that, we'll be able to explore from the same location and set up a base of sorts. It will make this exploration a lot easier."

"Same time?" I ask. No one mentioned time, just other planets.

Carl nods. "The wormhole connects to the same planet every time. It's in different locations, but the time appears to change as well. Near as we can tell, there's no limit to how far in the future or how far in the past it goes."

"So I might travel to the future too?"

"Yes, or the past. I suppose there's an infinitesimally infinitesimal chance you'll be in the present too."

Another tinge of nervousness shoots through me but quickly becomes excitement again. Time travel and visiting another planet? This is a lot more than I bargained for, but what a story I'll have to tell.

We chat for a while and I finally leave his office to finish my training classes. I've been going to them for a couple of weeks now. Most of it is science and survival preparation. What plants to watch out for, what animals, how the anchors work, what gear I'll have, and refreshers on surviving on my own should something happen.

They've sent several robots through and retrieved a ton of pictures and samples from the planet at this point. Apparently, they've been going into the wormhole for several months and have thoroughly prepared for my entry. After losing the first two scientists, they halted human entry for a while. All the knowledge they have does nothing but soothe my concerns. With how it's all laid out, I'll get to see some cool stuff and have a straightforward job to do.

After my last class, I head towards my room and immediately collapse on my bed. Tomorrow is the big day, the first of many trips into the wormhole. A good night's sleep is the last thing I need to ensure tomorrow goes smoothly.

△△△

Morning comes much too quickly, and I barely got a wink of sleep. The excitement of the next day was too much to bear, and I spent much of the night flipping through pictures of the wildlife on the planet. Before I knew it, it was time to get ready.

I showered, got dressed, and had a quick breakfast before heading towards the room that houses the wormhole generator. Carl and Fay were already there, and ready to get started.

The room is bustling with activity as at least a dozen people in lab coats fiddle with every square inch of the room. The amount of attention they spend on every little detail squashes my last remaining fear, and I feel confident in my decision to do this. Nothing can go wrong.

Carl helps me get into a dark gray jumpsuit and begins attaching various equipment to my body. First, a vitals monitor with a shield to survive the wormhole, a belt with a tether attached to the back, a backpack stocked with emergency rations and a first aid kit, a knife on my boot, and several pouches attached to my belt containing fire starters and flares.

The amount of equipment being provided for a two-hour trip seems excessive, but I'm thankful for the extra precautions. Should something happen, I'll be able to last a good while on my own.

"This book," Carl says, holding up a small green book, "has information on what is safe to eat out in the wild. Hopefully, you won't need it, but it's good to have. Just in case."

"Thanks, Carl," I say with a grin. He seems worried about me and takes extra care to make sure I'm well-prepared. I appreciate the gesture. Carl seems like a good guy.

Everyone clears out of the room, and Carl tugs at my tether one last time.

"Everything looks good," he says, then retrieves a metal briefcase from the corner and places it next to me. It contains the anchors and a diagram showing the layout I should place them in.

"Are you ready?" He asks.

"As much as I'll ever be," I say with a grin. I don't think any amount of preparation would actually make anyone 'ready' for this, but the excitement is overwhelming and I can't wait to take the journey.

Carl pats me on the back gently and heads towards the door before pausing and saying, "Good luck. Make sure to come back."

"I'll do my best," I say with a chuckle. Carl half-smiles and the door slides shut behind him.

I take a few deep breaths to calm the adrenaline rush flowing through me. It's about to happen. I can't believe I'm about to do something like this. I glance behind me at the window of the observation room. The scientists are gathering in a crowd, watching me intently and chattering amongst themselves. A couple of people wave at me and I raise a hand back at them.

"Are you ready?" The director asks over the intercom in the room.

"Yes," I say as steadily as I can. My body is trembling from the excitement and I'm doing my best to stay calm.

"Initiating wormhole generation," she says and the sound of heavy metal sliding echoes around me in the room.

I look back at the window again and see the blast shield slide to a close over it. The cameras in the walls and the lights have a similar shield close across them. They told me the wormhole would knock out all of their equipment, so this is necessary. I'm alone now, in pitch-black darkness.

A loud whir emanates from the machine in front of me, causing me to start. A purple light glows and the whir quickly turns into a pleasant and deep thrum as the vibrant purple wormhole erupts to life in front of me.

I want to stare at it for a few moments and let the beautiful swirling purple fill my vision, but the sound of metal scraping snaps me out of my daze and I grab the briefcase before it slides into the wormhole. The tug from the wormhole isn't overwhelming, but it's definitely noticeable.

Well, I'm on a two-hour timer now. It's time to go.

I reach for the lever that keeps the tether locked and start to pull it, but the sound of the wormhole changes from a thrum to a low whoosh. They never mentioned that happening.

I almost turn towards the wormhole, but a cold chill washes over me, freezing me in place.

Riley.

The voice sounds like it's coming from all around me. No, not around me. Inside of me.

Riley. Open the door.

What door? What's happening?

You must leave. There is grave danger here. Open the door and leave the room.

A bright red button is within arm's reach of me, right next to the tether. If I hit it, the wormhole shutdown will start and the room will unlock after a few minutes.

Leave now. Only death awaits you here. Riley, leave this place.

An overwhelming sense of certainty and calm radiates over my body as the voice fills my mind and consumes my thoughts. It's right, I shouldn't be here. I need to leave.

I reach for the button, and just before I make contact, another voice shouts. Deep and rumbling, accompanying another 'whoosh' from the wormhole, this time actually in the room.

"Drugh nar luthrg zet!" The voice shouts and I hear the sounds of two large bodies colliding behind me.

Release us, Riley.

Now I can tell that voice is in my head and it's an intruder. What the fuck is going on? Primal fear seeps into my soul, and my body screams at me to stay still.

I spin around quickly and drop the briefcase I was holding with white knuckles. It immediately starts sliding towards the wormhole, but I barely pay it attention.

A gaunt figure, hunched to avoid hitting its head on the ceiling, is in the middle of grappling with a massive blue man. The blue man isn't as tall as the other one, but his body is absolutely rippling with muscles. A stark contrast against the pale, thin creature. Against all certainty, the pale creature looks like it's actually overpowering the blue man.

Bright blue light flashes as the two collide and fight with each other. I notice it's emanating from the blue man and it happens every time he and the creature come into contact with one another.

The blue man slams his hips into the other creature with a dazzling burst of light and flips it to the ground. He mounts it quickly and draws a long blade from his belt and tries to drive it into the creature. The creature catches his arm and squeezes it tightly while trying to slash at him with its other hand.

A sound akin to glass shattering fills the room as another flash of light explodes in front of me before fizzling out. The light surrounding the blue man flickers like a dying bulb before disappearing completely.

The blue man avoids the deadly looking swipes and lets out a yelp of pain as he frees his arm from the creature's grasp. He slams the blade into one of the creature's arms and yells out.

"Fraeth!" The frustration in his voice is clear, and I'm positive that was a curse word.

I stare, unmoving. I don't know what to do. They didn't cover any of this in the training. I've had to break up fights as a paramedic, grieving families do all sorts of crazy stuff, but these are much larger than anyone else I've ever encountered. Oh, and they're also fucking aliens.

Riley. Help me. This blue being wants to consume you. It has come to take you, to claim you. I want to save you.

As the voice rings in my head, the blue man locks eyes with me. The fire of anger in his green eyes instantly turns to a look of desire. His glance is fleeting as he spins his attention back to the other creature, but the intent was unmistakable.

The two wrestle on the ground and the blue man gets the upper hand again. This time he has both his knees on the creature's arms, pinning them to the ground. The creature bucks under him and causes him to drop his blade. He lets out the same curse again and searches for the blade next to him without taking his knees or eyes off the creature.

The pale creature looks at me. Dead, sunken eyes. Pale skin and gaunt features. Its mouth flashes into a smile, revealing row after row of sharpened teeth. Something inside me, a voice deep inside my mind, my intuition, tells me to trust it. It's telling the truth, it wants to help me.

Riley. Please.

I slam my fist into the emergency shutdown and release the tether lock. Without thinking, I charge towards the blue man as he retrieves his blade and lifts it above his head. I slam my body into him and it knocks out all the air in my lungs. It feels like hitting a brick wall, but I make him falter, and the creature uses this opportunity to gain the upper hand. It grabs the blue man and tosses him noisily into the machine connected to the wormhole.

The room shifts appearances suddenly from the familiar deep purple to a vibrant turquoise as the color of the wormhole transforms. All three of us pause briefly at the sudden change, and the blue man uses this opportunity to drive his blade into the side of the creature; a bright light starts emanating from inside of it.

The creature lets out an ear-piercing shriek and throws the blue man across the room. The blade clatters to the ground beside me and I stare at it. It's unlike anything I've ever seen. A long, thin blade with wiring and tubes all along the hilt and base of the blade. A trigger is in the hilt's grip and the blade is still glowing as if it had just been blazing hot.

The creature releases another shriek, causing me to crouch down and cover my ears before they explode. I peek through squinted eyes and see the creature approaching me quickly. It reaches a hand out towards me and I think it's trying to help me up for a moment, but notice its free hand raised back with its claws extended, ready to eviscerate me.

Somehow I roll out of the way of its swipe and look around the room frantically for anything to help me. I spy the blade beside me again and snatch it up, leaping to my feet and pointing it at the creature, trying to keep my hands steady.

My fingers graze a trigger on the hilt and I pull it back, squinting my eyes. Nothing happens.

It's on me before I have time to react and just before its claws reach my soft flesh, the blue man crashes into it and knocks it towards the wormhole. The creature sways back and attempts to maintain its balance, but it's too late. It tumbles towards the wormhole and, to my horror, grabs my arm as it falls backward.

My life flashes before my eyes as I watch the wormhole grow larger and larger in front of me. The blue glow fills my eyes, and my body slides through with no resistance.

I fall helplessly towards the ground and land with a quiet thud on orange grass. My mind is in a daze and I'm having trouble figuring out what just happened or where I even am. The thoughts of the fight I just witnessed come rushing back in, and I jump to my feet quickly. The muffled sounds of the world around me come into focus again as constant shrieking fills my ears and the surrounding field.

The creature is standing several feet from me, releasing shriek after shriek as its skin sizzles in the sun's light and steam rises from its body. I glance at the sky and notice not one but three suns burning brightly overhead.

Riley.

The voice rings in my head again.

Help me. I must get to safety. I can protect you.

The sense of reassurance that came with the voice before is no longer present, and I resist the urge to give in to it.

"What are you?" I demand, drawing the knife from my boot. I don't think I'll be able to take it down if that huge blue man couldn't, but I won't go down without a fight.

Help me.

"No, answer my question!"

The creature responds with a shriek and closes the distance between us with blinding speed. Just before it reaches me, the blue man tumbles from the wormhole and lands on top of the creature. It would have been comical if they did not terrify me.

I quickly rip the shielding off my wrist monitor and hit the emergency button. It will send a signal back to retrieve me from the wormhole immediately.

HELP ME.

Not a request, a command. One I feel obliged to follow. I grip my knife tightly and move towards the blue man, stalking towards his back as he tries to squeeze the life out of the creature on the ground.

Just before I reach him, the creature lets out another shriek, and I break out of my daze again. This thing is toying with my mind. It tried to kill me earlier. Why would I help it?

The creature drives one of its clawed hands into the side of the blue man's chest and he lets out a howl of pain and rage before slamming his fist into the creature's face repeatedly. The creature presses its hand deeper inside and causes the blue man to tumble off of it. It leaps towards the wormhole above, but the blue man grabs its leg and slams it back into the ground.

With an unceremonious 'blip,' the wormhole disappears from existence. The emergency shutdown has finished. The cleanly sliced end of my tether slides noiselessly to the ground.

The creature releases another screech that makes me cover my ears and drop my knife. The blue man seems unphased and tries to subdue the creature again but is knocked away by an unseen force. That unseen force collides with me too and knocks me on my ass before slamming my head into the dirt.

I try to get back on my feet, but wave after wave emanates from the creature and pushes me further into the ground. The blue man is groaning and struggling to get closer to the creature but ultimately ends up on the ground.

After what seems like an eternity, an aircraft appears overhead. It's shaped almost like a falcon and sets down quietly nearby. The purple gleam of its body is blinding in the light of the three suns. A ramp lowers from the back and several large green men stand with large, sharp weapons in hand, waiting.

The creature quickly moves towards the

ship and disappears up the ramp. With it gone, the blue man can rise to his feet and stumble towards the ship. He must have retrieved his blade before coming through the wormhole because he draws it from his waist and limps slowly towards the ship.

The green men laugh at the blue man as he approaches and shout out several phrases in their language at him. Whatever they said must have been important, because he stops and stares daggers at them. The ramp closes, and the ship takes off, disappearing on the horizon.

"What the fuck," I say before collapsing back onto the grass. My mind feels exhausted, and I can barely think straight. It feels like something chewed on my brain for several hours and then left it on the floor overnight. I need sleep, I need to reset.

I'm still not safe, though. I raise up on my elbows and look towards the blue man. He's shuffling towards me slowly. Blood oozing out of the wound on his chest from where the creature stabbed him. He collapses a few feet from me and his body goes still.

Should I help him? I mean, that creature was clearly bad, and he saved me? I should help him.

I stand up and take two steps towards him before my legs give out and I slip into unconsciousness.

△△△

I wake up with a pounding headache and a dry mouth. My body feels like it has been thoroughly cooked by the sun, and I feel stupid for not trying to get into some shade before passing out. Thankfully, the three suns in the sky have become one and a half as they dip behind the horizon. I'm also thankful for the full jumpsuit I wore that kept most of me from being burned. The cool air feels good against my sunburned face and I take a deep breath.

The dryness in my throat causes me to cough violently, and after I regain control, I dig through my backpack. Thank god for the extra preparations. I pull my canteen out and take a long swig of, unfortunately, warm water. Now that's taken care of, I look around to take in my surroundings. Orange grass stretches for as far as the eye can see, with copses of purple trees dotted around. Some trees are close by, that's probably as good of a place as any to stay for the night.

I pull myself shakily to my feet and start trudging towards the nearby trees. I get about halfway before I stop and look back towards the blue man still lying in the grass.

"Fuck," I whisper to myself.

It is an ordeal, but I pull him over to the trees with me. He weighs just as much as he looks like he would. I would be a liar if I said I didn't give him a good once over. He's much larger than me and boy, is he in good shape. He has a few leather straps across his chest, a vambrace on one wrist, and tight leather pants with black boots finishing the look.

I fight his limp body for a few moments and finally get him propped up against one of the trees. His breathing is slow but steady. Maybe he'll pull through. I crouch down close to him and get a good look at the wound on his chest. It's large but doesn't look deep. After digging out my first aid kit, I bandage him up as best as I can. It's interesting to me that his blood is the same color of red as a human's.

I don't know what I expected, maybe green? Too many sci-fi movies, I guess. They're my favorite genre and now I'm apparently living in one. My body screams at me from every nerve that it's tired and to sit down, so I listen. I consider seating myself next to the blue man, but move over to another tree trunk and rest against it.

A power bar and some warm water make for a very mediocre dinner, but it's all I have. At least the bar is peanut butter and banana flavored, one of my favorite combinations. Of course, it tastes off as most power bars do. I sigh deeply into my canteen and scan the surrounding area. Thoughts of nasty creatures lurking in the orange grass fill my mind. Long, spindly legs pulling slimy bodies with gnashing teeth towards my scent. A shudder runs up my spine and I look towards the blue man. His chest is still rising and falling, thankfully, and I start to desperately hope he wakes up. I don't know what he's got planned for me, but it's better than being stranded here, I'm sure.

Stranded. I am stranded here either way. Millions, if not billions, of miles from home. This place looks nothing like the photos I saw of the planet I was meant to go to. Carl also mentioned that the time period could vary, so there's no telling what year I'm even in. The chance of rescue from the wormhole lab seems next to zero.

What do I care, though? No pets, no family left, no close friends. What's another planet except for a new adventure? That's a weak comfort at best. While it's true, I had no real attachments on Earth, I'm still concerned about never being able to return. Not that I can do anything about it.

Only one sun remains in the sky, so I gather up some branches at the base of a purple tree and some dry dead grass and build a small fire. The firestarter they provided me is very effective and starts the fire in one try. I pull off a few low-hanging branches and add them to the fire. I hope this burns long enough. The branches ignite immediately, but they don't seem to char quickly. Maybe that's a good sign. Loud crackling explodes from the fire, causing me to jump back. Dazzling mixtures of color rise into the air; sparks and embers of blue, green, orange, red, and purple rise with the smoke. It's mesmerizing.

A loud chattering sound, not unlike laughter, echoes across the field as the last sliver of sunlight dips behind the horizon. Another chill runs through me and I leap to my feet. I draw the knife from my ankle and hold it shakily in my hand. After a deep breath, I steady my hand and look around the area as best as I can in the flickering light of the fire.

I feel my ears straining as I listen intently for any sign of movement. The crackle of the fire sounds like it's amplified by a megaphone, and I have trouble focusing on any other sounds. More chattering comes from behind the tree the blue man is resting against. It sounds like it's right on the other side of the trunk.

One branch in the fire is sticking out and I hesitantly grab it, expecting it to be hot, but it's surprisingly cool to the touch. I lift it into the air, illuminating the area further, and walk towards the sounds carefully. The flashlight in my pack would let me see better, but creatures on Earth are scared of fire. Maybe they are here too.

My footsteps thud quietly in the dirt as I slink towards the tree. I glance down at the blue man for a moment and he shifts slightly in the light of my torch. Good, maybe he'll wake up soon. The chattering erupts from behind the tree again, and I grip my knife tightly as I round the enormous trunk of the tree. My knife at the ready, I slip behind the trunk and find... nothing.

My ears prick up again and I listen for sounds of movement, but hear only the crackle of the fire and the torch in my hand. After a few moments, I start to head back towards the fire but stop in my tracks when the cackling sounds above me. My eyes quickly snap to the branches several feet above me in the tree and I see a dozen eyes staring at me, each one glowing in the light of my torch.

Fear grips my core as I back away from the tree and lift my knife, ready to attack whatever is about to pounce on me. The pounce never comes. The eyes stare at me blankly and as my sight adjusts to the darkness, I can just make out the creatures in the purple tree above me.

Two birds, they look like owls except they each have six eyes and their beaks are long, like a hummingbird. They're pressed against each other snugly, each eyeing me suspiciously. I let out a quiet giggle and leave the two lovebirds to rest.

I return to my tree and lean back against the trunk. The birds chatter several more times, then go silent, leaving me with nothing but the crackle of the fire. I stare into it for a while and feel myself starting to doze. I want to stay awake and make sure nothing happens, but I won't make it far if I don't get some kind of rest. I give one more scan of the area and, satisfied that the fire will stay burning for a while, allow myself to doze off.

CHAPTER TWO

ZALTAS

Sharp pains in my chest wake me and I groggily look around the space I'm in. A small fire is burning several paces away, and the woman has passed out against another tree. I try to rise to my feet but find myself against the trunk of the tree as pain shoots through me and my hand subconsciously rushes to the wound on my chest.

Instead of wet blood, I feel mostly dry cloth. In the dim light, I can see bandages wrapped around me.

"Thanks," I say to the sleeping woman. At least, I hope she's sleeping. The thought of her being dead forces me to stand up and push through the pain. I take a few moments to steady myself and walk cautiously towards her.

I can see her chest rising and falling slowly as she breathes. She looks uninjured as far as I can tell. Good. The dancing light of the fire sends shadows moving across her face and it's hard to make out the details, but she looks just as beautiful as I remembered. When I first locked eyes with her on the other side of the wormhole, I knew I wanted her. I knew I would protect her, no matter what. I shake my head at myself and patrol the surrounding area of our makeshift camp. Orange grass and purple trees. No idea where we are. That can't be good. I was expecting to be back on Ethelox-12. I had not even noticed the planet was different; since I was so focused on the Alphur.

As I go behind the tree I was originally leaning against, I hear the familiar chattering of Nelthas above me and glance towards the branches. The creatures in the tree above are not Nelthas; they have too many eyes and their beaks are much too long, but their sound is unmistakable. Maybe a distant relative? Nelthas never sleep in places with predators, so this is a good sign, assuming they're related.

I leave the birds to their sleep and take a seat closer to the woman. I stare at her as she sleeps, wanting to rouse her. To talk to her, to hear her voice and see her moving. I hadn't been able to pay much attention to her during my battle with the Alphur.

Fuck, the Alphur. What was that ship it boarded, and what species were those creatures it joined? I've seen nothing like them. They appeared to be Flaxen but they were green, never heard of a species like that, and I like to think of myself as well-traveled.

Whatever they were, the Alphur being with them will not be a good outcome for anyone. I have to find a way to track it down. Figuring out where we are first is going to be the hard part.

The light slowly washes across the orange field as the sun peeks above the horizon. They were about to set when we first got here, I was out for a long time. Although, nights here could be short for all I know.

A light groan escapes the beautiful woman's lips as she stirs and I watch her closely as her eyes flutter open. They grow wide quickly when she sees me and she grips her knife firmly before rising to her feet.

"Hello," I say as gently as possible, "I'm not going to hurt you, don't worry."

"What are you, who are you? Where are we?" She responds, clearly panicking.

"I'm a Scovein, my name is Zaltas, and I do not know."

"I don't understand... why would I? You're a fucking alien. Of course I can't understand you. This is ridiculous, in and out. Two hours tops. Place the anchors and look around a bit, it's completely safe. Such horseshit."

"Oh right, you do not have a translator," I say and make a thoughtful noise, "This might be an issue."

"Yeah, sure buddy, whatever you say," she says with sarcasm dripping from her voice, "This is fucking wonderful, a nice little vacation we're going to have. Maybe I should have just gone with that other creature."

"That would not have been wise."

"Yeah, you're right, this is so much better."

"Can you understand me?"

"Okay, I'm sorry for losing my cool. This is scary, you know? You might be used to this but I'm certainly not," she says, her tone levels out slightly.

"Oh yeah, I'm completely used to traveling in wormholes and ending up on strange planets I have never heard of before. Happens daily."

"Sure, some coffee and pancakes would make my morning much better," she says, then laughs. She sounds nervous, but the laugh is genuine. Well, clearly she doesn't understand me and she's just pretending to chat with me to make herself more comfortable. Whatever helps.

"I will get right on that. Let me just head to the nearest store."

"You're the best, thanks," she says.

Thinking as hard as I can for any words I may know in her language, I can only come up with one. I've heard it hundreds of times from Drenas and Alyssa. I take a moment and try to form the syllables properly. Communicating this way is not something I'm used to. My face must have contorted oddly because the woman cocks her head to the side and stares at me with a confused look on her face.

"Bah nan," I say.

"All of that work for that? Are you okay? You look constipated."

I shake my head and try again, "Banana."

"Did you say banana?"

"Yes." I don't know what good this will do, but at least we're using the same language... sort of.

"I wonder what banana means in your language, we have that word too."

Well, I tried.

Another idea crosses my mind.

I place my hand to my chest, wincing slightly at the pain from the wound, and pat my chest lightly before saying, "Zaltas."

She stares at me absently for a few seconds before a look of recognition crosses her face.

She points at me and asks, "Zaltas?"

I nod and motion towards her.

She pats her chest and says a little too loudly and slowly, "Riley, RILEY, RIIIIILL-LEEEEEY."

"Okay, I get it. You are Riley," I say with a smirk.

"Yes, Riley!"

I can't help but laugh. If she only knew I

could understand her.

"Zaltas," she says, pointing at me and then points at herself and says, "Riley."

"Yes, yes, I get it. You're being a little patronizing now."

"Well, at least we've got some kind of communication going."

I think about drawing a banana in the dirt and saying 'banana' again to really blow her mind, but I think I'll save that for later. Right now, we have more pressing problems. Like where we are and how to get off this planet.

"We need to work out a plan," I say. "I know you cannot understand me, but talking to myself helps me think sometimes."

She makes a thoughtful noise and stares at me. I stand up and she takes several steps back. Her grip tightens on her knife again.

"Not going to hurt you, remember?" I say fruitlessly. I take a step towards her and she raises her knife in a defensive pose. She has some idea of combat basics, that's good. It would be better if I could explain things to her, though. I glance down at the canteen next to her feet; I could go for some water right now.

I take a step towards her and she draws the knife back, so I raise my hands and step back. I point at the canteen under her and make a motion like I'm drinking out of a cup.

She glances down quickly and looks back at me. I can see her debating what to do and she finally kicks the canteen towards me.

"Thanks," I say and pick it up. I want to drain the whole thing, but I don't know if she has any more or if this planet even has drinkable water; so I have enough to wet my mouth and get a little fluid in me, leaving the rest for her. Now if only I could find some food.

I slide her canteen across the ground back to her, and she bends down to pick it up. She takes a couple of steps away from me towards her backpack.

"Stay there," she says, still pointing the knife at me.

"Sure," I say.

She turns around and bends over, quickly placing the canteen in her backpack and fishing through it. I want to see what she's getting out of it, but I can't tear my gaze away from her luscious, round ass. I feel a tinge beneath my leather pants.

Riley retrieves whatever she is after and spins around before I can move my eyes away from her ass quick enough. Her face turns a deeper red, and she tosses two bars wrapped in metallic foil at me.

I retrieve them from the ground and look them over in my hand. They're tiny, maybe eight inches long and three inches wide, with a picture of someone on a two-wheeled vehicle on the front. 'PB&B' is the only thing printed on it. The back has a lot of numbers and chemicals listed.

"It's food," Riley says as she makes a motion of tearing open the wrapper.

"What kind of food, though?" I ask with a chuckle. Not that it matters. I don't have a choice, I need to eat something. Scovein eat massive quantities of food. We can only go about five days without eating before our bodies shut down. Any little thing will help.

I sit down by the tree and tear open the wrapper, sniffing the bar. It smells good, at least. I bite into it and the flavor is indescribably bad. It has a hint of the banana that we all know and love, but the other taste is disgusting. I choke it down and eat the second bar. The energy provided is much better than nothing.

"Yeah, they're not very good," Riley says.

I grunt in response. We've got to find a way off this planet. That ship that picked up the Alphur got here pretty fast. Maybe some kind of base is nearby. Lacking the presence of the Alphur preferably. Although I will need to track him down eventually. We probably have a few weeks before it amasses an army; they like to plot.

Shit.

The Melt Knife.

It is a stupid name, but I did not name it. Its creator did and let's say he's not a very creative person with anything besides technology. The knife does what the name implies. Incredibly well. It's also the only known weapon that can put down an Alphur permanently.

My hands grope at my waist hastily. My normal blade is in its place, but disappointment drags my face into a grimace as I find the empty sheath where the Melt Knife should be. I have to find it.

I look around the area, trying to get my bearings and spot what I think was our landing zone. Maybe it got pulled through the wormhole and is in the field somewhere. I stand up, but the pain from my chest hits me like a space freighter, and I lean against the tree.

This is too important to let a little pain stop me. After a little coaxing, I talk my body into standing upright. I feel a little shaky, but I think I can manage.

"I'll be back," I say to Riley, for no reason other than knowing I tried to tell her.

"Where are you going?" Riley calls out as I move further into the field.

"Melt Knife."

"I don't know what you're saying," she shouts, a little closer this time.

I look back to see her hurrying to catch up to me. That's good, it's probably best if she stays close. I do not know what this planet holds in store for us, aside from orange grass.

Signs of a fight mar the swaying grass in various spots. This was definitely where we landed, or something else was fighting here. I search the area and hear light footsteps approaching me from behind.

"What are you looking for?" Riley asks when I drop to my hands and knees to dig through the grass.

"My knife," I say simply.

"I don't think you'll find that here," she says.

I look back at her and notice her eyes flitting away from my ass.

"It feels like you can understand me, and that you're messing with me. Also, I saw you looking."

"There's no way that there is buried treasure here," she says with a smirk and exaggerated hand gestures.

"I'm glad one of us is having fun with this," I say and turn my head back to the grass, smiling to myself.

"Nice ass, by the way."

"I knew you were looking," I say without turning to her.

"I get half of the treasure."

"Sure thing," I say. I'm feeling desperate; the sun keeps creeping higher and higher. The second one is halfway up the horizon at this point. I have no idea how much time we've burned. I need to find that knife and then the Alphur.

I also need to figure out what to do with

Riley. Not being able to talk to her is going to cause some serious issues. We have to find her a translator.

My hands bump into something solid amidst the grass and relief washes over me when I wrap my hand around the hilt of the Melt Knife. I clutch it and stand quickly, holding it aloft in an exaggerated display of triumph.

"Finally," I say loudly towards Riley.

CHAPTER THREE

RILEY

Die. The word that came out of his mouth was unmistakable and the large blade he is holding tightly as he approaches seals his intent. He had been biding his time to take control. I should have stayed back, I should have run, I shouldn't have helped him. Stupid, stupid, stupid.

I can still run.

The wide-eyed smile of a maniac is on his face as he approaches me, and before he can take another step, I bolt off into the orange grass.

"Fraeth!" Zaltas' voice calls out behind me and I hear his heavy footfalls as he pursues me. The field is massive and there's nowhere to hide. Maybe I can slip behind a tree and dive into some grass? I don't know, but I have to figure something out soon. Those long legs will catch me quick.

My footing feels shaky as I run through the grass, which deep down I find odd, but the panic of being pursued overpowers my concern for the ground. It takes me a few seconds to even realize that I'm on an incline and the surrounding grass is growing taller and taller. It was up to my calves a moment ago, now it's above my knees.

As I run forward, the grass grows deeper and deeper, up to my chest now. Then up to my neck, I can't see where I'm going and stop briefly, but take off again when I hear Zaltas call out to me. He sounds close.

Suddenly, the ground disappears from under me and I feel myself falling through the air. I twist around and latch onto a rock protruding from the wall several feet down; it knocks the air out of me as I slam into a cliff face. Orange grass surrounds me from all sides except for the rocky edge I'm clinging to. The orange hue from the sun filtering through the grass is disorienting and I grip the rock tighter. I steal a glance down, which was a mistake, and am met with orange blades of grass stretching to unimaginable depths. The orange blades give way to blackness a hundred feet below me.

I hoist myself up onto the rock, which has orange grass somehow growing densely out of the top, and try to steady my panicked breathing. I pant wildly for a few seconds before sucking in several deep breaths and calming myself enough to think.

Okay, I can stay here for a little bit. Hopefully, Zaltas will lose interest and leave. Then I'll get my pack, assuming he doesn't, and figure out what the fuck to do from there. Being alone on this cliff in the vibrant orange light has really cemented the fact that I'm stranded on another planet. By myself, save for hostile aliens that want to do no telling what to me.

I want to cry, but I don't have time for that right now. I'll have a breakdown later when I'm safe somewhere. If I ever get somewhere safe...

No. I'm going to be optimistic. Those scientists at the lab are super smart, they'll save me.

Oh, but they didn't save the other two. They seemed to be fine, though, so that means there are friendly aliens on this planet somewhere. Right, I'm on the wrong planet. So that's strike two for the scientists. Fuck me, what to do, what to do?

Loud rustling emanates from every direction as a breeze rolls through the grass from the black depths below. A shudder rolls up my spine. Why is it coming from below and not above? Everything about this place is completely unnatural. How is the grass even standing up straight, being that tall? It should collapse.

Several pieces are within easy reach, so I grab one and try to break it off to get a good look at it. Try as I might, I can't get it to rip. What is this even made of?

"Du naet linde cul?" Zaltas shouts above me. He sounds panicked. "Fraeth, fraeth, fraeth."

I sit as still as I can and hold my breath. I thought I had fallen much further than I had. The grass above looks like an unbreaking canopy, but he sounded much closer than I would have imagined.

"Riley, du naet linde cul?" He shouts again.

This time he's met with a response, but not from me. A rattling howl echoes up from the depths below me and pure fear shoots through my body. I back as far into the cliff face as I can and stare wide-eyed into the grass, searching for any little movement.

Zaltas doesn't speak again. Maybe whatever made that noise scared him off.

Another howl surrounds me, and the grass sways violently in front of me. Sheer panic overtakes me and I scale the cliff. I'm not moving as fast as I'd like, but I have to balance moving quickly and not plummeting to my death or the jaws of whatever creature is lurking below.

A third howl, this time much closer, pushes me to my limit as I hurry up the rocky face. Thankfully, there were plenty of cracks the grass was growing out of for me to hold on to and climb. After what felt like an eternity, I see a break in the grass and grab the lip of the cliff.

To my horror, a large blue hand latches onto my arm and pulls me up to the solid ground. A horrible, ear-splitting grating noise comes from the depths behind me and Zaltas pulls me away from the edge, both of us dashing to higher ground. We watch mesmerized as the grass parts down the hill and a large, fleshy cylinder rises into the air. It's the same shade of orange as the grass, with dozens and dozens of mouths lining most of its surface. Each mouth is gnashing at the empty air in search of something to bite into.

"What the fuck?" I say, horrified.

Zaltas grunts in response.

The fleshy tube bends around in a circle several times before disappearing back into the orange depths. I've got to be more careful here. Getting so caught up in just surviving made me forget that I'm in an alien world. There's no telling what else lurks on this planet.

Surviving. Zaltas is still peering at the shifting grass where the monster last was; I still need to escape. I need my pack, then I'll have to travel more carefully. The way we came is safe, at least. I'll book it for my bag and disappear into another treeline. Hopefully, I can shake him.

I tense up in anticipation to run, but hesitate when Zaltas looks at me. The look in his eyes genuinely appears to be concern, but concern for what? My safety? Or that he doesn't get the satisfaction of doing whatever he has planned?

I start to bolt from him and head back towards our little camp.

His hand locks onto my arm, gently but firmly, and pulls me back against his hard body. He's way too fast for his size. I try to reach for the knife at my ankle, but he grabs my other arm and positions himself to clench me with one arm.

With his free hand, he takes the knife from my ankle and slips it out of view.

I try to wriggle free, but his strength is immense; I can't move at all. My hips buck wildly as I try to get any sort of momentum to kick him or shake free, but it's all to no avail.

The sound of metal sliding against metal fills my ears when Zaltas draws his blade. Adrenaline fills my body and I feel like I'm going to explode if I can't do something. But I can do nothing. I see the blade flash in the light as it moves past my head, but I can't see what he's doing.

I hear the blade sheathe again and feel a little relieved; that disappears quickly when he shifts me quickly and pulls my arms behind my back. Something wraps snuggly around them and I'm unable to move. He places me gently on the ground and wraps my feet tightly, then turns me over to face the sky.

Now I'm his, for whatever he wants to do to me. I'm trapped and there's nowhere to run, no way to run.

Zaltas peers down at me and the look on his face isn't malicious, but looks more like pity. Then again, he is an alien, so who fucking knows what he's thinking?

"Riley, la mytt dy asn," he mumbles. He drops the remaining blades of grass he had cut from nearby and hoists me up over his shoulder.

I bounce lightly up and down on his shoulder as he walks us back to our camp. Maybe being eaten by that monster in the grass would have been a better fate than whatever he's planning. I try to squirm out of his grasp, but his muscular arm tightens around my waist and presses me firmly into his shoulder.

The pace he keeps up on the way to our

camp is nothing short of impressive. Even carrying me, he doesn't seem to have any issues moving quickly. Once we arrive, he sets me gingerly on the ground and gathers up my backpack.

He holds it in the air in front of him and analyzes the straps for a few moments, then pulls the straps to their max length. He slings the backpack over one arm and flails his other arm behind him, trying to locate the other strap. After a few tries, he hooks it and gets the strap up just above his forearm before it gets stuck.

He's way too big for that backpack. Still, he tries. I wince as a quiet ripping sound comes from my backpack, and he freezes instantly.

I can't help but laughing. The absurdity of this entire situation is too much for me. I'm on an alien planet watching this huge blue man trying and failing to put on a backpack.

"Fraeth," he says.

Zaltas turns to me, and the look on his face causes me to laugh even louder. He looks so distraught.

This whole scenario eases some of my panic, and I feel more comfortable. Maybe it's because he seems so worried about damaging my bag. If he's that concerned about a simple backpack, maybe he will not do anything too horrible to me.

"Zurn del no, selkin," Zaltas says. He lingers on the last syllable of the word 'selkin' and tilts his head at me.

I start to shrug at him but remember quickly that I'm bound and say, "I don't know what to tell you, buddy. It's too small."

Zaltas grunts and fiddles with the straps on the backpack. He releases both of them from their clips and then ties them together and wears my backpack crossbody.

"Looks cute," I say. That was pretty smart.

Zaltas grins at me and says something I don't catch. Not that I'd understand, anyway.

He stands above me then flips open the top of the vambrace on his wrist. I hear a series of beeps as he taps on it. I thought it was just a leather vambrace, but apparently, it's some kind of computer.

After a few seconds of tapping, the vambrace lets out what sounds strangely like the error noise on a Windows computer. Frustration crosses Zaltas' face as he taps the screen repeatedly, and the noise sounds with every touch.

"Clicking it more won't fix it," I offer.

"Ner wylan."

Zaltas taps it several more times, and he's met with more error noises. The light reflecting off his face disappears. He sighs, closing the lid. I wonder what he was trying to do.

He looks down at me and begins to speak, but a loud whirring, followed by a boom, fills the field. Zaltas' head snaps in the noise's direction and he sighs, this time with relief.

I find myself on his shoulder, and he takes off running in the direction of the noise. That doesn't seem like the best idea to me, but I don't really have a choice at this point. I didn't see what caused the noise, but he clearly knows what it was.

"Where are we going?" I ask, knowing I won't understand the answer.

"Hylin ner tha."

"Oh, I didn't know there was a coffee shop here. Sounds nice. Are we going on a date?"

Zaltas chuckles and continues on into the grassy field. I swear he can understand me sometimes, but I know it shouldn't be possible.

I can't tell if I should be concerned or not. I mean, clearly, this entire situation is concerning, but Zaltas seems like he might be a better person than I initially thought. He saved me from a monster twice, and hasn't really done anything too bad to me. Aside from tying me up. I should give him the benefit of a doubt. Not that I have a choice, but pretending I'm deciding to do that makes me feel better.

CHAPTER FOUR
ZALTAS

Riley's body bounces up and down on my shoulder and I'm hyper-aware of her body every time it presses into me. That word came out of my mouth when talking to her. 'Selkin.' I know what it means. Scovein can't help but call their mate that when the connection is forged.

I search for the connection, it's weak but there. I feel the tiny thread connecting our being to each other. It will only strengthen. Eventually she'll feel it too. I've waited so long to find my mate and of course, when I do, I can't talk to them. Perfect.

"I'm going to get a white chocolate mocha and maybe some coffee cake," Riley says from my shoulder. She's set on the coffee thing.

"Whatever you wan," I start but I'm interrupted by a stabbing pain in my chest. My injuries are nowhere near healed enough, but I can't stop right now. Once we're safe somewhere, I can tend to them more. Hopefully. I don't know where we are. My vambrace is dead. The fight with the Alphur broke my Crystashield and drained the power.

I'm not sure if I'll be able to even recharge it here. There's no telling what time period we're in or what section of the galaxy we're in. Wormhole travel is strange like that.

That noise earlier, though, was unmistakable. A ship leaving the planet. I'm hoping to find more ships and ideally some friendly faces.

The orange grass gives way to rocky purple dirt and a slight incline with large purple rocks at the top. The other side drops off into a deep valley and, to my joy, there are buildings and several ships nestled in the center. I spy several being milling about the buildings. The same green ones that picked up the Alphur.

I set Riley on the ground next to one of the rocks and lean her against it gently. I point towards the buildings and then direct her attention back to me.

"They may not be friendly. Stay here and keep quiet. I need to go look," I say.

"Who are those people?" She asks.

I shake my head and say, "I don't know."

Riley makes a concerned noise and looks back towards the buildings. Her eyes go wide and she asks, "Are those spaceships?"

"Yes," I say with a nod.

Her eyes go wide again as she watches me. "Wait a minute, can you understand me? You nodded. Does a nod mean the same thing to you?"

"Yes," I say again with another nod.

"What the fuck, and you've let me prattle on about stupid shit. I didn't know you could understand me."

I shrug at her and smirk.

"Yeah, real funny, why can't I understand you then? Can you not speak English?"

I shake my head and say, "No, I have a translator installed."

Riley makes a quiet, thoughtful noise and asks, "Are we going into space?" Her voice sounds like a mixture of excitement and concern.

"Yes," I say with a nod.

"Oh, okay." Her response was not quite what I had expected. What is going on in that head of hers?

I point at her and at the ground beside her, "Stay here."

She shifts her body into the spot I pointed at and looks at me expectantly.

"I did not mean literally right there, but okay, that's fine," I say with another smirk. She seems goofy. I like that.

After making sure Riley is settled, I make my way down the slope as quietly as I can. Luckily, there are several large rocks along the way and I can stay out of sight of the base. The closer I get, the more I can take in. It looks temporary more than anything. I'm worrying that it's a raiding party. It's similar to the ones that Flaxens set up on Ethelox-12 when they were attacking rival tribes. Maybe these green men are much more akin to them than I thought. That would not be good. We may have to steal a ship rather than hitch a ride.

A familiar scent fills my nose as I get closer to the camp.

The smell of burning bodies.

I slide up to the side of one of the metal buildings and listen intently for any sounds of movement. After several seconds of stillness, I peek around the corner. Further into the camp, a fire is burning, several charred bodies are stacked in the flames, and I watch as two of the green men toss a large blue body on the fire.

Rage builds inside of me but I contain myself and stay quiet while I watch them. At first, I thought it was a Scovein they threw on the fire, but they were covered in tattoos, Scovein don't do that.

The green men remind me of Flaxen, with their crude mannerisms and stocky frames.

The two burst into laughter as the blue body catches alight and flames shoot further into the air. I slip closer to them and try to catch a bit of their conversation. The translators can translate hundreds of thousands of different languages. Hopefully, I'm not so far out that it doesn't work here.

"The blue ones burn so nice," one of the green men says.

"Yeah, them Khuvex go up good," the other replies with a guffaw.

"Shame about the ship."

"Khuvex are too smart, not that it did these ones any good."

They both laugh.

"Flesh is still flesh, and a blade is a blade."

"And loot is loot."

They both nod stoically and move away from the fire. I press myself as close to the wall as I can and crouch down behind several metal crates. The urge to dispatch them is overwhelming, but I stay my hand and let them pass.

"The pillaging part is nice," one says as they pass, "I love me some loot. But it's a shame no women were on the ships."

"Ay, that was a shame. Could go for a good ol' ravaging."

"Next time, maybe we can catch one of those human ships. Always packed to the brim, have our pick."

"Oh yeah, remember the one from last month, that was a good da..." The creature's voice cuts off as my blade sinks into its neck. Red blood runs down the blade and drips onto the ground from the hilt. I can feel the fire of anger burning in my eyes and slip the blade out quickly.

The other green creature simply laughs and says, "We missed one, eh? I'll get you taken care of, no worries."

He gets his sword halfway out of his sheath before my blade finds its mark in his chest. Confusion flashes across his face as I peer down at him. These disgusting green creatures really are no better than the Flaxen. They're large, but I stand a head taller than them. Its eyes grow wide as I pull my dagger up and out. It drops to its knees as blood pours out of the new hole in its body.

"There's no place for you here," I say. "It's time for you to try again in another life."

The creature tries to speak, but merely gurgles as blood rapidly fills its lungs. I want to let it suffer like it's probably done to so many others, but I slice its throat quickly and turn away.

The body thuds behind me quietly as I move towards the other side of the camp. Monsters like that don't deserve a second thought.

I saw two ships there earlier. I'm guessing one was the green beasts, and the other was the Khuvex they spoke of. A ship is a ship is what Idalas always says. So if you can fly one, you can fly them all. He's also a pilot in the Scovein military, so he may be a little biased at how easy flying ships can be.

I wish he was here. He was with me on Ethelox-12 when we were tracking the Alphur. I jumped into the wormhole in fear it would close before we could get to it. Idalas was close behind me. I wonder if he made it through, or if he's on Ethelox-12 wondering what happened to me.

"Please maintain distance from the ship,"

a woman says.

The feminine voice startles me and I look around quickly, dagger already in hand.

No one is around.

"Who is there?" I call out. No one is present except me and the two ships. One of them is beat up and looks like it could fall apart at any moment, the other is golden and gleams in the sunlight. It looks flawless.

I slide closer to the golden ship. The landing zone is open and I need to get behind some form of cover.

"Lethal force will be used. Retreat from the ship," the voice says again, right next to my ear. It's coming from the golden ship. An automated defense.

I relax, but only briefly, because a large, golden gun slides from the wing above my head and angles its barrel directly at me. I can see the head of the electromagnetic charge inside of it, ready to turn me into a steaming crater.

With great haste, I move towards the rear of the ship to appease the computer. I round the back and find the ramp down and several more guns. They immediately lock onto me and follow my every movement as I move further from the ship. They are not as big as the other gun, but the corpses surrounding them suggest I should not relax just yet.

Six of the green beast's bodies are littered around the base of the ramp, blackened and cauterized holes dot their torsos. The ship is not playing around. I suppose that's why they were complaining about the Khuvex ship earlier.

Well, looks like the rusty derelict is going to be the only way off of here.

This time, I cautiously approach the other ship and wait for any kind of warning. All is quiet. I go to the rear entry and the ramp is down on this one too, so I head inside. The cargo bay reeks of rotten meat and unwashed organics. My stomach threatens to unload its meager contents, and a retch escapes my lips.

I try to force myself into the ship, but the smell is overwhelming and I cannot make myself go forward. After quickly retreating from the cargo bay and back into the fresh air, I stop to debate my next move.

We can coop up in that disgusting mess and hope it doesn't fall to pieces when we leave the atmosphere. Maybe the interior is better than the cargo bay? Or much worse, I can't imagine their rest facilities are remotely clean. I sneer and take a deep breath of the fresh air. The smell from the cargo bay still lingers in my nostrils. I really hope that goes away.

Or. I can try to disable the security system on the other ship and we can take that nice and shiny ride into space. Disabling it from the exterior is probably impossible. Maybe the computer is capable of reason. A.I. is nowhere near complete, but most ships have a pseudo-A.I. capable of understanding different situations. Maybe it will communicate.

I've got to decide something. I need to get back to Riley. This base is small and I would have noticed others around, so she should be fine, but there could be returning patrols or other creatures about. I wish I didn't have to leave her tied up, but I could not risk her running again. That thing in the grass was more than enough to set me on edge.

After a brief glance at the smelly wreck in front of me, I head towards the other ship.

"Back again? Please maintain distance from the ship," the female voice says again, more sternly than before.

I approach the front of the ship slowly, and not knowing what else to do, hold my hands out to the side to show I mean no harm.

"Hello," I say carefully.

"That is close enough."

I stop moving and wait for any further instructions from the ship. It feels like a painfully long time, especially after two more guns emerge from its front and zero in on me. How many guns does this thing have?

"Where is Ditharan?" The ship asks.

"I don't know who that is, I just arrived here."

"Ditharan is the Khuvex that pilots this ship."

"I don't think he made it," I say cautiously.

"Explain."

"The green things, they killed several of the Khuvex it appears. They were burning their bodies," I say. It feels odd being so blunt about this, I normally would be a little more tactful informing someone that someone they were close to died. But ships don't have feelings.

"Ditharan is…. dead?" The ship asks, pain clearly present in its voice.

That's odd, a ship shouldn't be capable of showing emotion like that. Is the ship an A.I.? How far into the future did we wind up? Scovein technology is highly advanced compared to other civilizations, and we were nowhere near a true A.I., especially one that could exhibit emotions. No, it must be a personality module.

I feel bad for not being more graceful in the announcement. I know it has to just be mimicking the emotions, as they're programmed to, but it seems sincere.

"I apologize for my bluntness. We have been through a lot recently. Yes, it appears Ditharan has perished."

"How many bodies were in the fire?"

"Six."

"They're all gone."

We stand in silence for a couple of minutes. Thoughts of Riley being trapped and alone fill my mind and I begin to move the conversation along, but the ship speaks again.

"Who was responsible for his death?"

"I assume the green beasts that have been about."

"The Skeldi. Are there more than the six I have eliminated? I should have destroyed the other two ships instead of allowing them to depart."

"There were two burning bodies, but they are no longer amongst the living."

A quiet hum emanates from the ship that almost sounds like a sigh. I tilt my head and watch it closely as the guns aimed at me move.

To my relief, they point towards the ground and slide back inside the ship.

"Thank you for avenging my friend," the ship says.

"You are welcome," I say hesitantly.

"My name is Aurelia."

"Zaltas."

"In the event of Ditharan's death, I am to transfer ownership to Dytharan. Who is also, unfortunately, dead," Aurelia says, her voice breaking on the word 'dead'.

"I'm sorry," I offer, not really knowing how to console a ship.

"They left no further instruction past that, so I will default command to the nearest Khuvex."

"Who is th..." I start, but a loud hum from the ship and the tingling of an unseen wave passing through me stops my voice.

After the moment passes, I ask, "Who is the nearest Khuvex?"

Maybe we can hitch a ride with them at least.

"You."

CHAPTER FIVE

RILEY

Zaltas has been gone a while. The suns have crept across the sky a good distance. Maybe an hour? It's hard to tell here.

An involuntary grunt escapes my lips as I pull my hands again. I've been trying to get free of his bindings since he left, but he's got them tied snugly. I haven't decided if I want to run or not, but I'm getting uncomfortable in the position.

I roll over onto my side and pull myself into a ball. Pulling my legs as close to my body as I can, I try to pull my arms under them. My feet being bound makes it much more difficult than it should be. A sharp twinge in my calf signals me to stop, but I ignore it and keep pushing my arms as far down as I can get them. I smash my knees into my chest and with a little wiggling; I get my wrists under my feet.

The twinge in my thigh explodes into a full-blown cramp and I make that mixture of saying 'ow' and grunting that come with a sudden cramp. My legs straighten out slightly out of habit and my feet press into the binding on my wrist.

I try to fight through the pain and pull my arms around so I can stand up and ease the cramp, but the grass bindings catch on the treads of my boots and won't move.

I'm stuck.

"Fuck, fuck, fuck, fuck," I say repeatedly as I roll around on the ground. I've reverse hogtied myself. I'm completely fucked now. Zaltas needs to hurry up. Pulsing, sharp pain blasts through my body from my calf and completely takes over my thoughts.

I don't care what he has planned. Please hurry back. I need this pain to stop. I'm going to eat so many bananas when I get home. Fucking potassium deficiency.

After rolling around frantically, my body finally hit a position where my calf quits screaming at me and I lay motionless. Please, just go away.

The pain subsides and leaves the familiar dull ache of a recent cramp and I try to move my leg and finish pulling my arms under me. Another sharp tinge radiates from my calf and informs me that this is a bad idea. I retreat to my previous position and stay unmoving again.

Heavy footsteps echo off the rocks around me and I wait in quiet anticipation for Zaltas to arrive and free me. The footsteps multiply tenfold, and it sounds like an entire army is about to be upon me. I don't know what else to do besides roll myself against the rock and hope for the best.

Luckily, the cramp appears to be gone, except for the dull ache. I take this opportunity to thrust my arms under me hard and quickly. They slide under my feet and I see my glorious fingers in front of me. Still bound, unfortunately, but now I should be able to untie my feet.

I press my body into the rock as the footsteps grow almost unbearably loud. It's odd. There are no other noises, no voices, no growls, just footsteps.

As if responding to my thoughts, the purple rock I'm currently pressed against lets out a low groan like a person waking up after a deep sleep. The rock rumbles and shifts behind me. It was the sound of rocks shifting, not footsteps. I quickly roll away from it as it raises up into the air.

The only thing I can think of is that a

giant alien is about to smash me with a boulder. I shut my eyes and screw up my face, waiting for the impact. Instead, I hear another groan, then feel something large and wet slide across my face.

I gasp and open my eyes to see a massive black tongue coming for my face again. I try to move out of the way, but it connects with my forehead and drags sideways across it. When the tongue retreats, I get a good look at my assailant.

The purple rock I was up against now has a face and six stumpy legs. It's standing above me and looking at me curiously. I can see it debating what I am and whether I'm food. I hope it decides I'm not.

Its face is rather dopey and reminds me of a cow more than anything. It licks me one last time, lets out a low grumble, then trundles down the slope towards the orange grass several feet away. It instantly grabs a large mouthful of grass and thoughtfully chews on it as it looks around the area.

Other rocks in the area rise and join the first cow/rock/turtle thing in grazing. Some of them stop and analyze me briefly but none lick me again, thankfully. They're kind of weirdly pretty. Watching them calmly eat grass and make that low grumbling noise at each other is rather serene.

After the last creature makes it to the grass, I fiddle with the bindings on my feet. I get them off pretty quickly and stretch my legs. That's much better. The dull ache in my calf feels a little relief with the stretching and now I can run if I need to.

My hands are another story. I try to bite the grass free but don't have any luck tearing it with my teeth and just stare at it impotently, trying to will it to untie itself. One creature bellows loudly, and a thought crosses my mind. I wonder if I could... very carefully... get one of them to bite this off. I watch as one bites off a large swathe of grass.

That could be my wrist, though. Those huge teeth could easily crush through my skin and bone. Maybe that's not the best option. Oh, stupid Riley, I have my knife. I crouch down and pull it out of the sheath, holding it with both hands. Now, how do I spin it around to cut the grass?

Before I can fully commit to any plan, a familiar voice calls out behind me.

"Riley," Zaltas shouts.

"Any luck?" I ask him hesitantly. I still feel like I should escape him, but something makes me want to trust him. It feels like I'm connected to him somehow, it's almost reassuring. I noticed that feeling disappear when he left me, but now that he's back, it's there again.

Could be mind control like that other monster. I'm not sure. It doesn't feel the same. Maybe it's just because he's so hot. I may have been in serious peril for basically the entire duration of the past day and a half, but I've still noticed. Those muscles go on for days, and those abs look like a washboard. So what if he's blue and I can't understand him?

Zaltas stops within arm's reach of me and looks at my unbound feet and still bound hands holding my knife. He shakes his head and says, "Nerthyl."

"Okay?"

Zaltas looks at the knife and back at me again, taking a step backward. The urge to fight and run wells up inside of me, but I squash it down and slide the knife back in my sheath.

"Nerthyl, thes i giny haliyn," he says as he hurries towards me and jams something behind my ear. It feels like a slight pinprick and warmth rushes across my body from the spot he touched me. He injected me with something. I know that sensation very well from all the vaccinations I had to get to be a paramedic. Being able to feel it coursing through me, it has to be something strong.

"Did you just drug me? What the fuck?" I ask, pulling my hands to the back of my ear where he pricked me.

"I know it hurts, it will go away."

"It doesn't hurt, just feels weird. What did you inject me with?"

"It did not hurt? That's odd. They usually do. It was a..." he says, but I interrupt him.

"Wait, I can understand you?" I question him in disbelief.

"Apparently."

"Apparently," I say mockingly. "What was that?"

"A translator."

"So, now I can suddenly understand your language?"

"Mine and about two hundred thousand other ones."

"Why didn't you give this to me before?" I ask. I'm a little irritated he made me go all this time when translators were a thing.

"I didn't have one. I found this on a ship... well, my ship."

"Your ship?"

"It is now."

"Did you steal it?"

"No, it gave itself to me."

"What the fuck is going on?" I truly do not know what's happening anymore, not that I had a clue to begin with.

"I know little more than you do. We are in a place I've never been. But, we have a ship and we can talk now, so we are making some progress. Let's get off this planet."

"Why should I go with you? You tied me up and carried me around like some caveman's conquest," I say. I sound more irritated than I am. Some fleshy cucumber thing would have probably eaten me by now if it wasn't for Zaltas.

"I tied you up because this planet is incredibly dangerous, as you have seen, and you tried to run off immediately after almost dying."

My face felt warm and not just from the sunburn. I break eye contact and look at the cow creatures. Trying to run after almost getting eaten was probably stupid. I planned to be more careful that time, but maybe I shouldn't have been so hasty to run after he saved me.

"What are those?" Zaltas asks, joining me in viewing the rock cows.

"No clue, but they seem friendly."

Zaltas makes a thoughtful noise then says, "I will cut those bindings if you promise not to run."

Yeah, what other choice do I have? Stay here with the cows and twenty-story tall penis monsters in the grass? I almost crack a joke about staying with the giant penis monster, but I don't even know if aliens have penises, so what's the point?

I look over at Zaltas while he watches the rock cows. My eyes linger a little too long on his bulging blue shoulders and I run them further down his body. Well, he has nipples, so I'd assume he's a mammal. I drift further down his body, take a brief break on those abs, then trail further down. His leather pants are tight and I don't see how he's able to move so freely in them, some advanced fabric or other, I'd imagine.

My gaze stops several inches below his belt at the very large bulge tucked into his pants. My face burns hot this time and I look away quickly, staring at the ground. Definitely has a penis.

What am I doing? Now's not the time to worry about Zaltas' apparently massive cock. Say something, it's feeling very awkward now. I've been quiet too long. He didn't see me looking, or did he? I don't know.

My face gets hotter.

Oh god, I told him he had a nice ass earlier when he was bent over. I was half-joking, but mostly serious. It was nice, firm, and round. I thought he couldn't understand me. Now my face feels like the surface of the sun.

"Are you okay?" Zaltas asks, his head tilted and a look of concern on his face.

"Yes," I mumble.

"Your face is much redder than before. Is that normal? I'm not up to date on human anatomy."

"Yes, I'm fine."

"We should go to the ship."

"Okay."

"Do you want me to remove the bindings? You will not run?"

"I won't run," I say sheepishly.

Zaltas draws a blade from his waist and delicately but quickly slices the grass on my wrists off. My wrists itch immediately and I scratch them vigorously, letting out a quiet sigh of relief.

Then a thought popped into my head.

"Wait, how do you know I'm a human? How do you know what humans are?"

"I've met two."

"What? How?"

"Two more have come through the wormhole before you, albeit on a different planet."

So the other two girls met aliens too? They never mentioned that to me. Did they even know?

"Where are they now?"

"They are happy and probably far away from here. Look, we can discuss this later. We need to leave. That thing that came through the wormhole is incredibly dangerous. We have to find it and kill it."

I start to ask more questions, but just nod instead. I'll wait until we're safe somewhere to rail him with questions.

"Okay, let's go," I say with as much confidence as I can muster.

Zaltas moves ahead of me and heads down the incline to the buildings below.

"Bye, have a good breakfast," I say to the rock cows. An echo of grumbling and 'mrughagh' noises follows behind me as I descend the slope.

Zaltas checks behind him, looking at me several times as we approach the group of buildings. I know he's making sure I haven't run off. Which, honestly, offends me a bit, but I haven't really given him a reason to believe I won't yet. The urge to run is still there, but I believe it's in my best interest to stay with him.

We go between two buildings and enter a clearing with a fire burning in the center. As we approach it I stop in my tracks when I notice what's burning inside of it.

"Are those... bodies?" I ask cautiously.

"Yes," Zaltas says.

A shudder runs up my spine and I take a couple of steps back.

"Did you do this?" I ask.

"No, it was something called the Skeldi."

"Skeldi?"

"Another species, they attacked another group and stole their supplies and killed them all."

"That's awful," I say absently. The flames dancing on top of the charred remains sends another shudder through me and holds my attention longer than I'd like.

"They were disgusting creatures," Zaltas

says. "I dispatched two of them and the ship had an automated defense that took out the others that were still present."

"You dispatched two? Like killed them?"

"Yes."

"Why not try to talk to them and ask for help? Maybe the ones they killed were bad guys?"

"I do not believe so."

"How would you know?"

"I heard them discussing the attack and how they longed for women to rape, specifically human women. How they had done it before. I do not know Earth customs but by Scovein accounts that is not a good thing."

Another chill runs up me. Some things seemed like a humanity only thing. I would have thought if aliens existed, they'd be more advanced. Technologically and with societal norms. Less likely to do horrible things. Raping and pillaging seemed like a concept that would be unique to humans. At least Scovein do not abide by it, I'm assuming that's what Zaltas is.

"It is not a good thing," I say as I follow Zaltas past the fire and towards another large clearing with two spaceships sitting in it.

I let out a quiet gasp as we pass by two green humanoids dead on the ground, the surrounding area stained with blood. I'm guessing the two Skeldi he 'dispatched.' It's honestly something I've seen enough to get used to, not the aliens, but the bodies. As a paramedic, I saw my fair share of bloody scenes and had to get elbow deep in them. It's just shocking to stumble upon one so suddenly. I normally had a heads up and a little time to prepare myself mentally when I was on the job.

"You could have warned me," I say, glancing back at the two corpses one more time.

"About what?" Zaltas asks.

"The bodies."

"Death is a normal part of life. I did not think it warranted a warning."

"Maybe here, maybe for you. On Earth, we rarely deal with burned bodies and bloody messes suddenly and frequently."

I guess that's not completely true. I'm sure some people on Earth deal with that daily depending on the country they live in. When I was a paramedic, I saw things like that pretty frequently, just not in such large quantities. I should probably count myself lucky for not having to deal with that constantly.

Zaltas grunts thoughtfully and says, "There are several more behind the ship."

"Thanks."

One spaceship looks like it's actually made of rust and has several pieces hanging off it by wires and cables. I know nothing about building a spaceship or maintaining one, but that doesn't look normal. A growing pit in my stomach tells me that this is probably the ship we're stuck with.

Instant relief washes over me as Zaltas turns toward the shiny, golden, massive ship that looks in pristine condition.

"Whew," I say involuntarily.

Zaltas looks at me and tilts his head.

"I thought we were getting on the other one," I say.

"We can if you want to, but I do not recommend it. It is a much better ship than the gold one," he says, stone-faced.

"No, that's okay." Why would anyone choose that ship over this one?

I see a flash of a grin on his face as he turns away from me and heads towards the back of the golden ship. Was he just fucking with me? Was that sarcasm? Do aliens have sarcasm?

We take almost an entire minute to walk to the rear of the enormous ship. Its wingspan has to be at least the size of a football field. The buildings here look very temporary and aren't super tall but they paired with the incline really hid the ship from our view. The Skeldi must be good at sneaking around.

The back of the ship is littered with more green bodies with neat round holes burned through them. It would fascinate me under other circumstances, never having seen wounds like that, but I hurry up the ramp behind Zaltas instead of lingering.

The first part of the ship appears to be a cargo bay. It's immaculately clean and organized. Stacks of shiny crates are secured to the wall with various straps, and each crate is labeled with its contents. 'Meals', 'Medical', 'Repair', 'Entertainment', and 'Ammunition'. Each label has a list of detailed contents under it and I read through the medical list for a few moments before I realize everything is written in English.

"Why is this all in English?" I ask Zaltas as he walks up the stairs in the back of the cargo bay.

"It's not. The translators work on the written word," he says before disappearing in a door at the top of the stairs.

I guess that makes more sense than aliens knowing English. As much sense as anything can make right now, anyway.

Through the door at the top of the stairs is a short hallway with six doors. Three on each side. I watch Zaltas touch a pad to the side of a door and it slides open. He glances inside and, satisfied, turns to open another door.

I touch the pad closest to me and a rough sound plays from the pad, followed by a flashing blue light. I try again and am met with the same result. After a third try, I give up and move beside Zaltas to glance in the room he has opened.

It's a bedroom. Crew quarters. An enormous bed sits against one wall and a few shiny metallic rectangular cuboids, with no discernible features, line the rest of the walls. Another door is in the back of the room.

"One bedroom," Zaltas says stoically. "Guess we will have to share a bed."

"There are six bedrooms on me, each has its own bed and bathing facilities," says a female voice from all around. I glance up at the ceiling, trying to locate the source of the voice.

"Thanks Aurelia," Zaltas says before turning to me. "I was just joking, there are plenty of bedrooms. Take your pick."

"Mhmm, I'm sure you were joking," I say with an exaggerated eye roll. Knowing he has at least some kind of sense of humor makes me feel much more comfortable. "What was that voice?"

"The ship. Aurelia," Zaltas says.

"A ship that can talk? Is it an A.I.?" I ask excitedly. I always loved sci-fi shows, movies, books, comics, and any other media I could get my hands on. Being on a spaceship was exciting enough, but it having an A.I. I can interact with heightens my excitement even further.

"No, it's a pseudo-A.I. It just mimics emotions and is conversational, but it's all programming. True A.I. is nothing but fiction."

A huffing sound echoes through the hallway and Aurelia says, "I am a fully functioning A.I. I have learned and evolved over the past two decades. I am not mimicking anything."

Zaltas' face screws up and he looks confused. Maybe some other species out there created A.I. and he just didn't know about it. The universe is a big place. Surely he doesn't know about all of it. More to the point, a real A.I.! I never in my wildest dreams thought I'd be experiencing all of this.

"How is that possible?" Zaltas asks.

Aurelia goes into very technical detail about her creation for a couple of minutes. Every other word she says flies over my head and while

Zaltas appears to be listening intently, I get the feeling he's not understanding most of it either.

Zaltas nods and says, "Okay, thanks. I did not need an entire rundown, but I appreciate the effort."

"You are welcome," Aurelia says.

"What year is it?"

"The year in S.U.Y.A.T is ten thousand three hundred and twenty-seven."

"What the fuck?" Zaltas proclaims.

"What is S.U.Y.A.T?" I ask.

"Standard universal year after Tryglitharanica," he replies flatly.

"And that means?"

"Each planet has its own calendar. The S.U.Y.A.T. is the common year across the universe."

"Well, what year is it supposed to be? It was twenty twenty-one on Earth. I don't know what that is in S.U.Y.A.T."

"Three thousand nine hundred and forty," Aurelia says cheerfully

"We're six thousand years in the future?!" I ask in disbelief.

"It appears so."

"It is currently six thousand and sixty-one years later than three thousand nine hundred and forty S.U.Y.A.T.," Aurelia offers.

"Thanks," Zaltas says with a head shake.

Six thousand years in the future... everything I knew is gone. Maybe. I don't know the conversion of Earth years to universal years. Maybe one year on Earth is a thousand on the universal scale. It could not be that bad. Maybe, or it could be worse. Much worse. Earth and humans could not exist anymore. Stinging tears burn the back of my eyes and a lump forms in my throat. I start to ask more questions, but Zaltas leaves.

I swallow the lump in my throat and press my eyes tightly together for a few seconds and take some deep breaths. The panic and fear recede enough for me to function and I follow Zaltas. I'll save my total mental breakdown for when I'm alone in bed. Aurelia mentioned bathing facilities, a hot bath, some crying, lots of crying, and a soft bed sound like the perfect end to the day.

Zaltas heads down the hallway and into a larger room. It has a large table with several chairs around it and what appears to be a very well-equipped kitchen lining another wall. Everything is immaculately clean and shiny. The walls have several colorful splashes of red mixed with the chrome of the furniture.

It's odd how much the kitchen in an alien spaceship resembles one on Earth. A deep grumble followed by a dull ache fires off from my stomach. Oh yeah, I haven't had anything substantial to eat in a while.

Zaltas opens a large door next to the sink and a pale light bathes him in illumination. I sidle up to him and peer around his bulky frame at what was hidden behind the door. Dozens of shelves are covered in an eclectic mix of colors sealed in transparent containers. Jugs and pitchers take up an entire shelf, each full of a different colored liquid. It's a fridge! Easily five times bigger than one on Earth, but the chill wafting out of it and the food storage containers are unmistakable.

I don't recognize anything in there. A lot of the containers appear to be filled with vegetables or maybe fruits, but none of it looks familiar. My stomach grumbles again. Surely some of this is safe to eat and hopefully tastes good.

"What is al..." I ask, but a loud rumbling noise startles me and I look around in a panic. Are we being attacked? I turn my sight to Zaltas for guidance.

Zaltas puts a hand on his stomach and

says, "It is about time we found some food."

Zaltas stacks up ten of the containers and moves them to the table before returning to grab a pitcher of brown liquid. He seats himself and watches me patiently. I can see the look of urgency in those beautiful green eyes, but he says nothing. Is he waiting for me to get something or to come sit down? I look over at the stack of containers he has. Each one looks like it's holding half a gallon of food easily. Is he actually going to eat all of that or is that for both of us?

"Get what you like, let's eat, then we can finish exploring the ship," he says with a hint of urgency in his voice.

"Shouldn't we get somewhere safe first? We're still on a strange planet that clearly has hostile people on it," I say. Food sounds great right now, but I am still concerned about our safety.

Zaltas waves a hand at me and says, "Aurelia is more than capable of fending off anything on this planet. We will be fine. Sustenance is important."

"I can defend against anything on the planet except for Nurlaglins," Aurelia offers.

"What are those?" I ask, images of hulking monstrosities ripping the wings off of the ship and peeling back the hull to grab at me fill my mind.

"Nothing to be concerned with, let's eat," Zaltas says hastily. "We can discuss whatever you want after."

If a giant ship is concerned about a creature, we probably should be too, but Zaltas is apparently set on eating first.

I look back into the fridge and pick up a container divided into two sections. One side has some kind of diced vegetable or fruit and the other has what appears to be a slice of deep red meat. Zaltas clears his throat behind me, and I quickly grab a pitcher of blue liquid and close the door.

As I approach the table, Zaltas picks up one of his containers and turns it over in his hand, looking at it closely. He presses something on the side and sets it down. The interior fogs up with steam, hiding whatever is inside, and beeps rapidly after a few seconds.

I sit myself down on the other side of the table and watch his container. After the beeping stops, a quiet click sounds. Zaltas removes the latch holding the lid on and a puff of steam rises from the open container. The smell of grilled sausage and onions fills the area, and my mouth waters.

I find a button on the side of my container and press it. The container fills with steam and beeps. After a click, I carefully open the lid and the red meat inside is now a more appetizing brown with char marks along the edges. The diced green stuff has darkened slightly and is also slightly charred.

My gaze turns back to Zaltas to see if he will indicate how it will taste. His first container is already empty and a series of beeps are coming from a second as he watches it closely.

Guess it's okay.

I tap my finger on the meat and rub the juice from it on the inside of my wrist, then do the same with the vegetable on the other wrist. I watch for a few seconds for any adverse reaction. Nothing changes on my skin. Normally, I would do a few more tests to make sure it's safe, but the smell is intoxicating and I can't fight the urge to eat any longer.

The meat is cut into cubes and easy to pick up. The flavor explodes in my mouth, a mixture of saltiness and sweet followed by a slight burst of peppery heat. It's delicious.

The vegetable, I'm assuming it's a vegetable anyway, tastes mostly like roasted brussel sprouts. Something I hated as a kid but have grown to love as an adult. I'm very pleased with my hasty decision at the fridge.

I only ate about a third of the container. It had enough food for three people. Grabbing the container of blue liquid, I pop the lid off and sniff it. It smells slightly sweet and fruity, though I can't place what fruit it might be.

Zaltas makes a satisfied sound. All ten of his containers have been completely emptied, and he's drained most of his pitcher already.

"What is this stuff?" I ask, holding up the pitcher. "And what is this food?"

"No idea," Zaltas offers helpfully.

"The mixture includes: Carbonated Water, Citric Acid, Tatromine, Sodium Citrate, Parathan Granlo, Sucralose, Caffeine, Sorbic Acid, Benzoic Acid, Niacinamide, Acesulfame Potassium, D-Calcium Pantothenate, Pyridoxine Hydrochloride, Cyanocobalamin," Aurelia says and continues to list off a dozen more ingredients.

"Thanks," I say. Not that any of that had any meaning to me. I recognized a few of the ingredients, namely caffeine, which sounds great right now. Having a meal in me and sitting down in a comfortable chair has made me realize just how tired I am.

I take a sip of the liquid. It tastes like some vague berry flavor. Not the best thing I've had, but good enough. The familiar fizz of carbonation is comforting, and I have several more sips.

After I feel fully sated, I lean back in the chair and look to Zaltas for what's next. I really want to explore the rest of the ship, but apparently it's his now, and I don't want to make him mad.

"Are you going to eat that?" Zaltas asks, motioning towards the rest of my food.

"No," I say. How could he possibly have room for more food? I slide the container across the table. He catches it without missing a beat and empties the contents at an impressive speed.

Another satisfied noise escapes from him. I expect him to lean back and undo his belt, but he gathers the containers and dumps them in the sink by the fridge. A burst of steam erupts from the sink as he steps away from it and a quiet whir echoes in the room.

"Ready to see the rest of Aurelia?" He asks.

I make a grunting dad noise when I stand up and sheepishly say, "Yes."

We go into another hallway. It appears much like the one with the bedrooms, but only has two doors on each side. The hallway dead-ends at another larger door. This one is covered in bolts and locking mechanisms. Whoever built it tried to hide the mechanics in ornate decorations, but they still stood out.

Zaltas opens both doors to the right, and each reveals a room with a single couch and a large window revealing the area around the ship.

"Kind of barren," I say.

"Aurelia, do these relaxation rooms have full neural integration?" Zaltas asks.

"Yes," Aurelia says.

"What does that mean?" I ask.

The room we're currently looking into changes suddenly. The couch sinks into the floor and the window stretches to take up the entire wall. The window darkens and becomes almost impossible to see out. A fountain materializes out of the floor and water dances merrily from its golden bowls. Ornate benches appear on each side of the fountain and the sound of soft, alien music tinkles in the air as the lights dim and give the room the appearance of twilight.

"What the hell?" I ask in wonder.

"Neural connection, they're called relaxation rooms and can transform into almost anything the user desires," Zaltas explains, unimpressed.

"That's incredibly cool, like a holodeck?"

"I do not know what that is."

"It's like this…" I say absently as I look around the room.

I focus my thoughts on making a statue of myself appear in the center of the fountain, but nothing happens.

"Why can't I change it?" I ask.

"You have not been allowed to link with me," Aurelia says.

"Connection for Riley is allowed," Zaltas says.

"Full name required."

Zaltas tilts his head at me expectantly.

"Oh, Riley Bernardi," I say to the air.

"Your name is Riley Butts?" Zaltas asks with a quiet chuckle.

"No, it's Riley Bernardi?" I say, utterly confused.

"Riley Butts."

"Riley Bernardi. Bernardi."

"I don't understand how I'm saying that wrong. Butts."

"You're messing with me, aren't you?" He has to be.

"Adding Riley Butts to the neural database," Aurelia says.

"It's Bernardi!," I say loudly and brace myself for whatever is involved with a neural link.

Nothing happens, that I feel anyway.

"Riley Butts added to the database. What level of control?"

"Six," Zaltas says.

"Level six authorized."

"There now you should be able to use almost anything on the ship," Zaltas says.

"My name isn't Butts, it's Bernardi..." I continue to insist.

"Sometimes names do not translate properly and end up translating to the closest word in the other's native language," Aurelia states.

"So my last name in Scovein is Butts?" I ask Zaltas.

"Apparently so," he replies.

"And Khuvexian," Aurelia adds.

"Great," I say with a sigh. "Why is it translated as Butts to me when you two say it then?"

"It is likely that your name is not recognized as a name in any known languages."

"It's Italian!"

"Italian language unknown."

I give up. I guess it is what it is.

Zaltas moves across the hallway and opens another door, revealing a plain room that is blindingly white.

"Neural decon," he says quickly, closing the door and opening the fourth.

It was a medium-sized room with several tables and workbenches. The walls in the back were lined with all manner of weaponry. Many of them resembled swords, axes, daggers, and other melee weapons from medieval times. In stark contrast, the rack beside the first was covered with guns. All shapes and sizes with tubes and antennas sticking out of them every which way. It was hard to tell how you would even hold one. Last, some gigantic machine was in the back corner with a door on the front of it.

"Armory," Zaltas says, as if he's seen it a hundred times already. He steps into the room, and once the sense of wonder fades, I follow him inside.

Zaltas digs through a few crates tucked in a corner and mutters under his breath. He pokes around one workbench and pulls a large box from the shelf above it. It has a few wires running out of it directly into the wall of the ship. Something clicks and the lid flips open, revealing a smooth black interior and nothing else.

"Will this charge a Crystashield?" Zaltas asks.

"I don't even know what that is," I respond.

I feel slightly foolish when Aurelia speaks and I realize he wasn't talking to me.

"Crystashield is a forgotten technology and the voltage to charge it is unknown."

"So it technically can charge it?"

"Yes."

"Set the voltage to six thousand three hundred and twenty-two."

"Voltage charge set."

Zaltas removes his vambrace and presses it into the box. The black interior melds itself around the vambrace and the vambrace's lid pops open, showing an illuminated screen.

"What a sight for sore eyes," Zaltas says. I watch the screen and a small bar appears at the bottom and slowly fills with red. Once it is completely full, the vambrace rises slowly from the box until the interior is smooth again.

Zaltas retrieves his vambrace and puts it

on. He taps the screen and a light blue light flashes quickly, completely enveloping him, then fading away. He presses it again and the same light flashes, but rushes down his body before disappearing completely.

"What is that?" I ask, unable to watch quietly any longer.

"A Crystashield. Armor. The Alphur broke it during our fight," Zaltas replies as he closes the lid on his vambrace.

I'm guessing an Alphur is the thing that attacked me through the wormhole.

"That's incredible, it's a personal force-field?"

"At a basic level, yes."

Zaltas draws one of the blades from his side and squeezes the hilt. The same blue light envelopes the blade before retreating and dissipating.

"Your sword has a force-field?"

"It is a dagger, and yes, it makes it sharper."

"And keeps it from breaking... that is way too big to be a dagger," I add.

"To you."

"Fair enough."

Last, Zaltas removes the dagger covered in tubes that he was so desperate to recover earlier. He analyzes it briefly before tucking it back into his belt.

"What is that? You were super concerned about it earlier."

"The Melt Knife."

"Did you name it yourself, that's very creative? Does it melt things?" I say with a grin.

"I did not name it, no," he replies with a smirk. "Yes, it melts things. If by melting things you mean enveloping them in the fire of a burning star."

"Huh?"

"It generates the power output of a star at a focal point on the blade."

"That sounds very dangerous," I say, subconsciously taking a step back.

"It is. So do not mess with it."

"A whole star, hmm?"

"One second's worth of energy from a star."

"Seems less impressive. Why do you have it?"

"That is still an indescribable amount of

energy. It's to kill the Alphur. The only thing that can kill it, as far as I know."

"Do you stab it and activate the star power?"

"Yes."

"Do you yell out star power activate?" I ask, imagining a scene from a cartoon I watched as a kid. A smile flashes on my face.

Zaltas' face cracks into a smile and he just shakes his head.

"So wait, the thing you're wanting to drag me along to hunt down can only be killed by a fucking star?"

"Yes," Zaltas says before leaving the room and approaching the last door in the hallway.

"Why is this happening? Why did you two come through my wormhole?"

"Let's get into orbit, then I'll answer questions."

I'm tired of waiting for answers. I've gone with the flow for long enough and am tired of being clueless. I'm used to being independent and having control over my life. I can't do that without information. He took a break to eat and suddenly he's too concerned with leaving the planet to answer questions?

Before I can speak my mind, Zaltas opens the last door and enters. My mind goes blank again with wonder at the sight. A spaceship's bridge, just like in the movies. Panels, displays, buttons, switches, lights. An enormous window looking out of the front. Even has the spinning chairs mounted to the ceiling.

"Take a seat," Zaltas says as he sits in a chair at the center of the room.

Not knowing exactly where to go, I take the closest one to him. It's incredibly soft and comfortable.

A little yelp escapes me as the seat shifts under me and forms around my ass, thighs, and back. It immerses me in perfect comfort, and I sigh with relief.

Zaltas is staring at me quizzically and I say, "Sorry, the seat moved and startled me."

He pokes around the console in front of him and I watch intently as he opens and closes several flaps on the console and flips a few switches. He leans in close to the console and turns his head sideways, looking across it. Seeing him work is fascinating. I can't wait to feel the rumble of the engines, the pressure of takeoff, the sights of space rushing to greet us.

Zaltas hits a few switches, and nothing

happens. He looks over his shoulder in my direction, avoiding eye contact, and sweeps the room before returning to the console. Another couple of button presses, and he places his hands on the console and starts drumming his fingers.

"Do you know how to fly a spaceship?" I ask. I thought it was a long startup process, but now I'm starting to realize he probably doesn't know how to fly a ship that's six thousand years in the future.

"I know how to fly a spaceship," he says, stressing the word 'a'.

"Just not this one?" I offer.

"Just not this one."

Zaltas looks over his shoulder again, this time making direct eye contact with me. His stern face, paired with his searing gaze, feels like it's going to burn a hole through my very core. Until he grins at me, revealing a flash of pearly white teeth.

Something inside of me stirs and I feel warmer than usual. I shift uncomfortably in my perfectly comfortable seat and smile back at him shyly.

I've never let men intimidate me. Socially, at work, or romantically. But something about him is making me nervous. Not in a scared for my life way, but in an 'if he asked I might take him up on it' kind of way.

Riley. You're billions of miles from home. You're probably thousands of years from home. Now's not the time to be thinking about sex. Or is this the perfect time to think about it? I really don't know how I should act right now. Look at him, that chiseled face, that perfect smile. I can see the rounded top of his perfectly sculpted shoulder sticking around the chair slightly. Even his short black hair is perfectly maintained and looks luscious.

I should be panicking, scared, fighting for my life. But something about him has started to comfort me, to make me feel safe. The closer I am to him, the better I feel. It's almost like a connection between us, something inescapable and unseen, but ever-present. Thinking back, I've felt it since the rock cows, but didn't even realize it was there.

Or maybe it's just all in my head and I'm becoming delusional with the stress and lack of proper rest.

Zaltas' eyes grow a little wider and he cocks his head slightly. I just now realize I've been making unblinking eye contact with him for much too long. My face burns hot and I find something on the ceiling to look at.

CHAPTER SIX

ZALTAS

She is definitely an odd one. Were Emily and Alyssa this weird? I cannot recall. I spent little time with them one on one. Maybe it is just nerves on her part. Maybe she is feeling the connection. That blank stare on her face was mildly alarming, but there was a hint of desire in there.

The thread connecting us feels thicker now, but still not completely solid. I wouldn't imagine she is noticing it yet. It might not even matter to her.

I grin to myself as she averts her gaze to the ceiling and turns back to the console in front of me. Well, I've tried several things to start the ship. Idalas is full of shit. A ship definitely is not a ship. I guess Aurelia will have to take over for now. I will get a course from her later on piloting.

Idalas, Eldas, my brothers. I fear I may

never see them again. Trapped in the future, they are long gone at this point. A slight tinge jolts my heart at the thought. They will have lived their lives by now, no doubt to the fullest. Surely they missed me. Who would not? But I am on my own course now. Eldas had settled down with his mate already and Idalas was basically mated to the military. So was Drenas, and even he found a mate. It is my time now.

I have longed for fresh adventures, unfamiliar sights, new worlds. For my mate. I have found all of it. I will miss my brothers, but most Scovein live in the present and I am no different. They will live on in my memories. I hope they managed to get by without me present to torment them.

Maybe I will have contact with them again someday. If not, it was a pleasure knowing them and I will persevere. I will forge a bond stronger than the universe has seen. Riley tilts her head at me and smiles slightly. Everything will be fine as long as I have her. Turning back to the controls, I tap a couple of more buttons before looking to the ceiling.

Maybe this far in the future there are not even manual controls. A silly thought, surely a ship could not be advanced enough for combat. Then again, she is an A.I. Fully formed and functional, as she says. Who knows what she's capable of?

"Aurelia?" I say to the ceiling. I never know where to look when talking to a ship. It does not really matter, but it feels unnatural just talking to something without having a focal point to look at. My brain always chooses the ceiling.

"Yes, Zaltas? Do you need assistance piloting me?" Aurelia says, a little smugly.

I glance over my shoulder at Riley, who merely smiles at me.

"Yes," I say.

"Where would you like to go?"

"Just into orbit for now."

"This planet has a large asteroid belt in its orbit. Remaining there is unwise."

"Are there any Scovein settlements or outposts nearby?"

"The Khuvex currently inhabit the planet Dexterion," Aurelia says.

"And I'm a Khuvex?" They looked similar enough to a Scovein, maybe they're called something different in this time.

"Yes, would you like to proceed to Dexterion?"

"Make it so!" Riley chimes in enthusiastically. She is handling this better than I would have thought. I cannot tell if it's nerves, excitement, or insanity on her part.

"Dexterion is fine," I say. We will figure it out when we get there. No other logical options right now.

"Plotting course for Dexterion, distance sixty-seven point two light-years."

"Sixty-seven point two light-years, doesn't that mean it will be a sixty-seven years minimum before we get there?" Riley asks.

"Estimated time of arrival: One hundred and sixty-eight hours," Aurelia says as the engines fire to life and an explosion of light and color appears on the flight deck before me. Holograms with display upon display showing star charts, controls, temperatures, speed, and all manner of information about Aurelia.

"Whoa," Riley whispers behind me. She mumbles to herself for a moment, then adds, "That's only a week?"

"Take off in ten seconds, please restrain yourselves," Aurelia says merrily.

Restraints slide out of the back of my seat and secure me in place. I grunt involuntarily as the belt presses into the wound on my chest.

I really need to clean it out and re-bandage it. There was a big crate of medical supplies; there should be some h1 serum somewhere.

I hear Riley yelp suddenly, then snort and giggle. I assume her restraints secured her as well.

The engine rumbles to life and the vibrations make my teeth chatter for a few moments, then the dampeners kick in and all goes still.

"Three... Two..." Aurelia counts down to launch.

Riley squeals with delight behind me.

"One."

The view in front of us shifts as Aurelia turns us towards the settlement. The beat-up buildings sink into the ground as the window is filled with clouds lazily drifting overhead. We lift off and the clouds slowly inch closer and closer before instantly dispersing and revealing the vast emptiness of space. The windows tint to almost black as Aurelia swings our view across the three suns and lines up for warp.

Blast shields close across the window as all the light converges on a single point and becomes blindingly bright even through the tinted glass. My eyes squint closed until the blast shields fully seal and the room is bathed in the comparable darkness of artificial lighting.

"Warp speed entered successfully," Aurelia states.

The restraints release, and I rise from my chair to check on Riley.

"That was it?" She asks, standing up. She is clearly disappointed.

"What were you expecting?"

"I don't know, g-force and more than ten seconds?"

"Spaceships are equipped with dampeners to keep you from feeling anything."

"That's no fun."

"The speed of a spaceship entering warp would liquify carbon-based life-forms in twelve-point three seconds," Aurelia says a little too cheerfully.

"Oh," Riley says. She looks over at the blast shield and adds, "Can't even look out the window! At least we're in space."

"Not much to see out there, just blinding bright light."

Riley makes an odd, thoughtful noise and motions for me to follow her. She heads out of the flight deck, and I watch her closely as her hips swing from side to side. Beckoning me, taunting me. A tingle shoots from my cock and it twitches in my pants.

"Not now," I whisper to myself and follow Riley off the deck.

She leads me into the kitchen and sits down at the table, pulling another chair aside and motioning for me to sit.

I did not expect her to lead me to the bedroom, but I am still a little disappointed.

I have a seat and look at her expectantly. I have a feeling I am about to get interrogated.

CHAPTER SEVEN

RILEY

"It's time for questions," I say as Zaltas gets comfortable in his chair. "We're in warp and going to be for a week. You have plenty of time now."

"I do not have a problem answering your questions now," he says with a smile.

"Where are we?"

"I do not know."

Knew the answer to that one, don't know why I asked.

"What year is it on Earth?"

"I do not know. I do not know where Earth even is."

"The current year on Earth is five thousand two hundred and seventy-five," Aurelia says.

"It's thirty-two hundred years in the future?" I say in disbelief. My heart pounds loudly in my chest. The small sliver of hope I had was destroyed in a single sentence.

"Are humans still there?" Maybe I can return to some semblance of normal life at some point. I didn't have anyone back home I was really close to, so the shock of never being able to go back is more missing normalcy than anything. That's why I didn't back out of going into the wormhole, didn't have much going on, anyway.

"Earth was re-established in the year five thousand two hundred and forty-seven. Humans currently inhabit it."

"What do you mean, re-established?"

"According to records available, an ice age three thousand and twenty-six years ago caused humanity to flee the planet. They returned two thousand nine hundred and ninety-eight years later once the ice age had ended."

So, everything is gone gone. Even going back there would be completely different from how it was in twenty twenty-one. I honestly don't know how to feel right now. I feel like I should cry and panic, but the urge isn't there.

Knowing humans are still there waiting if I decide to go is comfort enough for me, I suppose.

"How far away is Earth?"

"Three hundred and thirty-six light-years."

I stand up and pace the room for a moment to collect my thoughts. Should I go to Earth? That makes the most sense, right? I wouldn't know anyone, though. It would be cool to see what it looks like now. What if it sucks? I might be better off wandering the stars. Oh, I don't have a spaceship. I could hang out with Zaltas?

I spin around to look Zaltas over and catch his emerald eyes flick up to meet mine. My cheeks burn slightly. Busted, sir. On Earth, I'd have called someone out for looking at me that way, but Zaltas. It feels like it's okay. I kind of enjoy knowing that he's into me. I should do the bend and snap. No, that's stupid. I'm not trying to attract him. Elle says it works flawlessly and he wouldn't be able to keep away from me. Or am I trying to attract him? I don't even know what my own mind is thinking.

"Are you okay?" Zaltas asks as I quietly giggle to myself.

"Yes, just lost in thought," I say.

"Do you have anything you want to ask me, or can Aurelia answer all of it?"

Zaltas winces and presses his hand against the now filthy bandages on his chest. I feel horrible and like a completely shitty paramedic for forgetting that he was injured. The straps on his chest intersect the bandage and he acts like he's fine. No, I'm making excuses for myself. I should have noticed.

"Oh no, I can talk to Aurelia. You need to rest. Do you want me to look at the wound? I was a paramedic."

"I do not know what that means," Zaltas says, "but no I am fine."

"I was a healer, I guess?"

"That would be handy if we were still stranded on the planet, but this ship has a large crate of medical supplies and should have some h1 serum."

I start to ask him what that is, but he heads towards the cargo bay. He's moving a little slowly, I hope that isn't infected. It didn't look deep, but puncture wounds can be tricky to gauge by eye. I watch him disappear behind the door at the end of the hallway, sneaking a peek at his ass as the door slides shut. I feel bad for even thinking about that while he's in this state, but it's hard not to look.

"What's h1 serum?" I ask Aurelia.

"H1 serum is an injectable liquid composed of tetraglycologicide, nanoletrino, chlorotaraglin, and water."

"Thanks, I mean, what does it do?"

"It repairs injuries."

"Any injuries?"

"It will not regenerate amputations, death, or fully heal burns, but most other injuries, yes."

"Diseases?"

"No. However, h5 serum will cure any affliction besides Narythiral Flu and Lux Disease. It still will not regenerate amputations and cannot revive the dead."

Hmm, being in the future has some benefits. Nice to know there's a cure-all available. Or well, a cure-most. Aside from the bloodthirsty aliens, the future is not so bad. Healing potions, self-cooking meals, spaceships, A.I. and at least one friendly alien.

Zaltas returns through the cargo bay door and nods at me before turning into one of the bedrooms.

A sexy, friendly alien.

My gaze lingers a little too long on his door before I snap back to reality.

"Do you desire Captain Zaltas?" Aurelia asks. Her voice was almost sing-songy, which I would have normally found funny, but made her question much more embarrassing.

"No, shhhh," I say hastily.

A sound not unlike 'mhmm' plays in the room and I can't help but laugh at the A.I. in a spaceship in the year five thousand, acting like a human in middle school. My embarrassment fades quickly and I resume pondering my situation.

"Are the Khuvex friendly?" I ask, suddenly nervous about arriving unannounced on an alien planet. Again.

"They built me, so I am inclined to say yes. However, there are good and bad ones, much like any other species."

"Even Skeldi?"

"Allegedly, there are some good ones."

"What exactly is the Alphur?"

"Hmm, unknown. No official records exist."

"Zaltas is acting like it's some tremendous threat. How are there no records of it?"

"Official records referring to them appear to have been removed a couple of thousand years ago. Several mythological texts exist about them, though."

"Well, we've got a week, tell me about them."

"The stories are brief and there are only mentions of them. Here is an excerpt from the Green One's text 'Descriptions of events during conflicts':

The army had a large number of soldiers.

It attacked the base camp outside of the Capital.

A weapon was deployed to restrain the entire army at once.

The Alphur was captured and interred in the Holding Center.

That is all the mention in that text of the Alphur. Further records of observation during its capture were available at one time but were deleted two weeks after their input."

"Wow, that's a super descriptive and helpful story. It really had me on the edge of my seat," I say.

"I thought it was lacking most storytelling fundamentals and could have been more descriptive."

"I was being sarcastic," I say with a giggle.

"What is sarcastic?"

"I would never be sarcastic, Aurelia," I say as sarcastically as I can manage.

"I do not understand, you just said you were being sarcastic."

"That was sarcasm, it was an example."

A quiet clicking sound, almost like fingers drumming on a table deep in thought, echoes through the room for a few seconds.

"Are you okay?" I ask. I'm worried I broke her somehow.

"No, I am not okay," Aurelia replies angrily, voice dripping with venom.

"I'm sorry, what's wrong?" I ask, sitting up in my chair. I'm suddenly very nervous. Maybe I should go find Zaltas.

"I was being sarcastic, was that correct?"

I breathe a sigh of relief and lean back in the chair. "No," I say grinning. "The tone of sarcasm is more derisive than angry."

"I will give this some thought and try again later."

"Okay," I giggle. "Is there any more mythology on the Alphur?"

"There are several more texts from the Green Ones. Would you like to hear more?"

"Are they any more detailed than the one you just read?"

"Yes," Aurelia says, drawing out the 's' sound. "Of course, they are more detailed."

"Was that sarcasm?"

"Did I do good?"

"Yes, that was perfect," I say, shaking my head and smiling.

"They are the same writing style as the first text."

"That's not helpful then. Does anyone else have any stories?"

"It does not appear so."

"Maybe I should ask Zaltas about it, then."

"Please inform me of what you find out."

"Can't you just listen in too?"

"I have no access to the bedrooms, for privacy purposes."

"Well, I'll let you know."

"Thank you."

I knock on Zaltas' door and wait for him to tell me to come in, but I hear nothing. I knock louder and wait again. Still nothing.

"Zaltas?" I say loudly while banging on the door.

Worry sets in. What if he died? What if his wound was much worse than I thought and him removing the bandage to clean it made it bleed and he passed out?

After pacing in front of the door for a few seconds worrying myself, I knock on the door loudly and shout his name.

No response.

Please be okay, please be okay.

I put my hand on the pad by the door, and it slides up. Zaltas isn't here.

A clatter echoes across the room from the door to the rear and I hurry to it, pressing my ear against the door and listening intently. It sounds like running water, and I hear a quiet groan. He passed out in the shower. The running water will make him bleed more. Shit, shit.

"I'm coming Zaltas," I shout.

Just as my hand hits the pad by the door, Zaltas responds, "No."

But it's too late.

The door slides up, revealing Zaltas standing completely nude in the middle of the room. A torrent of water is falling from the ceiling all around him and hazy steam rushes towards me and into the bedroom.

Zaltas turns around hastily, exposing his bare ass to me. While I greatly appreciate the view, it was hard to really take in because of the absolute mortifying feeling that had overtaken me.

I had seen what he was doing. His hand wrapped around his massive blue cock. I know what that groan was, and it certainly wasn't from pain. My body ignores my brain's feelings and reacts to the image burned in my mind. I feel the heat of arousal emanating from my core and slight dampness.

"Oh, fuck me, sorry," I say quickly and leave the room. Poor choice of words, or maybe my body took control of my voice for a second. The primal fire building inside of me is almost unbearable, and it came out of nowhere. I've never been turned on that quickly in my life.

That cock, though. Huge and vibrant blue. More than enough for any woman. Plenty for me, that's for sure, with extra to spare. Riley stop.

But why? We're both adults. I mean, I think he's an adult. I don't know alien biology, but he sure looks like one. Especially with that weapon he's been hiding in those leather pants.

I shake my head and go towards the kitchen, but turn into one of the other bedrooms instead. Before the door slides shut behind me I hear Aurelia.

"So, what did you find out?" She asks.

"Not what I was expecting, but what I suspected anyway."

"I do not understand."

"We'll talk later Aurelia. I need a nap," I say with a feigned yawn.

"Okay, sleep well, Riley."

"You too," I say absently.

The door to the bedroom slides shut with a very pleasant whir and the smell of a brand new car fills my nose. I inhale deeply and sigh with contentment as I look around the pristine room. The bed is made nice and tight with the blanket tucked in at the foot. Just like I like it.

An overwhelming urge to collapse on the bed and sleep for six days battles my willpower relentlessly, but I fight it off and head into the bathroom. A quick shower, then I'll have a nap. We've got a week until we arrive at, umm, the Khuvex planet. Dexter something? Anyway. Shower.

The room features a sink and mirror, along with a large open space enclosed in glass. Identical to the one I just witnessed Zaltas pleasuring himself in, I bite my lip and stare at the empty shower. A pang of desire hits my core. I'm getting distracted, let's see, that small pad on the wall above the bench must be the controls. I place my hand on the pad and it illuminates, displaying a wide assortment of wash options.

Flipping through all the pages would take an incredible amount of time if the 'one out of three hundred and thirty-seven' at the bottom is the page indicator. I make it through ten pages, each of which has thirty items before sighing deeply and saying, "I just want a normal shower."

The pad blinks in front of me with a pleasant chime and water falls from the ceiling behind me. Warmth fills the area instantly and steam rises from the floor. The smell of fresh water hits me and my body feels relaxed.

"Perfect," I say.

I shimmy out of my filthy jumpsuit and undergarments, tossing them on the bench, and step into the shower. The water refreshes me down to the essence of my being and my mind goes blank as the heat embraces me.

All of my worries. All of my panic. All of the dirt. All of my fear. It all melts away and swirls down the drain with the water.

I take another deep breath before releasing an immense and almost orgasmic sigh of relief. Something so simple as a shower has comforted me more than I could imagine. I think just knowing at least a shower is something universal makes me feel a little less out of place. No matter what happens, at the end of the day, I'll be able to take a hot shower.

A pair of hands press firmly into my back and I let out a quiet gasp. I almost turn around, almost scream, almost fight him off, but I don't. I lean back into them and enjoy the sensation of his hands sliding up and down my back. Massaging me deeply. The slipperiness of skin on skin has always done it for me and this is no exception.

I shouldn't let this happen, should I? My brain says no, my body says yes, my gut tells me it's meant to be.

I start to pull away but lean back into his hands again and they slip down my back and I shudder as they wrap around my side and trail my hips to the inside of my thighs. They slide up my stomach and cup my breasts, running underneath each ever so gently. Another shiver runs up my spine and I feel myself getting wet, and not because of the water.

The smell of lavender and sweet creams fills the room. It's absolutely intoxicating, and I could think of no other perfect scent for this moment. I let out a quiet moan as his hands reach my neck and delicately glide around them. They slide up the back of my neck into my hair and his fingers dig into my scalp firmly.

They massage my head thoroughly and I even feel him untangle some of my hair. The smell of lavender and sweet cream grows stronger and this shower suddenly feels a lot less sexual and a lot more utilitarian.

I spin around, it's my turn to rub on him, but my eyes start stinging and I press my hand to them quickly. My hand is covered in suds and I say, "Wait, wait, I got soap in my eyes, ah, it burns, hold on, sorry."

I tilt my head back into the water as his hands retreat and rinse my eyes out. After a few seconds, they feel much better, though still burning a little. I won't let a little pain stop me from finishing what he started, though.

"We shouldn't be doing this, but it feels so right," I whisper before spinning around to face him.

No one was there.

A tremor rolls through me again, this

time not of desire but of being creeped out. Is the ship haunted? Are there ghosts in space? Someone was definitely touching me. Or am I just delusional and horny and imagined the whole thing?

I jump back and almost slip on the floor as two robotic rubber hands descend from the ceiling. A robotic voice says, "Shower mode: normal. Eighty-five percent complete. Would you like to continue?"

"Are you fucking serious?" I say. Embarrassment floods my body and replaces any other emotions I was experiencing earlier. "I thought you said you weren't in the rooms, Aurelia?"

"Answer not found. Shower mode: normal. Eighty-five percent complete. Would you like to continue?"

Oh, I guess it's just automated. The thought of something else washing me like that, especially just a machine, kind of creeped me out. I feel even weirder because it turned me on, and that I'm still mostly aroused. But.... it was really great. I mean, it's almost done, might as well let it finish, right? I'm not being lazy, just letting the computer do its job. That's what it's here for!

I glance around the room, looking for what I don't know, and abashedly say, "Yes."

The rest of the shower wasn't nearly as sexy now that I knew it wasn't Zaltas, but still refreshing. The water stops and after the ceiling finishes dripping, I look around and realize that there are no towels. How am I supposed to dry off? I also notice that my clothes are missing from the bench and a sudden jolt of panic hits me.

"Oh... umm," I whisper. I was so ready to fuck Zaltas' brains out, I don't know why the sudden disappearance of my clothes feels like such a big problem. I suppose without the heat of arousal, I'm thinking clearer.

The opening in the glass of the shower melds shut and panic further sets in, what's happening now?

Before I can move, a wild vortex of warm air engulfs my body. It hits me from every direction and I unconsciously shield my eyes. It disappears as suddenly as it came and I'm completely dry. A quiet click echoes in the room and the glass opens again, releasing me.

"Please do not move," the monotone voice instructs before I can step out of the shower. I stand still and brace myself for whatever else is about to happen. I feel hands digging gently through my hair and soft bristles running through it. Once the machine finishes brushing my hair, it says, "Normal shower complete."

"Well, apparently towels are a primitive idea here, now where are my clothes..."

The bench my clothes had been on... now has my clothes sitting on it again. They're folded and look much cleaner than before. Is everything on this ship automated? Must be nice, never having to do any chores. Wish that was my normal life.

Except, it is my normal life now. Maybe, anyway. Unless Zaltas boots me off the ship. From how he's treated me so far, I don't see that happening. Earth and its chores can suck it. I grin at myself before yawning loudly. I really want to get some more answers from Zaltas, but I need a brief nap at least.

I slip my clothes back on, put my belt and knife holster on one of the metal boxes, and collapse onto the bed. My jumpsuit isn't the most comfortable thing, but this bed sure is. I snuggle up to the massive pillows and let the fluffy blanket envelop me. Normally, I would lie in bed and think for a couple of hours before being able to fall asleep. Not this time. I passed out almost instantly.

△△△

"Good morning, or whatever it is," I say to Zaltas. He's seated at the table with a pile of empty containers and a couple of empty pitchers. I hope the food lasts the rest of the trip, with the way he eats, we might be out in a day.

"Hello," he replies, looking into each container to make sure he didn't miss any food.

"Don't worry, I won't eat all of mine," I say with a grin.

"Good morning, Aurelia," I add, feeling slightly bad for forgetting about her.

"Greetings Riley. There is no morning in space," she replies.

"I figured as much, thanks," I say, shaking my head. She's getting snarkier as time progresses. Is it my fault or Zaltas'? Who knows what's rubbed off from him.

"You are welcome," she replies merrily.

I open up the fridge and am surprised to find it's mostly been restocked. I guess food production is automated on Aurelia too. There were huge crates labeled as food in the cargo bay, but they didn't look like they were hooked up to anything, just boxes on the floor. Curiouser and curiouser.

Grilled chicken, or whatever tastes similar, and some kind of vague apple-flavored mush.

I eat a decent amount and pass the rest to Zaltas, who finishes it happily. We sit at the table in silence for several minutes while I search for something to say. The sudden intrusion I dropped on him yesterday was still fresh in my mind, along with the slightly too steamy shower I had afterward. He doesn't appear bothered in the slightest, but I still can't find anything to say, so I leave.

That just made things feel more awkward. I slip into one of the relaxation rooms. It just has a couch, white walls, floors, and ceiling, and a window displaying various planets passing by at a rapid speed. It's dizzying at first, but after I sit on the couch and watch for a few minutes, it becomes more relaxing.

"Aurelia?"

"Yes, Riley?"

"I thought Zaltas said it would be all white outside?"

"It is not actually white, it just appears that way because this entire dimension is made of light."

"What do you mean?"

"The Travelista dimension is made of light. I do not know how else to elaborate."

"Are we in another dimension?"

"Yes."

I am utterly confused. Did the wormhole take us to another dimension too? But that's not right, she said it's made of light.

"Why are we in another dimension?" I ask.

"FTL travel is impossible in our normal dimension, so the warp drive shifts us into the Travelista dimension to traverse our universe."

"Okay," I say. I still want to know more, but I feel like it will just hurt my brain and I move back to my original question. "But this window isn't all white. I can see planets clearly."

"That is not accurate to what is outside of me at the moment. It is just an approximation of things we have passed. We are traveling at a much faster rate of speed than it appears through the window."

"Oh," I say, not knowing what else to add.

I zone out on the view in front of me for several hours before finally getting bored. Bored of space travel, I never thought that would happen to me. This room can transform into whatever I want. I wonder how in-depth it can get. Is it just what I imagine or is it like a close guess at what I'm wanting? Let's mess with this.

I envision a statue of myself made of gold

in front of me. It appears almost instantly forming up out of the floor. I reach out and touch it, my fingertips are met with cool, smooth metal. I wrap on it with my knuckles and it echoes with a 'ding.'

The rest of my day is consumed with amassing and disposing of an eclectic collection of statues, vehicles, plantlife, water features, music, smells, and colors. When I finish, the ceiling is hot pink, the floor is black, and the walls alternate between hot pink and black. One wall is taken up mostly by a window displaying flickering blue flames reaching to the ceiling.

Statues varying in height of me line the walls in various poses. A huge neon green lion statue takes up most of the center of the room, with my face of course, while water pours from the ceiling into neon green ponds at the base of the lion, or as I've been calling it, the Rilion. The closest thing to classical piano music I could find tinkles in the air and the smell of cinnamon buns covers the room.

I lean back into the plush black armchair and admire my handiwork. A yawn escapes me and I stretch with a groan. My eyes feel heavy and I wonder how long I've been here. Should have made a clock to go in the room, too. I yawn again and imagine a neon digital clock with pink numbers on one of the black walls. When I open my eyes, it's there.

Ten p.m.? Shit, I've been in here all day. Or have I? I don't even know what time it was when I got up.

"Aurelia?"

"Yes?"

"How long have I been in here?"

"Fourteen hours."

Shit, I did spend all day in here. I wonder what Zaltas has been up to. I feel kind of bad not interacting with him today. My hand strokes the side of my neck as I peer at the doorway. I should find him.

Before I even move, the door to the relaxation room slides up and Zaltas pokes his head in and glances around.

"This is what you have been doing all this time?" He asks.

"Yes," I say self-consciously. It was fun, though. I rode a jet-ski on basically a water treadmill. Can't be embarrassed about that, right?

"It is," he pauses and makes a thoughtful noise, "Interesting."

"Thanks."

"That is a lot of statues of yourself," he

says, entering the room and looking around.

"Yeah, it feels like I'm a pharaoh or something."

"Pharaoh?"

"Neverm…" I start to say, but Aurelia interrupts.

"Pharaohs were a type of ruler on the planet Earth eight thousand years ago."

"Yeah, that," I say.

Zaltas stops in front of the Rilion and swaps between staring at it and at me before simply asking, "Why?"

"It's a Rilion!" I say enthusiastically. Zaltas appears more worried than amused. I guess it's not as funny if you don't know what a lion is.

"Is it just a coincidence a Rilion looks like you or is that why you chose it?"

"It's a coincidence," I say, not wanting to explain what a lion is. Maybe I can find a picture somehow, and then I'll go over it.

A space beside the Rilion becomes wavy as something forms out of the ground. A large cylinder slides out of the floor and bends as it nears the ceiling, pointing directly at the two of us. The color of it shifts to a vibrant blue. Is he making a penis? Really? Men are apparently the same, no matter where you are.

Mouths form along the sides of the cylinder, and I realize quickly what he's made. It's that dick monster that attacked us on the planet, except at the top of it is Zaltas' face with a goofy smile staring down at us.

"Seriously?" I ask, bursting into uncontrolled laughter.

"It's a Zalturional," he says, looking at me for approval.

"I don't get it," I say.

"Aurelia told me that monster was called a Nushurional. It has my face, a Zalturional."

I laugh again, he's much smarter than I thought. Apparently, he got the lion thing and was just messing with me. A sudden rumble in my stomach interrupts my good time and reminds me I haven't eaten since this morning.

"I need to eat," I say.

"Me too."

"Zaltas ate thirty-eight minutes ago and does not actually need to eat. He is only choosing to," Aurelia chimes in.

"Mind your business," Zaltas says to the ceiling, and winks at me.

We have a quick dinner and retire to our

separate quarters. I'm glad he came into the relaxation room. It made me feel like things were smoothed out, and hopefully, I won't be as awkward tomorrow. I settled into bed and fell asleep quickly.

My dreams were hot, and I mean hot. Featuring Zaltas and myself in the middle of a tropic jungle, both wearing nothing but small leopard print loincloths. Water rushed loudly from the waterfall behind our treehouse and the heat of the jungle made us sticky with sweat, but we didn't care as we tore into each other's bodies. The taste of his lips lingered on mine as I sat up in bed quickly.

My body is still throbbing for relief from the dream and I decide to get out of bed. I make my way to the shower and toss my clothes on the bench before climbing in. I start the shower on the normal setting and find a manual option. After clicking manual, water flows from the ceiling, creating a nice cloud of steam. A long tube descends from the ceiling with a showerhead on the end. I grab hold of it as the water cascades across me and my body sends another pulse of desire through me. I tap some buttons on the side of the showerhead and the stream changes to various flows and finally lands on the pulse setting. One of my favorites from back home.

After my very long and... relaxing shower,

I head to the kitchen and have breakfast with Zaltas. He's in a good mood but not very talkative today, so we eat mostly in silence except when I blurt out, "Did you know you can kind of control the shower, too?"

"Yes, with the controls?" He says.

"No, I mean, like in the relaxation room."

One eyebrow slides up his face, and he cocks his head, waiting for me to tell him more.

"Not as in-depth, I guess, but I made a chair appear in the shower."

"Were you getting tired in there?" He asks.

"No, I was... mmm just needed a relaxing shower."

Zaltas contemplates me, then says, "I could see how that would be nice to have." His words were clean, but I could sense the dirty undertones.

"Keep it in your pants, sir," I say with a shy smile.

"I meant nothing of that nature, I meant I could see the appeal in sitting while showering."

"Oh," I say, a little more disappointed than I should be. "My bad."

"Are you finished with your meal? I have something I wish to show you?"

"Yes, what is it?"

"Come with me," Zaltas says and heads towards the relaxation room.

He opens the door and steps to the side to let me go in first. The room is super bright, and the ceiling resembles a blue sky with white clouds drifting lazily across it. It looks like we're at a small cafe in some nondescript city on Earth, sitting on the patio. The walls are animated, showing a city street stretching into the distance, with vehicles driving along the intersecting roads. They don't look exactly like cars, but they're very close. People that resemble humans are milling off in the distance, just far enough away to not be able to see them clearly.

The sounds of a city surround us and the smell of coffee and baked goods fills my nose. It honestly feels like I'm back on Earth. As close as I'll probably ever get.

"Zaltas, this is wonderful," I say, smiling at him.

"I had Aurelia help me set up close approximations of Earth in twenty twenty-one based on what was available."

"You two did a great job," I say. They really did. I could hang out here for hours.

"I remember back on the planet. You said

you wished to go to a coffee shop for a date."

I blush, probably much more noticeable now that my sunburn has faded. Is this supposed to be a date? It's also very sweet. He remembered that from such a hectic time.

"That's super sweet of you," I say and have a seat at the small table in front of us.

Zaltas sits across from me and we end up chatting for hours. He tells me about his brothers, their encounters with the Alphurs, and the two human women he had met before that came through the wormhole. I wish I could have got more information from him about the other humans, but he didn't seem to know much about them or was withholding it.

I tell him about life on Earth, my job, my life until now, the job I took going into the wormhole. I lamented not being able to return to Earth and a sense of normalcy, but have mostly come to terms with what my future holds. Zaltas told me about how Scovein only live in the present and onward and how he will miss his brothers but will not mourn their loss.

"Cherish whatever memories you have from Earth," he says. "But do not mourn the loss, you got to experience it and it continued on even with you gone."

That makes me feel a little small and less

comforted, but I kind of see where he's coming from. I mean, I guess the Earth technically continued on, just frozen for a couple thousand years in between. He's right, though, no sense in craving a return. I should look at what I have now and the future.

"You know, you're right. I'll try to think of it that way," I say with a grin and stand up. "It's about time we let this place close down for the night."

I wave my arms around the empty cafe patio. Unfortunately, food and drinks aren't something the rooms can create, so no coffee was ordered. It also can't make living things, so we've been alone this whole time. That's been nice though, no disturbances. I'm sure Aurelia has been listening in, but she hasn't said anything.

The blue sky has faded to black, and stars are twinkling overhead. We head towards the door and both pause at the same time before turning to one another. My hand finds its way to his bicep and I stroke it and give it a good squeeze.

"This was fun, Zaltas. Thank you. I feel good about everything now."

"I had an enjoyable time as well," he says. That dopey grin flashes on his face. That paired with those green eyes is too much for me.

I reach up and put my hand behind his neck and pull his lips into mine. Something inside me sparks, and a jolt runs through my body. It feels like it flows out of me and into him, startling me. I pull away from him quickly and regret doing that. It feels right, too right. My head is feeling fuzzy and I don't know what to do at this point.

"Thanks," I mumble and bolt out of the relaxation room and into my quarters. I climb into bed and stare at the ceiling, deep in thought for no telling how long. At some point, I slipped into sleep.

ΔΔΔ

The next few days, I did my best to avoid Zaltas. I felt horrible for doing it. He did nothing wrong, but I feel too overwhelmed. Zaltas realizes this and gives me my space. Aurelia tried to pry a few times, but quickly gave up when I wouldn't tell her more. She's apparently hooked on gossip.

I don't ignore them, though. I say hi, ask how they are, then keep to myself. I just really don't know what to say to Zaltas at this point. I've never been the best at expressing my feelings or even really allowing myself to get close to someone. Something about that kiss, that electric tingle, felt real. Like an actual tangible connection, and that's too close.

Or is it? Should I get over myself and apologize to him? Probably. I'm the one that kissed him too, that's what makes it worse. If he initiated, I could just dump off the problem on him, but I'm the problem. I'm the cause of it. I have to talk to him. I have to. This could be just what I need.

I spent most of today in bed, okay all day, turning these thoughts over and over in my head, trying to find the words. I know now that I want to talk to him, but what do I say? Sorry? Is that good enough?

We'll be at the Khuvex planet in the morning. This week has been wild, but our journey is about over. Even though I've been a recluse the past few days, I've enjoyed spending time with Aurelia and Zaltas. It's been surprisingly peaceful and relaxing, mostly. If my brain would chill the fuck out. I'll sleep on it and maybe I'll know what to say in the morning.

I wiggle my way under the covers of the bed and get cozy before realizing I still had my jumpsuit on. I should take it off, I'll sleep better. I always got mad when I fell asleep with clothes on. It always felt like I could have had a much better night's sleep and wasted it by being clothed.

Fuck it. I'm already comfortable. The soft pillows under my head and the soft, warm blanket on top lulls me to sleep quickly.

$$\triangle\triangle\triangle$$

"Riley?" A voice echoes in my dreams.

I look up to see Zaltas standing above me in all of his glory. Completely nude. Bulging blue body on full display, just for me. Cock rock hard and throbbing. Just for me.

I don't hesitate. I reach out and wrap my fingers around his girth and tug it gently. The fleshy warmth in my hand sends a ripple of heat through my body. I never realized how badly I could want someone.

"Riley?"

Zaltas is towering above me, head tilted back and eyes closed, enjoying my hand as it strokes his cock gently.

"Riley?" Louder this time. I feel pressure on my shoulder and a gentle shaking, but Zaltas has his hands to his side.

My eyes snap open and I find Zaltas standing over me again, unfortunately clothed this time. My arms are stretched across the bed towards him, with my fingers touching my thumb, leaving a sizable hole in the center. The flames of embarrassment consume my face and I sit up quickly and tuck my hands under my butt.

"Yes?" I ask as calmly as possible. The dream is still fresh in my mind, still warm in my body.

"You were not answering, so I came in," he says.

"Okay."

"Here is your backpack. I restocked it with medical supplies."

Zaltas sets my backpack on the bed. It looks much cleaner than before too.

"Thanks," I say, grabbing a strap on the backpack and pulling it towards me. The familiar hilt of a knife sticks out of one pouch on the side.

"We'll be at the Khuvex planet in about thirty minutes," Zaltas says as he exits the room. He looks back at me and gives me a once over before moving into the hallway.

"Zaltas, wait," I say hastily. He stops in the doorway and tilts his head at me.

"Yes?"

"I'm sorry."

"It is fine."

"No, I feel horrible and…"

I falter and say nothing for a moment before steeling myself and saying, "Come here."

Am I really going to do this? I want him. It feels right. There's no harm in it. Right? My body is screaming at me to do it, but maybe I shouldn't.

Zaltas approaches the bed slowly. I can tell he's not sure of what I'm wanting, but I can see the look in his eye of what he's hoping I want. Lucky for him, that's what I have in mind.

"Thirty minutes, huh?" I ask, giving him the most sultry look I can manage.

"Yes," he says, watching my fingers as they grip the zipper on the front of my jumpsuit and slowly slide it down. Once my cleavage is in abundant display, I pull my shoulders inward and glance down before looking back up at him.

Zaltas' face is betraying little emotion, but his steely stare is shifting between my eyes and my cleavage. I can see the struggle in his eyes as he tries to focus on me. Good, right where I want him.

One thing that is betraying him is the ever-growing bulge in his pants.

I pat the bed and Zaltas climbs in beside me without hesitation.

Hands intertwine, and I pull him against me. Our lips touch and press into one another. The warmth floods into me and lingers as he pulls away. The taste of his lips and the electrifying sensation that hangs around signals to me that this is the correct decision. Just like the first time, except now I'm going to go with that feeling. I pull us together again and bury my tongue into his mouth, sending him into a frenzy.

Zaltas' hands run down my back and mine caress his. I try to reach across his entire length, but my arms are too short and a hint of jealousy spikes my arousal. His hands cover every square inch of me without issue, and I desperately wish mine could do the same to him.

I push him onto his back and climb on top of him, caressing every nook and cranny of his hard chest and finally getting to feel the stones he calls his abs. Zaltas turns his head back slightly and closes his eyes as I rub every inch of him I can, sliding my hands under the straps across his chest. Pressure on my hips grows as he tightens his grip on me and I begin to grind myself on his waist.

A quiet cracking sound fills the room as I slide the zipper of my jumpsuit down slowly, stopping just below my navel. Zaltas' eyes open widely and his hands dive into the opening. The warmth of flesh on flesh sends a chill through me and each stroke of his massive hands feels electrifying. They run up my back and slide down under my tits before cupping under them and sliding across my pebbled nipples with the slightest touch.

A tremor rolls through me and I slide myself down his body until I feel his bulge buried beneath my ass. The soft fabric of my jumpsuit brushes against my shoulders as Zaltas pushes it back off of me, desperate for a full view. I'm more than happy to oblige him.

I continue to grind on top of him, rocking my hips ever so slowly, directly on top of his growing bulge. The mass of flesh under me, waiting for me to have it, sends more ripples through my body and I feel myself getting wetter by the second.

Rising to my feet, I stand over him and remove my jumpsuit. I toss it to the side and undo my bra, revealing my tits to him for the first time. The fire in his eyes erupts into a blaze as he sits up and his hands reach towards me, gripping my hips, then rubbing up and down my thighs.

I playfully bat his hands away and say firmly, "Off." Motioning towards his pants.

My underwear joins the rest of my clothes in a pile, and I look down at him. Zaltas is completely nude, pants and straps off, tossed to the other side of the bed. I didn't even feel him move. Impressive. But not nearly as impressive as the massive, hard cock jutting into the air below me.

Crouching down, I grab the base of his cock and take it all in. Girthy, long, veiny, blue, and glorious in its size. I seat myself with his cock between my legs and my ass on his thighs. I squeeze his cock gently with my hand before sliding my hand up to just below the head and back down again. One long, smooth motion.

Zaltas lets out a quiet groan and hastily pulls some pillows under his back so he can enjoy the show comfortably. A show I'm ecstatic to put on for him.

Two hands on his cock and I pump it slowly, watching his expression for what he likes. Every movement I make causes his face to contort in pleasure and the sounds he lets slip sends me into overdrive. I can feel myself positively dripping, and I want to make this last. I want to toy with him; I want him to toy with me. But I can't. My body wants it, it wants it now.

I press his cock against my slit and rub myself up and down his length. Deep, pulsing pangs of pleasure crash through my body as the head of his cock touches my throbbing clit and I let out an involuntary gasp.

A look of concern flashes across Zaltas'

face but is quickly replaced by pure satisfaction as I nestle the head of his cock into my lips. His hips press upward as his body begs to be inside of me, but I raise slightly and squeeze his cock firmly.

"No, I'm in charge," I say sternly and massage his cock for several more seconds. I want him to destroy me, but the reactions I'm getting from him are giving me far too much pleasure to release control. Not yet. I use his shaft as my personal toy, rubbing my throbbing clit against it and pressing it into my folds. As more of my wetness coats him, it slides more and more effortlessly, the gentle friction pushing me over the edge and driving me into an insatiable frenzy.

Zaltas starts to speak, no doubt a perfectly formed quip on his tongue, but I cut him off by pressing his head inside of me. His words are replaced with a quiet groan and all clever thoughts are cast from his mind. The only thing left is me and my body. He's mine, for the time being.

My walls stretch to accommodate him and I'm honestly a little surprised that the weapon he calls a cock fits inside of me, but my body makes it work to my immense gratification. I get most of the way down before I meet resistance and have to throw in the towel.

My body squeezes tightly against his cock as I raise up, almost letting him spill out of me, before slipping back down his length again. The sensation is overwhelming. More tremors roll through me as the pressure inside of me builds with each movement.

Zaltas' hands make their way back to my body and maneuver themselves to one of my tits and the side of my neck. One hand caresses my neck gently, feeling almost like a feather brushing against it, while the other teases and torments my hard nipples. The hand on my neck works its way down my body and pinpoints my clit. A finger delicately presses against it and teases it lightly. I can't take it much longer. The pressure inside of me builds to an almost unbearable level with each touch from him and every thrust pressing deep into me.

I hadn't noticed, because of the mind-blanking pleasure pouring through my body, but I had stopped moving and Zaltas had taken over. His hips rising and falling as he drove his cock deeper and deeper inside of me. I felt his thighs press against my ass. He had managed what I failed, to get himself all the way inside of me. And it feels incredible. My breathing becomes erratic and heavy. Everything feels better than it has any right to.

It feels like my mind has blanked and my vision dulled. All that is present inside of me is pleasure and his massive cock slamming deep inside of me. The pressure inside of me increases to unsustainable levels and I finally let go. Electric tremors radiate from my core and wave after wave crashes against me, threatening to knock me unconscious, but I hold on and ride the dizzying wave as it ripples through my body in unending ecstasy.

Just as my orgasm starts to wane, I feel Zaltas' cock somehow get harder inside of me and his breath grows shallow. He groans in the most pleasant way as his cock pulses deep inside of me, filling me up with every drop he has to give. The warm explosion inside of me is icing on the cake and sends another shiver up my spine, causing me to collapse into a quivering mess on top of his chest, unable to stay upright any longer.

We lay together, still and silent, for several moments as I try to steady my breathing. I focus on the rise and fall of Zaltas' chest and the steady thumping of his heart. His arms wrap around me and he squeezes me tightly while we bathe in the afterglow.

Once I regain my composure, I whisper, "That was the best sex I have ever had. Ever. Hands down."

"Same for me, selkin," he replies quietly. His hands rub up and down my back, this time more lovingly than lustfully.

I wish we could stay here like this. A good long nap after such a good fucking seems called for, but Aurelia's voice interrupts us from the hallway.

"Dropping out of warp in five minutes," she calls out.

Zaltas doesn't budge. He seems perfectly content to lie here, too. After a few moments, I decide to be the one to ruin the mood.

"We should get ready," I say.

"Probably," he replies unconvincingly.

I relish the moment a few seconds longer, then roll off of him and head towards the bathroom to clean up quickly. Before I make it past the bed, he snags my hand and gently pulls me in for a kiss. The warmth of his lips lingers on mine as I go into the bathroom.

After cleaning up, I go back into the bedroom to find Zaltas gone, along with his clothing. Mine are stacked neatly on the bed and I get dressed quickly.

I pick up my backpack and pull my knife out of it. I look it over quickly, then slide it into the sheath on my ankle. Stealing one last glance at the bed, I head out of the room. I'm going to contain myself next time, have some more fun with him. Though, the memory of that feeling of him inside me will be hard to resist and not rush to.

Zaltas and I look at each other silently in the kitchen. He has a dopey grin on his face and I can feel the same thing on mine. Something is different now, not in the normal way that things change after sex with someone. No, this is much different. I feel close to him, closer than I should. We have known each other so briefly and been able to actually speak so much less time, but... there's something there. Something connecting us. It feels almost like a physical rope, tying our beings together. Connecting us in the best way imaginable.

It sounds silly. I almost wonder if I'm high. Maybe the atmosphere on the planet had messed with my brain and made me feel some kind of cosmic connection with the universe and others. Try as I might to wave it away with doubts, the connection is there.

"How's your wound?" I ask Zaltas as I sit beside him at the table. The memory of our encounter is still burning brightly in my mind. I was so consumed with desire that I didn't even notice the state of his wound.

He slides one of the straps on his chest over, revealing smooth, undamaged skin.

"It is fine," he says.

"Looks more than fine to me," I say in disbelief. No scarring, no scabs, nothing. It looks like he wasn't even injured.

Zaltas grunts in acknowledgment and says, "They did not have h1 serum. They had h5 serum. A large upgrade, it seems."

My backpack clicks quietly as I undo the latches and flip the top open. Several clear containers are filled with silver cylinders. I retrieve one and turn it over in my hands. The cylinders have a glass vial situated in the center filled with a light blue liquid, a small button on the back makes it resemble an ink pen more than anything. Stamped on the side in black is 'h5'. The rest of my pack contains fresh bandages and my survival kit.

I pull out my canteen and it sloshes merrily, filled to the brim. Several of the containers from the fridge are stacked inside the pack, too. Instead of diced vegetables and raw meat, they are split into three parts. One has some kind of dried plant matter, the middle looks like water, and the right has jerky made of who knows what.

"You've got me well stocked, thanks," I say with a smile. "You had me well-stocked earlier, too. Packed to capacity." I add with a wink.

"I do my best," Zaltas says with a 'pleased with himself' smile. He flips open the lid on his vambrace and taps the screen. His face turns into a scowl.

"What's wrong?" I ask.

"No other Scovein communicators are responding to me, I have sent out several dozen signals."

"We are in the middle of unknown territory in space," I offer.

"Yes, but the communicator can reach several hundred light-years. We should be within range of some Scovein settlement if we are so close to Earth."

"Close to Earth, three hundred light-years," I say absently. I guess closeness in space is relative.

"Three hundred and thirty-six," Aurelia says cheerfully.

"Thanks, Aurelia," I say.

"Dropping out of warp in thirty seconds. Dampener failure chance point zero five percent. Please secure yourselves."

Without warning, restraints pop out of the chairs and secure us both snuggly.

"Did she say there's a chance the dampeners will fail?" I ask Zaltas, slightly alarmed.

"There is always a chance they will fail,"

Zaltas replies with a grin.

"I don't like that."

"I do not think anyone does."

"Warp disengaged. Entering atmosphere in ten seconds," Aurelia says.

"Do they know we're coming?" I ask.

"I have informed them of Ditharan's death," she says before pausing briefly. "And that Zaltas is the new captain. Landing clearance has been granted. A detachment of guards will meet us at the landing pad."

"Should we be concerned?" I ask Zaltas.

He merely shrugs at me.

"Great."

"Atmosphere entered. All clear. Landing in two minutes," Aurelia says. The restraints disappear back into the seats and Zaltas immediately heads to the bridge.

"Where are you going?" I ask, hurrying behind him.

"To the flight deck, I would like to see what a Khuvex settlement looks like."

We enter the bridge, or flight deck, I guess it's called, and both stare in wonder at the sight before us.

The blast shields on the window have been retracted and reveal a view of a sprawling and gleaming city. The buildings stretch into the white clouds, and each one appears to be made of shimmering gold dotted with white ivory. The buildings all spiral upwards, giving the city an otherworldly look. It almost resembles termite mounds, but much prettier.

"It's so beautiful," I say quietly, unable to tear my gaze from the gorgeous view laid before me.

"It is, selkin," Zaltas replies.

I've heard him use that word before, selkin. I wonder what it means. It doesn't translate, apparently. Like my last name... what if he's calling me a turd or something?

The entire city is on a massive island surrounded by orange water. Large ships float lazily across the sea, coming and going from the banks of the island.

Seconds later, we settle down on a flat golden surface, and I look to Zaltas for direction. He keeps watching out of the window and says nothing. The platform we're on sinks into the ground and the only reaction he has is a slight head tilt as he watches intently.

We are plunged into darkness for a second

before bright lights illuminate the area we're in. The ship sinks further into the ground, revealing a large garage. Hundreds of ships line the walls, tucked neatly into cubbies of varying sizes. We move towards an open spot and our platform rotates so we are facing outwards and slides us into the hole.

"Landing procedure is complete," Aurelia says. "Good luck."

"What do you mean, good luck?" I ask.

"I do not know how the Khuvex will react."

"Can you protect us? You have those guns."

"My weapons systems are disabled due to the docking procedure," she replies.

"Awesome," I say as sarcastically as I can muster.

"Is it awesome?" Zaltas asks. "It seems like a problem to me."

"No, I was being... nevermind."

I shake my head at him and he leaves the flight deck.

We get to the cargo bay, and Zaltas lowers the ramp. I pull my backpack tightly to my shoulders and brace myself for whatever is about to come.

Four very large, very well armored, and very intimidating humanoids stand at the bottom of the ramp. They're all wearing hulking, spikey silver armor with glowing green eyes and spears taller than Zaltas are gripped in each of their hands. They stand unmoving and statuesque, waiting for us to make the first move.

Instinct screams at me to grab the knife from my ankle and ready myself for a fight, but I take my cues from Zaltas and hold steady. Zaltas walks down the ramp and stops several feet in front of the armored creatures. He keeps his hands to his side, clearly ready to grab a weapon if necessary, but his posture stays relaxed.

I want to hide behind him, it seems the wise thing to do. I'm definitely outgunned here, they all have a couple of feet on me in height, and probably a couple hundred pounds too, but I step beside Zaltas and stand up straight. I try to exude confidence, like Zaltas, but it's one hundred percent faked. I would be fucked if anything goes sideways. I know it, and I'm sure they do too.

Zaltas shifts himself slightly, putting himself between me and them just barely. Enough where he could leap in front of me almost instantly. It's at this moment I notice the smell drifting off of him. Sweet like vanilla with a hint of wood, maybe cedar. My mind wanders at the worst time and I snap myself back to reality. How have I never noticed that smell before, it's wonderful?

My thoughts are interrupted as Zaltas says, "I am Zaltas. This is Riley."

"Aurelia informed us that Ditharan has died," one creature says in a booming, robotic voice.

"Yes," Zaltas says without further explanation.

"She said he was killed in glorious combat with the Skeldi and that you avenged his and the other's deaths."

"Yes," Zaltas says again.

"You are the new captain of Aurelia?" Another of the creatures asks in an identical voice.

"Yes," Zaltas says again, the sound of his voice hinting that he's tired of them asking questions they already know the answer to.

"You succeeded where Ditharan failed and eliminated the Skeldi pirates?"

"That has been made clear. Do you have any questions that you do not already know the answer to?" Zaltas asks.

The four creatures look at each other, then back at Zaltas before the first says, "No."

"Okay, what now then?"

"Welcome to Dexterion," a third silver creature says as cheerfully as a robotic voice can.

The four of them turn in unison and march out of a door at the side of the landing pad. It seals shut behind them and they leave the two of us alone with the sounds of machinery whirring.

"Umm," I say, the adrenaline of a coming fight still coursing through me. It's hard to think straight. I thought for sure shit was about to go down. "What?"

"That's a very well-thought-out question," Zaltas replies.

"Were those robots?"

"No, Khuvex in armor. Probably, anyway."

"Probably?"

"This is new to me, too."

"Oh, right. You're handling this a lot better than I am, you know?"

"How so?"

"You don't seem concerned about being in a weird place... and time."

"I am concerned. There is nothing that can be done about it at the moment, though. So worrying about it is unnecessary."

"Okay buddy, wish I could have that mindset."

"It will be fine, selkin. Do not worry. Now, we need to find whoever is in charge and figure out how to track down that Alphur. Aurelia informed me they do not know what that is, that makes it much more dangerous."

Zaltas heads towards a different door than the one the guards disappeared into. This one is much more ornate and welcoming. I can't bring myself to move. The fear of the unknown has gripped me again and I'm suddenly very nervous. Being in the wilderness on that other planet was one thing. Sure, there was orange grass, purple trees, and weird monsters, but surviving in the wild doesn't really change. Food, water, shelter. That's all you have to concern yourself with. Well, and not being eaten by something.

An alien city, though. Social systems, judging eyes, potential pitfalls in speaking to others, accidental insults, direct insults, laws and rules. There's so much that can be different and so many things I could mess up by accident. I could say the wrong word to someone and wind up in prison for a decade. That could happen in different countries on Earth. I can't imagine how it'll be on an entirely different planet.

Zaltas looks over his shoulder at me and says, "Come on, selkin. We have a city to explore." A flash of a smile crosses his face and I feel instantly at ease. I swear that man has some spell on me, but I'm not sure I even care. I feel a connection with him that is completely unexplainable and makes no sense to me, but it's there. I feel like he has my back, no matter what.

I hurry up to him and stop at his side. He looks down at me and I can see the burning passion in his eyes. The desire and heat coming off of that gaze threatens to melt me on the spot.

CHAPTER EIGHT

ZALTAS

Try as I might, I cannot seem to tear my eyes away from her. She is really the most beautiful thing I have ever seen in all of my many travels and all of my years. The desire for her runs hot through my body and our connection grows stronger with every passing moment. The thread connecting us is thicker and thicker and I cannot help but wonder if she feels it, too.

Especially after we had sex on Aurelia. The thread is more of a cord now. The foundation is forged completely and sturdy. I cannot get the image of her body on top of mine out of my head. I desire it again. I want to give her more pleasure. I want to make her feel everything she could ever need to feel. I want to taste her, but she did not allow me to do that. I will make sure next time I do.

A smile spreads across her face and I turn

my attention back to the door in front of us. I have been to many cities that are foreign to me and while there have been problems before, most of the time if you keep to yourself and do not interfere with others, things go smoothly. I will have to stick close to Riley. I suspect that Khuvex and Scovein are one and the same. Aurelia said I was Khuvex when we first met, but that could have been a reading error.

If that is the case, assuming we have not gone in a different direction over a couple thousand years, which is possible, we should be relatively safe in the city. Regardless, I will make sure Riley is safe. My selkin.

The door splits in the middle and slides off to each side, opening into a small room. A panel on the wall lists dozens of floors with dozens of subsections. The panel spans from floor to ceiling. It must be a power lift. I guess that technology has not advanced as much as one would think.

"Is this an elevator?" Riley says, stepping to my side. She lightly places her hand on my forearm, and I am momentarily distracted by her soft touch. The warmth emanating gently from her hand sends a tingle through my body from the spot she is touching.

"An elevator is a thing that takes you up and down," she says.

"Yes, it is a power lift," I reply, regaining my composure. It is funny how such a tiny creature could have so profound of an effect on me. Though, I have always longed to find my mate and heard from others about how you undoubtedly know and it is undeniable. I would move the very cosmos for her, and she does not even know it.

We step into the power lift and the doors seal shut behind us. A pleasant feminine voice says, "You are docked at pad ZZ289."

"ZZ289," Riley whispers to herself.

Amidst the far too many buttons on the panel is a slightly larger one that says 'surface'. I reach out to press it and Riley quickly pushes it before I can. She beams up at me and watches the numbers on a display tick by as the power lift moves us through the complex.

Being in this close proximity to her, in this tiny compartment, is almost unbearable. I can smell the scent coming off of her. Lavender and sweet cream. My favorite combination of scents. I want to have her, every inch of her. I want to bury myself inside of her, give her everything I have, and make her yearn for nothing.

A trilling noise interrupts my thoughts and causes my hardening cock to soften slightly as I am brought back to the current situation.

That is good. These pants are too tight for any of that and they do little to hide my arousal. I shift slightly, trying to mask my bulge as much as possible, but it's almost impossible to conceal. These pants are for ease of movement and battle, not comfort and fashion.

I look towards Riley and make eye contact with her wide-eyed stare as her eyes snap up to mine. She grins suspiciously and turns her attention back to the now opening doors. Was she looking at my cock?

Bright light greets us as the doors slide open and we step out onto a white stone-paved pathway. An uncountable number of people are walking by and sitting around the vast courtyard. Riley gasps quietly. Green, vibrant trees shade most of the courtyard, and Khuvex and many other species lounge on the benches under them. Golden lamp posts rise from the ground in equal spacing throughout the entire area, each of them off at the moment.

Four paths intersect in the center of the courtyard, one leading towards us and the landing pads, the others leading off in different directions towards the city. Riley is wide-eyed and looking around in every direction. Her gaze is dripping with curiosity. I feel some of the same. I recognize the Khuvex from the other planet, but I do not recognize many of the other species.

Most of the people around are Khuvex, but several other species are dotted amongst them. A group of Nuldarians walks by, their orange patterned skin and tall lanky bodies hard to miss amidst the sea of others. They look much the same as in my time. A distant cousin of the Green Ones. If I can find a lab staffed by Nuldarians, they would be the best shot at getting home. They are just as intelligent as Green Ones and can figure out any problem.

The entire scene is borderline overwhelming. I like to think of myself as sociable, but being in this situation and having so little information is hard to handle. I should have quizzed Aurelia on more things instead of jerking off in the shower.

That memory suddenly came flooding back, the look on Riley's face. She knew what I was doing. I cannot help but chuckle. The embarrassment was there, but it was fleeting. What is done is done and there is no point in dwelling on it.

"What are you laughing at," Riley asks, still scanning the area with great interest.

"Nothing," I say.

"Well, what now?"

"We find whoever is in charge and see if

we can track down the Alphur. Hopefully, get some help to take it down."

"If those guards were what the Khuvex normally look like in a battle, they should be very capable."

"I would think so."

A tall, thin blue woman walks by us. She has her five sets of arms tucked neatly behind her as she passes. Riley stares and her eyes follow her closely. The woman notices and smiles down at Riley, waving two of her right arms as she goes by. Riley waves back and returns the smile.

"What is that?" She asks me quietly.

"I do not know," I say.

Riley makes a thoughtful noise and looks out at the crowd again. She gasps loudly and I try to see what she was looking at, but she takes off running.

"Riley, wait,ten-foot" I say, but she's several yards ahead of me already.

She weaves through the throng of people quickly and mumbles out several apologies as she bumps into a few of them. She's much smaller than a lot of them and I have to struggle a bit more to get through.

Finally, clear of the crowd, I find Riley standing in front of another female human sitting on a bench.

Riley says something I cannot hear, and the human on the bench shakes its head. A weird flicker rolls across its body and the hairs on the back of my neck stand up. I carefully approach the two and take Riley by the hand, holding it firmly, and peer down at whatever creature is before us.

"What is going on?" I ask Riley, not breaking eye contact with the creature.

"I thought it was another woman, er, human woman. She said she's not," Riley says, unable to hide the disappointment in her voice.

A broad and short purple man sits on the bench next to the creature that looks like a human woman, and I watch cautiously as the human's skin trembles and morphs into a short, stout, purple female. Shapeshifters, that is unsettling.

"Um, well, thanks anyway," Riley says as she backs away. She squeezes my hand tightly and pulls me with her. Once we are out of earshot, she whispers to me, "I didn't know shapeshifters were a thing."

"I did not either," I say. I had heard stories but never encountered one. It is unsettling.

"They didn't speak, which I thought was

weird. I asked if she was from Earth and then if she was human and she just shook her head at me and smiled constantly. Very creepy."

"That is disturbing," I say, glancing back over my shoulder at the now empty bench.

We walk out of the courtyard and head down a random street. The roads are lined with shops of all sorts, selling every variety of item you could imagine. Weapons, armor, food, clothes, guns, beds, drinks, and several things I have never seen before.

Riley stops in front of one of the shops, a metal bikini is on display on a mannequin. She cocks her head to the side and looks back at me.

"What would this protect against?" She asks, turning back to the mannequin.

"Errant seed, I suppose?" I say.

"Ew, Zaltas, why?" She shakes her head.

"I do not think it's meant for protection."

"The whole window is full of armor. Why wouldn't it be?" She asks, motioning towards the assortment of armor on the mannequins.

I point up at the sign above the door and smirk as her eyes follow my finger.

"Sextraterrestrials?" She says slowly.

Riley laughs, "I was trying to figure out

why armored pants would be crotchless."

"Well, now you know why they are."

Riley laughs again. This time it's followed by a snort before she says, "Could you imagine the sound. CLANG CLANG CLANG CLANG."

That imagery is too much for me, and I burst into laughter too.

A diminutive red-skinned man followed by a towering green female walks out of the door as Riley thrusts into the air, saying 'clang' again. Both of them have discreet brown packages tucked under their arms. The man shuffles the package under his other arm and the distinct rattle of metal can be heard.

Riley stops what she's doing and her face turns a bright red as she turns her back to the couple. The woman drapes her arm over the man's shoulders and they retreat silently down the sidewalk with their sex armor in hand.

"I can't..." Riley wheezes out before she laughs again. She buries her head into my chest and laughs hysterically into me. I can feel the dampness of her tears streaming down my side and I laugh again, too. Although I feel a little bad for the couple that was just looking for a good time; Riley's laughter is infectious and I cannot stop.

She throws her arms around my waist and presses herself deep into me as her shoulders heave with laughter. I put my arms across her back and hold her tightly as both of our chuckles fade. The sense of hilarity fades quickly into something much more sensual. I can almost see the tension between us in the air. It hangs like a heavy fog surrounding us.

Riley slowly releases my waist, hand trailing slowly across my sides as I release my grip on her. The urge to caress her back is too great, and I let my fingers gently run up her back. Our eyes lock and the burning desire in hers is unmistakable. I feel like she is going to drag me into this store and buy us our own armor.

Thoughts of the Alphur penetrate my thoughts and bring me back to the problem at hand. We really need to find some help and track it down. It has only been a couple of days, so it should not have done much damage, but the longer we wait, the worse things will be.

I am enjoying this time with Riley far too much. I should not allow us respite, but push ahead. It is hard, though. I want to please her and make sure she is comfortable. Perhaps easing into things will be best in the long run. There will be danger and difficulty soon enough. I do not desire to put her in the path of it, so hopefully I can find somewhere safe for her here. She can wait while I dispatch the Alphur.

Our eyes lock and thoughts of the Alphur melt away.

CHAPTER NINE

RILEY

I have half a mind to drag him in there and buy our own sets of armor. When in Rome and all of that. Our eyes linger on one another for what feels like forever. I just now noticed how blue they are. Deep and inviting, like pools of water at the bottom of a long drop. Refreshing and inviting, ready to ease your pain during a hot day.

His scent hits me again, further inviting me into him. The smell is like a drug to me. I can't get enough of it. It's at this moment that I realize... I do want him. All that he has to offer. Powerful, caring, huge, enjoys my humor, smells amazing, sexy as anyone I've ever seen. What's not to want?

My fingers find their way to his chiseled-from-granite forearm and I stroke it gently before bringing myself back to reality. We're in the middle of the street in a completely alien city. What am I going to do? Try to take him right here on the sidewalk?

I return my hands to myself and ask, "So, where to now? Can we go into some stores?"

"We do not have the time. We have lingered too long as it is. The Alphur is out there and very dangerous. We need to find some help," he says rather unconvincingly.

I take the tone of his voice as an invitation to press the matter further.

"Just one store, then we can. Neither of us have been here before. It will just take a couple of minutes. We need to ask for directions anyway, right?"

Zaltas grunts thoughtfully and says, "You are right, I get to choose the store."

"Okay," I say. I really wanted to check out some of the food shops or maybe a clothing store, but I have a sneaking suspicion we will be looking at weapons.

Zaltas motions for me to follow, and we hurry across the street to a shop with several mannequins on display. This time they are fully-clothed. The door slides open as he steps up to it and I run inside after him.

The interior of the shop is much, much

larger than I expected. The outside looks like any other shop on a town square. Glass display windows and a singular door. The neighboring stores were only about twenty feet away, but instead of going straight into the store, we were met with a staircase that went up one story. The back of the building stretched hundreds of feet and could easily fit Aurelia inside.

Display after display of clothing was scattered in every direction with seemingly no rhyme or reason. All shapes and sizes of mannequins were set out, decked in the latest fashion trends. Cylindrical rooms with doors on the front were seated in the center of each sectioned off area of the store. The lights shift from warm to cool colors as we wander past each display. I'm guessing to simulate how the clothing would look in the environment it was made for.

The strangest thing is that there is not a single shelf with any clothing on it. No price tags, no checkout counters, no employees. Just the mannequins and the cylinders. It would have been creepy if not for the vast amount of people perusing the store.

I watch a ten-foot tall man with deep blue skin and massive yellow horns coming halfway down his back approach one of the cylinders. It stretches to accommodate his height and width, then the door on the front opens. I steal a glance at the interior, and it appears completely empty. Zaltas joins me and we stand silently watching.

The door on the cylinder closes and, after a minute or so, reopens, revealing the man in a very sporty-looking green jacket with loose black pants and massive green boots. He looks down at his body and then notices us staring at him and flashes a confused and slightly annoyed look at me.

Not knowing what else to do, I flash a smile at him, paired with a nod and a thumbs up. His scowl turns into a smile and he goes back to looking at his new outfit.

"Looks better on the mannequin," Zaltas whispers to me before going further into the store.

"He looks lovely," I say with a grin. "Why did you want to come in here? I figured you'd take me to an armor store or weapons or something."

"I like clothes," he says simply.

I grin at him again, "You wear so much, I should have known."

Zaltas looks down at his barely covered chest and shrugs at me.

"This is battle attire, I'm a much nicer dresser usually."

"Oh, sure."

"You are one to talk, Ms. Jumpsuit."

"Hey, this is my work outfit."

"Your only outfit."

"Oh, right. I should probably find some new clothes somehow, in case this one tears."

"More jumpsuits?"

"Oh, hush," I say with a head shake. Shirtless, leather pants, and boots over here, making fun of my clothes. Although, the view his current outfit gives isn't something I'm going to complain about.

"What kind of currency do they take here?"

"What makes you think I know that? Do you just enjoy hearing me say 'I do not know'?" Zaltas says with a stern face that quickly cracks as he smirks at me.

"I keep forgetting, you have more of an idea what is going on than I do."

"Not really," he says as he circles a mannequin.

The mannequin is four-armed and wearing a black leather jacket with buckles hanging off the sides. The pants are tight-fitting but not as much as the one Zaltas is currently wearing. Large black boots with thick soles and more buckles finish the outfit. A typical 'bad boy' outfit. Zaltas would look kind of hot in it.

"That's a style on Earth," I say. It's interesting seeing something so familiar on a mannequin trillions of miles and thousands of years from home.

"That is strange," he replies.

"I agree."

"Maybe humans have had more influence on the universe than we know."

"That's comforting. I could still get a taste of home occasionally."

Zaltas glances over at me and a thoughtful look crosses his face. He heads over to the cylinder and it adjusts itself to his size and the door opens. I stand outside the door as he enters, and it closes behind him. After a few moments, he reappears decked out in the same outfit on the mannequin.

He flexes his arms and stretches them in various directions before doing a couple of squats.

"You pleased with yourself?" I say, rolling my eyes at him, clearly showing off his physique.

"What do you mean?" He asks, curling his right arm in so tightly I can see his muscles bulging through the jacket and straightening his left arm out to the ceiling. He tilts his body to the right, taking on a stereotypical bodybuilder pose.

"You are clearly showing off."

"I am not. I am testing the flexibility of the material."

Zaltas turns his back to me and bends over fully. He touches both of his hands flat to the ground and peers at me from between his legs.

"Yeah, okay Zaltas," I say with another eye-roll, but I was really trying to not look at that glorious booty on display before me.

"What do you think?" He asks.

I look back at him, he's still bent over.

His question is returned with silence on my end. I get an eye-full this time, though.

"Well?" He asks, shaking his ass side to side.

"Yes, yes, you have a great ass," I say, purely mesmerized.

"I meant the pants," Zaltas says, still staring at me between his legs.

"Oh… they fit you nicely," I say.

"Thank you," he says, returning to the upright position. Zaltas retrieves a neatly wrapped package from the side of the machine and turns it over in his hands.

"Wait, how did you buy that?"

"They still use credits. My vambrace has mine stored on it," he says, waving his armored arm in front of him. "It said I need to get an AICC to avoid future problems."

"What is that?"

"No idea."

"I guess we should both get them. And I need to earn some credits somehow so I can buy new clothes."

"What would you want?"

Suddenly put on the spot, I scan the room quickly and lay eyes on a pretty basic outfit. It's a pair of shorts, a black tank-top with a red jacket and a pair of heels. The heels seem like a bad idea, but the boots I've got on now are sturdy enough to last a while. I wonder if you have to buy the complete outfit at once.

"I like that," I say, pointing at the mannequin in the tank-top and shorts.

"Easy to move in and stylish, except for the shoes."

"I'd just wear my boots."

"I will purchase it for you."

"No, you don't have to do that. I'll figure something out. This jumpsuit is really tough and will last a while."

"I am insisting," Zaltas says before taking my hand and leading me to the cylinder.

He pulls me gently in front of him and stands me in front of the doors. The cylinder morphs to my size and the door opens.

"How do I pay?"

"You will need my vambrace," he says, removing it and handing it to me.

"What do I do?" I ask, but he pushes me through the door and it seals behind me.

The interior is well illuminated and a screen lights up on the wall in front of me. It has two selections. Manual and automatic. I tap manual first and a huge list of names appears before me. Words I couldn't even pronounce or recognize. I tap an arrow pointing to the left and thankfully it takes me back to the first selection. This time I select automatic.

The cylinder whirs to life as the walls rotate around me and a vibrant green light shoots across the ceiling, forming a grid. The grid slides up and down my body rapidly and the word 'human' appears on the screen with two buttons saying yes or no.

I tap on yes.

My clothes disappear from my body instantly and I shift to cover myself subconsciously.

"What the fuck," I say, my hands darting across my body.

"Please remain still," a robotic voice instructs from all around.

I fight the urge to move and stand still. Within seconds, I feel soft cloth against my skin and start to look down, but remember the machine's instructions and hold fast. My eye level shifts a few inches higher as I feel cushioning appear before my feet.

"Complete," states the machine.

Hesitantly, I glance down at myself. Red jacket, tank top, shorts, and heels. All perfectly fitting. More so than anything I have ever purchased before.

The display in front of me flashes a white light before becoming reflective, and I see myself in my new outfit. Perfectly form-fitting. I stretch my arms out to the side and do a quick squat to test the flexibility of the fabric. It hugs my every curve with each movement and offers no resistance. Absolutely incredible.

A small button flashes on the mirror that

says: 'Finish and pay.'

I tap the button, and a breakdown of the cost appears. The total flashes five hundred fifty-seven in red. Geez, I don't know how much a credit is in dollars but that seems expensive.

Turning Zaltas' vambrace over in my hand, I find a small button and press it. The lid flips open, revealing a screen with dozens of icons and meters on it. I have no idea how to use this. I need Zaltas' help.

Reaching for the door to the changing room, I notice there is no handle. I fit my fingers into the side of the door and pull on it. It doesn't budge. I give it a firmer pull and a light flashes on the display.

"Please pay before exiting. If you try to exit without payment, authorities will be called."

"Okay, then..." I say quietly, returning to Zaltas' vambrace.

This time, I notice a smaller window that says credit transfer requested. I tap on it and it shows 'five hundred fifty-seven requested,' balance available twelve million six hundred thousand and thirty-two.

"Holy shit," I whisper. Zaltas is loaded. I still feel bad letting him buy clothes for me, but not nearly as bad knowing he isn't broke.

I tap 'approve' on the vambrace and the screen in the changing room flashes 'payment received.'

"The payment method you used is outdated by four seven six three years. Obtain an AICC to avoid complications in the future. Purchase successful. Please leave," the robotic voice says.

"Wow, so thankful for my business," I say as the door slides open.

After stepping out, Zaltas comes up to me and I hand his vambrace back to him. I want to say something about how rich he is but hold my tongue. He slips the vambrace back on and looks me up and down.

"How does it feel?" He asks.

"Incredibly comfortable."

"You should do some stretching," he says, followed quickly by, "To make sure it fits properly."

"I did in the room," I say with a grin and a head shake.

"Oh, good," he says, not quite able to hide his disappointment.

A small package is at the bottom of the cylinder, and I bend down to retrieve it. I move slowly, making a show of it and ensuring Zaltas has plenty of time to get an eye-full. I can feel him watching me, and the heat of embarrassment fades quickly as satisfaction takes over. I know he's pleased with what he sees. I can feel it.

I arch my back slightly before returning to an upright position. I slip off my heels and dig through the package for my old boots. After retrieving them, I put them on and place the heels in the package.

"There, now where to?" I ask, turning towards Zaltas.

"I had hoped to ask someone for directions. I see no sign of anyone working here. It all appears automated."

"Yeah, it looks that way. Why not ask one of the Khuvex, they'd know I would think?"

Zaltas glances at the nearest Khuvex. A woman, with blue skin and a large bust, but closer to my height than Zaltas'. She's wearing a modest gray outfit hiding most of her figure and a cloak draped over her shoulders. She's quite pretty, her features are much like the other Khuvex with sharp jaws and high cheekbones. Her long black hair is tied in a utilitarian ponytail and held together with a golden clasp. Zaltas walks up to her, and I follow behind.

As we draw closer, she reaches out to

touch the clothing on the mannequin in front of her, revealing a very toned and defined arm. I bet she'd give Zaltas a run for his money in an arm-wrestling match. She rubs the fabric between her fingers delicately and makes a thoughtful noise. The mannequin is clad in almost nothing. What looks like a gold and ornate sports bra is the only thing on the mannequin's torso with a bright red and floor-length airy skirt hanging off the waist. Gold flats and a golden belt tie the look together. Much different from what she currently has on. Flaunt what you got, girl.

"Greetings," Zaltas says confidently. The Khuvex woman turns to him and looks him up and down.

"No thank you," she says, equally as confident, her voice deep and sultry.

I slip up beside Zaltas and stifle a giggle at the sudden and severe shutdown he just received. Zaltas glances down at me and shrugs. I laugh a little this time.

"We were hoping you could give us some directions," I say after a very awkward silence.

The woman looks at me and her face lights up in a smile.

"Oh, I am sorry. I thought you were after a mate. I did not realize you had one. That was distasteful of me," she says carefully.

"Thanks," I say with a hint of embarrassment. I'm far from embarrassed about Zaltas, but we haven't even discussed what we 'were' exactly, and being labeled a mate so casually was odd to me. Though it felt kind of right.

"You two are wonderfully paired. Made for each other, it seems. I can tell your bond is strong. Why do you not have tattoos, though?" She asks, looking at Zaltas.

Zaltas shrugs and says, "Not a Scovein thing to get tattoos."

"Scovein?"

"Yes?"

The woman laughs. "You have a wonderful sense of humor about you. Where do you need direction?"

She looks at me expectantly and I say the first thing that pops into my mind, "Take us to your leader."

The woman tilts her head and says, "I have not the time, but I can give you guidance."

"That is fine," Zaltas says, as I feel my face turn red.

"The Baron can be found at the Tycliandrian Palace. Outside of this store, you will make a left and journey down the road until you come to the eighth intersection. Go right and then take the third left. You will see the palace. It is golden and magnificent. Much like the Baron," she trails off and a shadow of a smile haunts her face.

"Thank you," Zaltas replies.

The woman snaps back to reality and says, "You are most welcome, safe journeys."

"Same to you," Zaltas says as we depart.

As we walk down the street, I notice the Khuvex females more and more. They don't stand out nearly as much as the men, because of their size. I hadn't really noticed them before because of the wide array of species present, many of them much more odd-looking than the blue and tattoo-covered Khuvex. Seeing them standing beside their male counterparts made me feel even more confident about Zaltas. Their size difference seemed of little concern to anyone else. Granted, they were probably a lot stronger than me, but I feel like I could bring my own strength when necessary. I've held it together this long! I'm strong in my own way.

Almost every building on the streets has a shop of some sort at the base. With the massive amounts of people wandering about the streets, I'd imagine the tops of the buildings are housing. We've passed four intersections now and have been walking for almost an hour; either these cities aren't broken up into blocks or they are much larger than back on Earth.

I steal a glance upward at one of the towering spirals. I know I should have stopped walking and stepped to the side. I hate when people are walking and not paying attention, but I feel like such a tourist and it didn't even cross my mind.

Something slams into me at knee level and I almost fall to the ground. Zaltas' firm hands grasp my shoulder and steady me before I spill all over the sidewalk.

My knee is aching already, and it feels like I ran into a concrete divider. I look down to access the damage and find three eyes in the center of a dark purple face staring up at me with a venomous scowl.

"I'm so sorry," I mumble out, quite embarrassed with myself.

"It's okay, sweetie," a deep, soothing feminine voice responds from the creature below me. What I thought was a scowl was actually a smile, paired with the scrunches and squinted eyes of a scowl. The creature pats my knee gently.

I wince at the light touch, and it stops patting me immediately.

"Oh, now I've injured you, let me help,"

she says, rummaging through her tiny backpack. She retrieves a small cylinder and removes a cap from it. A light mist sprays out of it and the relief on my knee is immediate.

"Thank you," I say with the best smile I can muster amid the embarrassment.

"Be careful out there," she says, patting my leg gently again.

I watch the strange creature disappear into the crowd as she continues on her way.

"What was that? It felt like I ran into a brick wall," I say to Zaltas.

"I do not know," he replies as usual. "What is a brick wall?"

"Like a stone wall, really hard."

Zaltas makes a thoughtful noise, and we continue on our journey. I randomly bend my knee all the way back as we walk, testing the injury I had received. It still feels like nothing had even happened. I wonder what that spray was.

We take the eighth right and the tone of the street shifts abruptly. The hustle and bustle of the shops and people milling about transforms into a lively throng of festive creatures. Many of them mixed together, laughing and chattering. Music thumps from each of the buildings and the light shifts dramatically from brightly lit and sunny to dim and electric.

The attire of the patrons has gotten much more eclectic, too. Vibrant colors cover almost every person wandering the area. Some even have glowing articles of clothing on. Memories of glow sticks and music festivals come to mind.

Blue, green, purple, yellow, orange, turquoise, burgundy. Ten feet tall, three feet tall, six feet tall. Two arms, twelve arms, five arms. Tentacles, hands, spikes, claws. All manner of species are mixed in a crowd that is almost hard to look at. It swirls and moves in front of me in a dazzling spectacle. I reach out for Zaltas and take hold of his hand to ground myself. He clutches my hand and leads me through the crowd. The warmth and strength coming from him makes me feel calmer and we wind through the crowd.

Hucksters stand by every doorway, trying to entice people to come inside, shouting all kinds of promises. The perfect night, the perfect man, the perfect woman, the perfect drink. Everything is available to anyone willing to step inside.

"We've got Baniqu, best outside of Zurak!"

"Food inspired by the Alkaline and drinks to match!

"Slyk bets and competitions. Winner takes all. Massive prize pools!"

"Sedation teases, come lose control and let your ladies and gentlemen show you unparalleled pleasure!"

"Chili pepper seasoned Zarthes. Real chili pepper from Earth!"

At the mention of Earth, I stop and feel the urge to go talk to the large, deep blue man with curly horns outside of a seedy-looking dive bar. Zaltas stops when I do and shoots me an inquisitive look.

The deep blue man sees me looking and perks up a little. Apparently, it's been a slow night for him.

"Real chili pepper straight from Earth," he says again, "We've also got fresh sliced bananas!"

The word bananas catches Zaltas' attention and he turns his gaze towards the man. I can see the gears turning in his head as he debates what to do.

After a moment's consideration, he says something I don't catch.

"What?" I can barely hear over the music and crowd.

"I love banana too," he shouts, "but we will have to wait."

"He said from Earth!" I say loudly.

Zaltas looks at me thoughtfully and says, "We can come back after we see the Baron. He will probably have more answers for you than this one." He motions towards the man by the door with his finger and shakes his head.

The man by the door looks visibly sad and moves his attention away from us to yell about chili peppers at someone else looking in his direction.

"Okay," I say. I'm a little disappointed, but I'm sure that guy has no clue about Earth. He was probably just told by his boss to say that.

We take the third left off of the party street and the lighting changes again, this time becoming bright and warm. The buildings on the road shimmer with a golden glow and the sounds of the previous street become muted and distant. After several feet, they disappear completely. The sounds of birds, or some other creature, chirping and singing fill the area. A large mixture of aliens wander this area too, but they're all dressed in shiny and professional-looking attire.

Well, as professional-looking as armor can be. They all move with a purpose, and hardly any of them linger. This road feels almost as busy as the last but in a more determined way. Most of the people here are clearly busy and have jobs to do.

At the end of the street is a large building, though not as tall as the surrounding spires, it is no less impressive. The golden spirals coming off of each corner perfectly complement the white walls surrounding the building. A huge golden gate is raised leading into the complex. It has a massive section of the city sectioned off with nothing but air above it. The street dead ends in the palace and we stop outside of the gates. A line has formed, people with business inside, and we take our place at the end.

Several guards check in with each person in line and move through them quickly. We had at least twenty people in front of us, but waited for less than five minutes. The guards were like the ones at the landing pad. Hulking, spiky silver armor with green glowing eyes and deep robotic voices. They carried the same spears as the other.

"What business do you have at the palace?" One guard asks in his metallic voice, gaze flicking between me and Zaltas.

"It is a long story," Zaltas says, "but we come from a… distant place and have news of a threat to the system."

"What place do you hail from and what is this threat you speak of?"

"Sulrast, and an Alphur has escaped in

this system."

"Sulrast? Alphur?" The guard replies with disbelief.

"That is correct. The Alphur is a great danger and must be hunted down and executed immediately."

The guard shifts uneasily which makes me feel uneasy, too. This isn't going well. I don't know what I expected. Thinking about it now, our story is pretty unbelievable. Should we even mention we're from several thousand years ago? Probably not. The guard motions towards a booth attached to the gate.

Two other guards show up, one of them in golden armor instead of silver and with red eyes. A supervisor?

"What is the problem here?" The supervisor asks.

"They say they are from Sulrast and an Alphur is here," the first guard says.

A metallic grunt of doubt echoes from the golden guard.

"So, you came from a planet that was destroyed three thousand years ago, chasing after a mythical creature?" The supervisor asks Zaltas.

Zaltas stares blankly at the golden guard.

Pangs of guilt rush through me, and I want to comfort Zaltas. Knowing Earth was still out there kept me a little sane. I couldn't imagine how I'd feel if it was completely gone. I reach out to him, but pause and stand still. I don't want to antagonize the guards accidentally.

"It appears that way," Zaltas finally replies, voice steadier than I expected.

Two of the guards press something on the side of their helmets and the third remains motionless.

"Well, what do we do?" One of the silver guards asks.

After a few seconds of the guards looking at each other quietly, the same guards asks again, "What if they are telling the truth, though?"

More quietly staring at one another followed by the guard saying, "That could be the case but the... oh, right." He quickly taps something on the side of his helmet and all three of them look at each other back and forth in silence.

Finally, all three guards tap the side of their helmets and the golden one says, "You will be allowed entry. The Baron will hear your concerns. Follow me."

"Thanks," I whisper to the two silver guards as we pass them. The one that apparently forgot to mute himself gave me a little wave and turned to the thirty people that had lined up behind us.

On the other side of the white walls are beautiful gardens with a trickling stream winding through. Small bridges cross the stream in various places, with one main path leading towards the main doors of the palace. Dotted throughout the garden are tables and chairs with many aliens sitting at them and discussing who knows what business. Most of them seem in pleasant moods and sip from large metal cylinders.

Identical, incredibly short men in neatly pressed suits rush between the tables. We pass by a couple of them as they scurry about and as far as I can tell, they are all exact copies of one another. There don't appear to be any discernible features. At least a dozen of them are running between the tables and smaller side doors on the palace.

Everyone in the garden is immaculately dressed, and I feel completely out of place in my red jacket and shorts. Zaltas doesn't seem too bothered by his attire and moves coolly down the pathway, head high and looking around at all the figures in the garden. A look of wonder crosses his face a couple of times. Clearly, there are some things he's never seen either.

One nearby table has two blobs with creepy human-like faces, who appear well-dressed as far as a blob can be, a cat person, and what appears to be just an ordinary horse. The horse has a lavender bow tie and green, ornate cufflinks above its hooves. A conical top hat sits on its head and it appears to be wearing glasses of some kind. I watch in awe as the cup in front of it lifts unaided to its , and the horse takes a drink before the cup sets itself neatly back in place. The whole situation is comical and I start to giggle but the horse shoots me a dirty look and I maintain a straight face as we head up the stairs to the palace.

The interior of the palace is just as ornate and golden as the exterior. Several groups of aliens meander about the massive entryway, but not nearly as many as were in the garden. The short, identical aliens quickly meet up with groups and lead them down side corridors. I try to take in all the details of the palace, but there are so many it's hard to know what to even focus on. A grand stairway is the focal point in the room. It leads up to a second floor then begins to spiral up and out of sight.

The hallways branching off to the side have large black doors on them and all are closed. To either side of the staircase are smaller doors leading who knows where, but that's where the little aliens are coming from.

I lean in close to Zaltas and feel completely safe as he drapes an arm over me. His scent overtakes me and I breathe him in deeply. We stand together and wait for whatever is to come.

CHAPTER TEN
ZALTAS

Feeling Riley pressing against me makes me feel more whole than I have in a long time. Perhaps ever in my life. Having her present with me makes me feel complete. I want to steal her way to the far reaches of space and live out my days being able to make her happy. The Alphur seems like a distant concern compared to her.

But, it is not. It is pressing and could decimate many systems. Alphur hold centuries-long grudges too. Chances are it will not forget us and will try to hunt us down, eventually.

Soon, selkin, soon we will be at peace and have nothing to answer to but each other.

One of the tiny creatures scurrying about approaches us and waits patiently for us to acknowledge it. I glance down at it, waiting to hear what it has to say.

"Sir and ma'am. My name is Lukto. If you will, follow me," the small creature says in a silky voice.

It quickly moves to one of the doors lining the hallway before I can respond. Riley and I glance at each other before following behind it. Another one of the small creatures zips past us quickly, saying a word of apology. Riley looks between it and the one in front of us inquisitively. They are completely identical in every way, face shape, color, clothing, mannerisms, movement, and voice.

The door in front of Lukto opens with a pleasant creak as it pushes its entire body against it. It moves slowly, but Lukto does not appear to be struggling. It seems almost deliberately dramatic.

A brightly lit, and golden of course, room greets us on the other side of the door. I have grown a little weary of the gold everywhere. It was dazzling at first but has become repetitive and honestly is starting to feel tacky.

"Greetings," a deep, gravely voice booms from atop an ornate throne. I shake my head at the sight of more gold, as the figure is also clad in golden armor. He does not have a helmet on at least, so his voice is not the grating robotic sound of the guards.

"I am Baron Parinien Talintherineclanica-linethes the Twelfth. You may address me as my full name, or as most prefer, just the Baron," he continues. The Baron stands and bows curtly before approaching us. I return the slight bow and nudge Riley as she stands wide-eyed.

Riley shrugs at me and whispers, "What?"

"Bow," I say quietly.

"Oh."

Riley bows deeply, head going almost down to her knees. The Baron appears absolutely delighted by her gesture and approaches her first.

"Ah, such a pleasure seeing the old ways. Traditions are important. We must not forget that," he says and bows deeply in return to her.

"My name is Zaltas, and this is Riley," I say.

"A pleasure," the Baron replies, still looking at Riley.

"Nice to meet you," Riley says, confusion marking her face.

The Baron leans in close to her and turns his head to look at me. He eyes me up and down and then straightens up and looks back down at Riley.

"Such a strong connection between the

two of you, I can almost see it," he says off-handedly.

Riley opens her mouth to speak but closes it quickly as the Baron continues, "So, a human, and you are a Scovein, hmm?"

He approaches me slowly, metal-clad feet clanking loudly on the white stone floor.

"You have heard of the Scovein?" I ask, caught off-guard by the question. Everyone has acted like we were completely unknown. The guard knew of Sulrast, but past that I have heard no mention of my people.

"As I should, Scovein are the Khuvex's ancestors."

The Baron lifts his head up and peers down his nose at me, revealing an intricate network of tattoos running up his dark-blue meaty neck. He stretches his arms out to his side and lowers them slowly. I have no idea what he is doing but cannot help picturing a falcian doing its mating ritual. Wings outstretched, orange neck puffed up, and dancing. The only thing that is missing is the wild calls of a horny female swooping in to take him.

"Hmm." The Baron returns to a normal posture and looks at me expectantly.

After a few seconds of awkward silence,

I finally ask what is on both mine and Riley's mind, "What are you doing?"

"I was under the impression that was the traditional Scovein greeting. Maybe my studies are lacking."

"I suppose they are a bit. I have never seen any of my people do that."

The Baron glares at me with an intensity that makes me brace myself for combat. I watch as his arm moves back and ready myself for action. The tense mood is quickly broken by a wheezing laugh and a firm slap on the shoulder from the Baron.

"Yes, yes. Well, I have made a fool of myself in front of an ancestor. Such is life."

"By ancestor, you mean we evolved into the Khuvex?"

"Yes. A very, very distant ancestor. Thousands of years, if the records are to be believed. After my display a moment ago, I am not sure if they should be believed."

"You seem to be taking the appearance of a several thousand year old person quite well," Riley says.

"Ah, right. I suppose that is a good question to start with on my part. How did you get here?" The Baron asks as he walks towards a...

golden table next to the throne with several comfortable chairs and a view out a massive window. "Come, sit and speak with me."

We take seats opposite the Baron and after appreciating the cushioning on the chair for a moment, I say, "A wormhole."

The Baron makes a thoughtful noise and says, "A wormhole? It took you this far into the future? I had only heard about them going a decade at the most."

"Apparently they go much further than that," I say.

"It would seem that way. Are you looking for respite? You are more than welcome to stay in the palace as long as you need."

"The main reason for us finding you is for assistance in capturing and executing a rogue Alphur that made its way through the wormhole."

Riley clears her throat beside me and shoots me a dirty look.

"Of course, we would be happy to take you up on the offer of lodging, too," I add.

"An Alphur? I have read stories of them, heinous creatures, but a singular entity is no match for the Khuvex. This system is one of the most secure in the galaxy."

I almost mention the dead Khuvex and

the Skeldi but decide to hold my tongue.

"Although, things have become tense lately with the Skeldi pushing into our borders. The loss of Ditharan, Dytharan, Taceyn, Blyran, Stereien, and Nulraian is devastating news to be sure."

The Baron stares wistfully out of the inordinately large window beside us. The look of regret haunting his face appears to be genuine, and I believe he might actually be honorable and trustworthy.

"The Alphur is not to be underestimated," I say after sufficient silence. "I have seen them commandeer entire armies for their purposes. This one left with a group of those Skeldi."

The Baron mutters something and says, "Off with the Skeldi? That could be problematic. Tell me, why would the Skeldi not just kill the Alphur? They have a penchant for that."

"They are almost completely invincible. I am not sure if there is any weapon in the current time that would even destroy one, short of launching it into a star. I have this from my time, though," I say as I slowly slide the Melt Knife from my belt and place it on the table. Two guards step from behind the throne at the sound of the metal sliding across the sheath and stare in our direction.

The Baron picks up the knife and analyzes it in his hands. His fingers wander the length of the blade and delicately touch the hilt before finding the trigger and resting upon it.

"I would advise you not to press that," I say cautiously. It would obliterate everything in this room. The blade is coded to only be activated by a Scovein or Green One's hands, but I do not know if a Khuvex would count as Scovein in this case.

The Baron places the blade in front of me and asks, "How is it capable of killing an unkillable creature?"

"Activating it releases a stream of energy equivalent to one second of power generated from an active star."

The Baron's eyes grow wide and he eyes the blade even more inquisitively than before.

"Fascinating."

"And deadly."

"Even being indestructible, how can a singular creature generate enough threat to warrant a full military response?" The Baron asks, still unconvinced.

"It has telepathic capabilities unlike anything you have experienced. It corrupts and penetrates the minds of any creature it is near, particularly bloodthirsty species."

"Like the Skeldi," The Baron says thoughtfully.

"I can attest firsthand to its powers," Riley says quietly. "It held sway over me and had I not been in an extreme situation already, I don't think I could have resisted it."

The Baron clicks his tongue and drums his fingers on the table for a few seconds, then says, "Lukto."

"Yes, sir," Lukto says, appearing beside the Baron out of seemingly nowhere.

"Show these two to one of the guest quarters," he says, adding with a smile, "Make it one of the nicer ones."

"Of course," Lukto says, motioning for us to follow it.

Riley stands and looks at me, unsure of how to proceed.

"What of the Alphur?" I ask. We cannot linger if we are not getting help here. We have to find someone that will listen.

"Let me deliberate over night and do some research. In the morning, I will give you my answer," The Baron says.

We have already burned a lot of time just

getting here. I have let myself get sidetracked by Riley. While she is worth it in every way, the danger present will only get worse.

I start to protest but decide to keep quiet. This is better than nothing.

"Thank you," Riley says as we leave the chambers.

The Baron raises a hand and disappears behind the throne.

Lukto scurries ahead of us at a surprisingly brisk pace for something with such tiny legs. Riley is moving at a light jog beside me as we wind through the hallways of the palace. The hallways are just as ornate and gold-covered as the entrance and throne room. Various works of art line the walls with statues of Khuvex men and women interspersed.

Riley makes several quiet gasps along the trip. Every so often, a massive window appears in the hallway with a view of different planets. Some kind of holo-screen I would imagine, they appear life-like and it's hard to not be drawn towards them. The one next to us shows a vast field with swaying purple grass, an orange cloudless sky, and gargantuan creatures grazing in the fields. Their mournful cries can even be heard as if they are muffled through the window. If I didn't know better, I would think we had teleported to another planet.

We pause in front of the window and watch the creatures move slowly through the field, tearing large swathes of grass out of the ground and chewing it thoughtfully. Their long necks taper up to tiny heads with small horns. Their long snouts jiggle with every chew. The cube-shaped bodies have at least a dozen thick legs supporting their frames, and I swear you can hear the thumping of their legs as they move about.

Lukto watches us, waiting patiently. He approaches the window and taps a screen near the bottom, causing one of the panes to shift upwards. The sounds of feet thudding and long cries fill the hallway along with the scent of trevelin trees and musk. It is not unpleasant, but not the best thing I have smelled.

"What?" Riley asks succinctly.

She hesitantly reaches out of the window and brushes her hand against some nearby grass. It bends under her touch and she retrieves her hand, staring at it in wonder. I am at a loss, as well. The palace did not appear large enough to house such a large enclosure. This one appears to stretch on for miles and it's the fifth one we have seen. The sky isn't the right color for this planet either, unless it has changed since we have been in the palace.

"Trade secrets," Lukto says with a grin as it closes the window again.

"You can't just let me do that and not tell me what's going on," Riley says dejectedly.

Lukto merely smiles and motions for us to follow it further down the hall. It starts around another corner.

"Apparently it can," I offer with a smirk.

"What were thos... nevermind you don't know do you?"

"Nope."

"Do you know how it works?"

"Yes, but I am not telling you."

"You liar," Riley says, shaking her head at me.

I shrug at her, and we follow behind Lukto.

CHAPTER ELEVEN

RILEY

He's just messing with me. He doesn't actually know how that works. That had to be real, right? But it couldn't be. The grass, though, I felt it. I could smell the area, I could hear the creatures. Does he know?

I stare at Zaltas expectantly as we progress down the hallways. He glances down at me for a moment, then looks back to Lukto. He's messing with me.

"How does it work?" I ask him again.

"Not telling you, unless Lukto does," Zaltas says slyly.

"And I will not," Lukto responds cheerfully.

I sigh dramatically and cross my arms in as exaggerated a way I can before putting on my best glare at Zaltas. He doesn't crack and just grins at me, causing me to break my glare and smile back.

"You don't actually know," I say.

"I might," he replies.

He doesn't.

"This will be your quarters for the night, or as long as you desire," Lukto says, pausing in front of an unnecessarily large golden door. The amount of golden surfaces in the palace was impressive at first, but is feeling gaudy. I hope everything in the room isn't gold and white. It would be nice to have some variety, but I have a sneaking suspicion it will be.

The door glides open silently and reveals a large room with several couches and what appears to be a television. A furry rug, made of no-telling-what, sits as the main centerpiece. The walls are thankfully a deep woodsy green, still with gold trim, but it's nice having some color for a change. The furniture is all dark brown with gold trim, giving a surprisingly earthy feel to the room.

"This room was furnished by Commander Zaltravian from Klektiral-3. It was the first room he stayed in at the palace," Lukto began talking about history and I feel bad for doing it, because he seems so enthusiastic, but I tune him out and look around the room.

Two brown chairs with a table between them sit in front of a stone fireplace that stretches up to the ceiling. A blue fire burns cheerfully inside, the crackle echoing through the room and the smell of burning wood mixes with a light floral scent.

I look at one couch and sigh dreamily. I'm ready to stretch out on a couch and nap, and that couch looks super soft and inviting. Lukto has been describing the history of the room for several minutes and all I can think about is getting on that couch. Preferably pushed up against Zaltas. Maybe a little teasing. Some caressing. My hand presses against the side of my neck lightly as thoughts of Zaltas and me on the couch fill my mind.

"...died right here on this couch!" Lukto says, waving a hand at the very couch I was just daydreaming about.

"What?" I ask, snapping out of my fantasy.

"She died on this couch," Lukto says, waving his hand at the couch again.

I want to ask who, but I feel bad enough for not listening to him. I don't want to make it clear that I wasn't.

"The bedroom is to the right, the left is the bathing facilities, and the rear door goes to the balcony. The pad by the door will control the view."

A bath sounds great. I wonder if they actually have a tub here. That seems like something a palace would have.

"Please, enjoy yourselves. You can call me anytime you need something," Lukto says, motioning to a pad by the door. He looks between the two of us and adds, "Whatever you need."

With that, Lukto leaves the room quickly and closes the door behind itself.

"I am relieved there are some colors in this room," Zaltas says, looking around the room.

"Me too! The gold and white was getting a little old."

Zaltas chuckles and says, "Yes it was."

"Who died on the couch?" I ask, staring at the couch that I so desperately wanted to lay on. The other couches are still nice, but this one looks so comfortable.

"Someone died on the couch?" Zaltas asks.

"Were you not listening to Lukto?"

"No, I stopped listening when it began listing the family history of the commander."

"Oh, I stopped before that," I say with a giggle. "Poor thing was just being thorough."

"To a fault."

"Be nice."

Zaltas grins and says, "I am always nice."

"Mhmm."

The room is lacking any kind of meal prep area, so we call Lukto for food. He brings us an assortment of items and we have a mini feast. Zaltas eats enough food for ten people, as I have seen him do before. I have a more modest meal that resembles steak and mashed potatoes. Lukto understood the concept of steak quickly and it tastes almost the same. The mashed potatoes took a little more explanation, but he brought me the closest I think I'll get on an alien world. It tastes mostly like plain veggie chips but mashed up and moist. Unfortunately, I forgot to mention the creamy texture added by butter and milk. At least I remembered the salt.

After eating, Zaltas and I sit on the couch next to each other. I tried to ignore that someone died on the comfortable-looking couch but could not bring myself to sit on it, so we ended up on another. It will haunt my dreams, not knowing how comfortable that other couch is.

"What now?" I ask.

Zaltas makes a thoughtful noise and glances at the door to the bathroom.

"I think I will have a bath," he says.

"A warm shower does sound nice," I say.

"I would prefer soaking in a tub with some froth and pleasant music."

"Are you going to use scented candles and have a drink too?" I ask teasingly.

"That sounds nice," Zaltas says. He gets off the couch and heads into the bathroom, stopping in the doorway to look back at me. "Well?"

"Well, what?" I ask, feigning ignorance. I know damn well what he means, and I am completely game. He messes with me, though, so I can mess with him, too.

Zaltas shrugs and disappears into the bathroom.

That didn't go as planned. I was hoping for some playful banter and a little playing dumb but he apparently wasn't having it. I sigh and go into the bathroom.

Zaltas is there, completely nude. That glorious ass is on full display for me, and he doesn't turn around as I enter. Sounds of rushing water fill my ears while steam quickly envelopes the room.The tub in front of him could hold five Scovein easily and is already mostly full of steamy water. Whatever he put in it smells just like him and is absolutely intoxicating. Vanilla with a hint of cedar.

He turns a knob on the side of the tub and the dozen faucets inside silence. I creep up behind him as slowly as I can and gently place my hand on one of his cheeks, giving it a firm squeeze.

Zaltas spins around and looks horrified by my presence. His hand quickly goes to cover his uncoverable cock. It would be comical how incapable of hiding it he was if this situation wasn't suddenly embarrassing.

"What are you doing in here?" Zaltas asks hurriedly, looking around the room in a panic.

"I thought... I thought you wanted me..." I stammer out, rapidly retreating from the room and utterly confused. Did I misread him earlier? He seemed rather clear about wanting me to join him.

My back hits the bathroom door with a quiet thud and I grope for the pad to open the door. The door slides open behind me and cool air hits my back. I step out and the door closes quickly, the warmth from the steam fading quickly.

I stare at the closed door, trying to process

what just happened. My face is still warm from embarrassment and I have no idea what to do at this point.

The door doesn't offer any guidance, so I turn away from it and peer around the room.

A quiet sliding sound from behind me signals the door opening, and I face it again. My eyes are met with Zaltas standing there completely nude, looking at me with utter confusion. His cock is on proud display in front of him and he does not try to hide it.

"What is going on?" I ask, not knowing what else to say.

"I thought we were playing a game," he replies. "You feigned ignorance, I feigned ignorance. We would end up bathing together. It sounded fun."

Apparently, he was having it and was much better at playing games than me. I don't even know what to say in response. I try to speak but nothing comes out, so I take action.

Sliding past his bulky frame, I graze his cock with my hand and stroll into the bathroom. Jacket off, boots off. I slip my tank top slowly over my head and shimmy out of my shorts. I take care to move slowly and deliberately. The desire to look back at him and relish his gaze is hard to resist, but I manage. Once my clothes are all tossed in a pile, I carefully dip a foot in the tub.

The hot water feels incredible and I can tell ultimate relaxation is near. Quiet padding grew louder behind me and Zaltas' large hands grip my waist. A shiver runs up my body at his touch and I lean back against him, feeling his stoney chest against my shoulders.

A warm, wet sensation sends another shiver up my spine as he plants a kiss on my neck. He pulls back with the slightest suction and a barely audible pop. I let out a quiet gasp, followed by an 'mmm' when he does it a couple more times. Each impact of his lips against my skin feels like a warm embrace in my soul.

I pull away from him, reluctantly, and dip myself fully into the tub. It is much deeper than I expected and once I'm seated, the water is up to my collarbone. It's wonderful. My body is conflicted as pure relaxation fights the immense arousal inside of me.

Zaltas steps into the tub in front of me and slowly settles himself down. I watch every inch of his body as it disappears into the water. The urge to move to him and mount him is almost irresistible, but this time, I'm not rushing to the finish line. I can control myself.

He lets out a satisfied sound and leans back against the walls of the tub. He's opposite of me and we look at each other quietly. The tension is almost palpable. Neither of us makes the first move and I keep waiting for him to approach me, but he leans his head against the rim of the tub and sinks further into the water. Sitting up, I could see all of his chest and then some, now just his collarbones are showing.

Unable to resist, I shimmy towards him as seductively as possible. He's trying to play it cool and not look towards me, but I see his eyes slightly open, and he's peering at me down his nose. I bet he's rock hard under the water, thrilled for what's to come.

I feel like a shark as I glide towards him through the water on the textured flooring of the tub. Hungry for my prey, ready to devour every inch of him. The throbbing in my core adds to the sensation of primal instinct guiding me towards his gifts.

Our bodies press against one another as I cozy up beside him. I'm guessing there's some kind of soap mixed in the water because the slipperiness of our skin in the water sends my body into a fit. I love that sensation. Skin gliding across skin, unimpeded and frictionless.

My fingers dive under the water, and I caress his thigh. Running down as far as I can reach and back up. With each motion, I get closer and closer to the inside of his hip. After four strokes,

I brush the inside of his 'v' with my finger and let it slide towards the base of his cock. I stop before making contact and run my hand down his thigh and back up again. This time, I connect with his cock.

Hard as a rock, just as I expected. I feel a grin slip up my face and as much as I want to tease him, I can't resist taking a handful. Fingers around his cock, I glide my hand up the entire length of his shaft. The lubrication present in the water is astounding, and the thoughts of things sliding in and out and across each other sends a wave of heat through me. My clit is already throbbing, begging to be touched and caressed.

My fingers twist gently around his head. This time I'm awarded with a quiet groan from Zaltas. He still has his head back, but he's barely hiding the fact that he's staring at me now.

Contorting myself slightly, I use my other hand to rub up and down his torso while I continue to play with his cock. My fingers wrap around the base of his head and slip back and forth under it, generating more groans from Zaltas and more pangs of desire from me.

The dips and grooves of his granite chiseled body feel heavenly as they slide under my fingers and I relish every sensation it gives me. I feel Zaltas' arm slip behind me and his hand places itself on my waist. It glides up and down my side, brushing my tit gently with each pass. I try to focus on what I'm doing to him, but his hand feels magical on my skin.

I draw myself back to his cock and slide down his shaft again. I go for his balls for a little light fondling and I'm surprised. There aren't any. I rub my hand under his cock back far enough to graze the bottom of his ass and back up. Not a thing, completely smooth. I do one more pass to be sure and this apparently feels fantastic to Zaltas. His cock jerks, tapping my forearm under the water, and he's staring at me with head raised now.

His hand wraps around my waist again and pulls me closer to him. His hand finds its way between my thighs and delicately brushes against my throbbing clit. All thoughts of his testicles, or lack thereof, disappear completely as an explosion of warmth swells inside of me. I let out an 'aww' when his hand retreats but gasp as he slides me onto his lap. His cock is pressed up against my slit, poking out from between my legs.

Zaltas' fingers dive back into the water and work their magic on my clit again. Light at first, gentle circles that increase in pressure as I get more and more aroused. I grind against his cock, up and down, with each pass he makes on my clit. I arch my back into him and let out a moan, then another gasp as one of his hands slides up my body and gropes one of my tits. He pinches my hard nipple lightly and his finger glides across my clit from side to side as his cock presses against my labia.

"Oh, oh," I try to speak, but I'm having trouble between breaths. "Zaltas, don't stop... that feels... so good."

He maintains the exact same pace and pressure, unlike most men, and sends me into an explosive climax. My body quivers on top of him as I bat his hand away and shudder. His cock tenses up between my legs as I try to pull them together and the head presses itself against my clit. I thought I had peaked but apparently not as this sent me into overdrive. Stars dazzled in my eyes as I trembled violently with his cock pressed into my folds.

Apparently, that was too much for Zaltas, too. I feel his hips buck under me, sliding his cock up and back down my slit, causing me to pull my thighs closer together. He lets out a quiet groan behind me. His cock jerks between my legs again and tenses up against my pussy. His head poking up between my thighs erupts under the water. I become vaguely lucid in the afterglow of my orgasm and quickly grab his cock under the water and give it a few squeezes and rubs while he jerks under me.

Once he's properly drained, I lean back on him and his hands find their way around my waist.

"Well, that was a fun bath," I say, tilting my head back against his chest.

"It was. I think we will need a shower now," he replies.

"Probably a good idea," I say, twisting my head to the side and planting a kiss on his cheek before climbing out of the bath.

CHAPTER TWELVE
ZALTAS

A shrill chime echoes through our chambers and I leap out of bed, scooping my blade off the table and readying myself for battle. The chime sounds again and Riley opens her eyes and glances around the room. A look of panic crosses her face when she sees me crouching by the door.

"What's going on?" She whispers. Her voice is steady, but I can tell she is struggling to maintain that. She climbs out of bed quickly and retrieves her knife from a package on the ground. My warrior selkin, I feel prideful over her but have to refocus on the situation at hand. "Is that an alarm?"

"I am not sure."

We should be safe in this palace, it appeared well fortified. The Baron could have had second thoughts on us, though.

The chime plays one more time.

Lukto's voice plays from unseen locations in the room, "Apologies, but it is drawing near breakfast time. The Baron would have you join him and hear what he has to say."

Riley sighs loudly with relief and tucks her knife away. The looming threat of battle lingers in my body briefly before I sheathe my blade and get dressed. I debate on wearing my battle attire, but choose the outfit I purchased. Riley seems to appreciate it and I like her thinking of me as a 'bad boy'.

By the entryway, the pad is lit up and I tap on the screen to accept the incoming call. Lukto is standing in the hallway on the screen and looks relieved to see me.

"Ah, good. Breakfast will be served in thirty minutes. Make your way to the throne room when you are dressed and ready."

"And how do we get to the throne room?" I ask. We turned so many corners I lost track after the tenth.

"One of me will happily assist in escorting you. Just ring when you are leaving," Lukto says before disappearing from the screen.

One of me? What does that even mean? While pondering the mystery of Lukto, Riley slips up behind me and puts her arms around my waist, squeezing me as tightly as she can manage.

"Hello, selkin," I say.

"Hi there," she says as she buries her face in my back and rubs against me. Her hair tickles, but I maintain my composure.

She releases me, and I get a good look at her. The most gorgeous being in the universe, now or thousands of years ago. My selkin. I cup her cheeks in my hands and stare at her.

"What?" She asks between squished cheeks.

"You are beautiful, the most beautiful and exquisite creature I have seen in all of my travels."

Her face turns a deep shade of red and she pulls her face out of my hands and turns away.

"Stop," she says shyly, with a smirk on her face. She looks to the ground and some of her hair spills across her face, masking it. My heart aches at the sight of her, in the best way possible.

"You need to know."

"Well, thank you," she says. She brushes her hair out of her face and behind her ear before looking up at me. My heart thumps loudly in my chest, and I wonder if she can hear it.

I draw her in close to me and we embrace each other tightly. I breathe in her scent. She smells incredible, though I miss the normal scent she has. Our bath together was laced with my normal fragrances. I use them for a reason, though.

"Last night was fun," Riley says, slightly muffled by my chest. I release her and she leans back and feigns, gasping for air before laughing.

"It was, very much so," I say with a grin. I want a repeat right now, but time is ticking down and we should probably see what the Baron's verdict is. "Let's go get breakfast and speak with the Baron."

"I am pretty hungry. You wore me out," she says, nudging me with her elbow and wiggling her eyebrows at me before opening her mouth and winking at me.

She is definitely odder than the other humans. I love it, though.

I wink back at her and open the door to the hallway. We step out of the door and both look to the left and the right, then at each other.

"Do you know where to go?" she asks.

"Nope," I say, reaching back inside to summon Lukto on the pad.

Very suddenly, Lukto appears below us.

"Are you ready for breakfast?" It asks.

"Lead the way," Riley says with a smile.

We only take two turns before we are in the main entryway and in front of the throne room doors.

"How did we get here so fast, it took forever last night?" Riley asks Lukto.

"We took the scenic route so you could get in the sights of the palace last night," Lukto replies.

"We could have found this ourselves," I say. There was no mention of a scenic route last night. We walked for at least thirty minutes and this time it was less than five.

"I did find it odd that you needed an escort for such a short distance," Lukto says cheerfully before departing.

"What a strange creature," Riley says.

"Yes, it is."

The door to the throne room creaks open, Lukto dragging it from the inside.

Riley starts to say something but is interrupted by the Baron's booming voice.

"Ah, my friends, come, have a seat," he gestures to an enormous banquet table set up in the center of the room. It is covered with dozens of golden plates, piled high with mounds of food. More than ten Scovein could get through. The table has four chairs situated around it.

The Baron takes a seat at the head of the table and me and Riley sit on the side. I glance at the fourth chair. I wonder if it is an extra or if we're expecting company.

"Commander Tarchond will be joining us shortly," the Baron says, following my gaze. "She is held up at the moment, so please help yourself to whatever you like."

I start to ask about the Alphur and what decision he has made, but the Baron turns his attention towards the food on the table. My stomach grumbles angrily. Maybe breakfast first is fine.

The Baron does not hesitate to pile food from everything in reach onto his plate, so I follow his lead. I have never seen most of the food on the table, but it smells good, and I am not a picky eater. Riley is being much more careful about what she selects and has a very paltry pile on her plate compared to me and the Baron. It amazes me how humans can function on so little sustenance.

I devour everything on my plate and go for seconds, then thirds. Reaching my max capacity, I spear a piece of deep-fried something. When my fork goes into it, a purple liquid leaks out of it and a fishy smell fills my nose. My stomach can barely hold anything else, but the scent makes me salivate and I take a bite. It is one of the best things I have tasted. Fishy, vermyldany, with a depth of flavor I could never hope to replicate.

"You have to try this," I say to Riley, spearing another piece and offering it to her. Purple juices drip off of it and onto her plate. Her face contorts oddly.

"No thank you, I'm full," she replies. She does not know what she is missing out on.

"Ah sigblod," the Baron says as he holds up a piece of the deep-fried item on his fork. The purple juice glistens delectably in the light. "One of my favorites. Deep-fried space squid is the more common term." He pops the bite in his mouth and chews thoughtfully.

"Space... squid?"

The Baron nods at Riley and after swallowing says, "Yes, one of the few joys that Skeldi have introduced to the galaxy."

Riley picks up a metal cup in front of her, the outside is frosty and a light haze floats out of the top. She sniffs it hesitantly, then her eyes grow wide, and she tilts her head slightly.

"Is this banana?"

"A banana smoothie," the Baron corrects her.

"You have bananas here? And smoothies?"

"Both are one of the many joys that humans have introduced to the galaxy," the Baron says.

I forget she is not familiar with other civilizations. She has taken everything so well, so far, it doesn't seem natural that she is from a planet with no intergalactic travel. Banana is one of the most popular flavors in probably the entire universe. Apparently, it still is thousands of years in the future.

"All of our bananas in the palace are sourced straight from Alyssa's bananas," the Baron says proudly.

I grin at the name. Glad to hear her business has stood the test of time. I would have thought the name would have changed to something more creative along the way, though. I scan the table and quickly locate another frosty cup and pull it towards me. The inside is the creamy yellow of a banana smoothie and the smell is unmistakable. I drink half of it quickly and pause to squint, trying to relieve the sudden sharp pain in my forehead from drinking it too fast. Once the pain subsides slightly, I finish the rest.

While the sigblod is delicious, it pales in comparison to the flavor of banana.

"Is that on Earth?" Riley asks.

"No, their headquarters is several thousand light-years from here. Though, I have heard that the family wants to move it to Earth once the planet is fully functional again."

"Fully functional?"

"Yes, it should be almost there, I would imagine. It has been around thirty years by this point."

Riley makes a 'hmm' noise and takes a sip from her smoothie.

The door to the throne room creaks loudly and Lukto's face appears in the growing crack. After some effort, the door fully opens and a Khuvex woman in shiny red armor walks into the room. She has a helmet tucked in the crook of her arm and an impressive-looking sword on her hip. She is much taller and broader than most of the Khuvex women we have seen so far, but she still has a curvy figure. Her black hair is tied up neatly in a bun behind her head.

The red armor is too flashy for my taste, but still cuts a nice figure. The sharp angular corners and the way it shifts with her movement point that it was custom-made and probably pricey. I kind of want a set for myself.

"Commander Tarchond, please have a seat. Help yourself to whatever you like," the Baron says. He leans back in his chair and looks around the table. He looks like I feel. Wanting to eat more but not having the space.

Commander Tarchond sits on the opposite side of the table and analyzes the food on display. The temptation on her face is unmistakable, but she proves stronger than I ever could be and says, "It looks delicious, but I am not hungry. Thank you."

"At least a drink," the Baron says, sliding a metal cup towards the commander.

She picks up the cup and sips it. "Thank you."

"You have been briefed on the situation at hand. Do you have any questions for Zaltas or Riley?" The Baron asks.

Good, it sounds like he is going to help us.

"Many, but most are not imperative."

"You will be escorting them, so maybe you will be able to sate your curiosity on the journey," the Baron says. "If there is nothing you need to know now, I release you into Commander Tarchond's care."

"Does this mean you will assist us with the Alphur?" I ask.

"Yes. After some research, it appears the myths might be much more than that. A lot of information on the Alphur has been purged from most archives, but the little that remained was concerning. You will have Commander Tarchond and her detachment to assist."

"How big of a detachment?" I asks.

"Large enough," the Baron says. "Commander Tarchond will take you from here."

The Baron rises and walks around the table, getting unnaturally close to Commander Tarchond. They look at each other for a brief moment, and geez, the tension in the air between them was almost visible. I half expected them to have each other on the table, then and there.

"Thank you, Laurelyn. Be safe," the Baron says almost inaudibly. He pats her firmly on the shoulder and leaves the room.

RILEY

Zaltas has a goofy grin on his face and says, "So, you and the Baron?"

Commander Tarchond turns her head away and pretends not to hear him.

"Do you wish to fly with Aurelia or would you prefer another transport?" Commander Tarchond asks after a slightly awkward silence.

"Aurelia, please," I say quickly, before Zaltas can press her more about the Baron. He's been talking about how much of a threat the Alphur is and all he can think about now is digging into the commander for gossip about her and the Baron. I can see it on his face.

"Yes, we will take Aurelia," Zaltas says, thankfully dropping the previous subject. Although, I doubt it's for good.

"Very well, let us be off," the commander says.

Zaltas snatches another cup off the table before we leave and sips it as we leave the palace. All that food, and he still has room. It's incredible.

"You should fill your canteen with this," Zaltas says as we walk through the gardens to the main gate. He raises his cup at me and takes a long drink from it.

I can't help but smile at him. "You think so?"

He makes a satisfied sound as he finishes the last of his drink and nods at me.

"I think water's fine."

"I'll take that," Lukto says below us, appearing out of nowhere and reaching for the empty cup.

Zaltas hands him the cup calmly, and I try to still my pounding heart. Lukto scares the shit out of me every time he does that. I know it's small, but I feel like I should notice it approaching, at least occasionally. Lukto runs off with the cup cradled in one of his arms.

"Lukto reminds me of Drenas," Zaltas says.

"Who is that?"

"He is a friend, another Scovein. He is always so serious. All the time, I have tried without avail to get him to lighten up."

"Lukto seems good spirited, how are they similar?"

"Drenas loved sneaking up on people. He acted like he did not do it on purpose, but you could see it in his eyes. He got pleasure out of startling people. I feel like Lukto does too."

"I'm surprised you don't do that."

"It would be amusing, I cannot move that silently, though."

"Is he as big as you?"

"Drenas is slightly larger than me."

"How on Earth... in the universe? Hmm... How could something his size move quietly enough to sneak up on people?" How on Earth probably doesn't hold the same weight out here as it did back home.

"I never figured that out, but he was very good at it."

I giggle at the image of Zaltas cooking in a kitchen and a large man sneaking up on him. Zaltas gasps and drops his spatula, clutching his chest and looking offended at the other Scovein. Zaltas is wearing a floral apron. I let my imagination run a little wilder. There's nothing under the apron either. After cursing at Drenas, Zaltas bends down to pick up the spatula and reveals his ass through an opening in the back of the apron.

"What are you grinning at?" Zaltas asks, a

small smile on his face too.

"Nothing," I say, shaking my head.

Instead of taking us out of the main gates, the commander takes us down a stairwell past two guards, who salute her as we pass. The bright light of the palace garden gives way to dim blue lighting and we enter a long, wide corridor that winds off into the distance.

Zaltas follows along quietly, but I can't help but ask, "Where does this take us?"

"To the landing pads, the military moves through these tunnels to arrive in trouble spots rapidly or to deploy," the commander says matter-of-factly.

"Trouble spots, like in the city?"

"Yes."

"Does that happen often?"

"Often enough to have these tunnels," Zaltas chimes in.

"Yes, at least once a week. We have a wide variety of species congregating in our city. Some of them have blood feuds with others and things can get nasty when they meet. Last week, a group of ten Rhondals encountered two Glunthers. You can imagine how that went."

"Oh sure," Zaltas says, clearly not knowing what she's talking about.

Commander Tarchond nods stoically and continues, "There was very little left of the Rhondals. The entire store it happened in was basically black afterwards."

Two people obliterating ten? I wonder what they look like. They must be huge.

"Well, I hope we do not have to deal with any Glunthers anytime soon," Zaltas says.

"As do I. They are difficult to restrain once they get heated. You would think something so small would be easily contained, but that is not the case," the commander says with a chuckle, breaking her stern demeanor.

We stop in front of a large door and she presses a pad next to it. The door slides open, it's another power lift. Once we're all on board, the commander presses a few keys and the lift shifts sideways, startling me. It rises and drops as it continues to move sideways. The motion isn't strong inside the lift, but it is a little disorienting.

Much to my relief, a chime sounds as the lift stops moving and the doors slide open. Unfortunately, we do not get off, but two Khuvex guards board with a stout creature roughly my height. It's wearing what looks like a full hazmat suit and wheezes loudly.

The lift takes off again and stops rather quickly. The three newcomers depart and we continue on to the landing pad.

Aurelia is pleased to see us, and her ramp lowers as soon as we step off the lift.

Her voice echoes warmly throughout the landing pad, "Welcome back Zaltas and Riley."

"Hello, Aurelia, did you have a good night here?" I ask. I hope she wasn't too lonely.

"Yes, some of the other ships in the pad are humorous. We spent the night swapping stories."

"I'm glad you had a good time," I say with a smile.

"Was your time on the planet productive?"

"Yes, this is Commander Tarchond. She will be joining us for now."

"Hello, Laurelyn," Aurelia says.

"It is nice to see you again, Aurelia," the commander replies.

"You two know each other?" I ask.

"Yes, Ditharan and I traveled together on a couple of missions. It is a shame to hear what happened to him. I am sorry, Aurelia," the commander says sullenly.

"Thank you," Aurelia says quietly. "But, we must press forward. Time is fleeting for us all, even a computer. Living in the past will only burn away the few precious moments we have left. I will always care for Ditharan. His memory will live on with me, but I will remember him fondly instead of with regret and sorrow."

"Well said," the commander replies after mulling over Aurelia's words.

Zaltas grunts in acknowledgement and I place my hand lightly on his back. He looks pained and relieved all at the same time. I know he's struggling with the loss of his friends and brothers. I had no one else. I just mostly miss the routine I had on Earth. There's a strange comfort in a good routine. With no family or close friends to mourn the loss of, it makes me feel slightly guilty that I can't relate to what Zaltas is going through.

"Words to take to heart," Zaltas says, straightening himself up and climbing the ramp into Aurelia.

We all sit around the kitchen table. Being back aboard Aurelia was more comforting than I would have imagined. She felt like the closest thing to home that I had at the moment. She and Zaltas. My home and companions.

"The... Alphur, has been located," the commander begins.

"Really, how?" Zaltas asks.

"I was getting to that," she says, slightly frustrated. "We hooked in with Aurelia and got the signatures for the other ships that were present on Duntarylls-12. One of them remains on Duntarylls-12, one was destroyed during a raid on a space station in this sector. The other five are currently in the same system as the space station. They have not moved in a couple of days. We fear that the initial attack on the station was a test of its defenses and they are waiting for reinforcements for a full-scale attack."

"No, the Alphur would not do that. It will infiltrate the station and take it over from the inside," Zaltas says hastily.

"Then the first ship attacking the station makes no sense. Though, Skeldi rarely make sense."

"Perhaps they sensed something amiss with their group and split off?"

"That is possible, though. The attack on the station was suicide. Even a Skeldi would know that."

"Definitely curious."

I listen intently to their conversation. I

know nothing of battle tactics, Skeldi, space stations, or Alphur. I wish I had something to contribute. Then something dawns on me.

"Maybe they were resisting the Alphur and it forced them on a suicide mission?" I offer.

"That is possible," Zaltas says to me with a smirk. "It is still odd that it would attack a space station it clearly has an interest in. Is there anything else in that area?"

"No, just the space station. It is a central intake hub for the region and a lot of trade goes through it. Most ships stop there when they enter the sector for refueling and restocking," the commander says.

"That will be its target then."

"The station is only two light-years from here, so we can arrive quickly. My detachment is ready to leave immediately."

"Coordinates upload received from Khuvex detachment Starclimb. I am fully stocked and fueled. Departure at your ready, Captain Zaltas."

"Anyone need anything before we leave?" Zaltas asks.

Commander Tarchond shakes her head and I say, "Nope, all good."

As good as I can be, I haven't really considered what our end goal actually was. The thought of facing down the Alphur again is terrifying. My mind has suppressed that entire memory very well until now. That voice in my head, the sunken, pale face. Those teeth. Shivers rise the length of my body and a small lump of panic forms in my chest.

Zaltas' arm slides around me and squeezes me tightly. Instant relief washes over me. I'll be fine, we'll be fine. The Khuvex seem competent and strong and Zaltas will be beside me.

"Initiate take off," Zaltas says to the ceiling.

"Communicating with landing pad… take off confirmed. Travel to surface commencing," Aurelia says.

The entire ship shifts slightly as the landing pad detaches and gravity bares down on us as the lift pushes us towards the surface. The lump of panic moves to my stomach and grows with every second. Deep breaths. Breathe in, breathe out. Stay calm.

"Surface reached. Initiating take off sequence. Please secure yourselves."

Restraints slide out of the seats and secure the three of us.

"Dampener failure chance at point zero

five percent."

I hate hearing that.

Aurelia's engines come to life and a deep rumble quickly disappears as the dampeners kick on.

"Launching in: three, two, one."

My lungs fill with air and I brace myself. I've done this before and I don't know why I'm suddenly so nervous. The looming threat of the Alphur must weigh heavily on me.

"Atmosphere breached. Commencing warp in ten seconds. Please remain seated."

Like we have a choice, these restraints are snug, to say the least.

"Destination: two light-years. Travel time: five hours."

Zaltas places his hand on my knee and squeezes it gently. Calmness radiates from him and into me, and his touch makes me feel at peace. Commander Tarchond is busy analyzing the gloves of her armor and picking at unseen blemishes. She seems like she's in her own little world right now.

"Warp reached. Seven of seven ships with Starclimb have signalled that they are in warp."

The restraints retract into the seats and

Zaltas asks, "Seven of seven ships? How many people are in Starclimb?"

"Fifty-six," the commander says proudly. "All under my command, and for the time being yours. We will eliminate this threat quickly and efficiently. We have an eighth ship that should arrive in the next hour doing reconnaissance. It has been instructed to maintain contact with the station but not inform them of what is happening."

Seems kind of shitty to not tell them about the danger, but I don't know much about battle tactics or hunting people.

"I hope we eliminate it quickly," Zaltas says. "The Alphur is dangerous, even when grossly outnumbered."

"I have been informed. I trust my detachment to get the job done. I was briefed on the Melt Knife? Was it?"

"I did not name it," Zaltas says, grinning.

"I trust you will wield that during the battle?"

Secretly, I hope Zaltas will turn it over to one of the Starclimb members, but I know he won't. He feels responsible for bringing the Alphur here and responsible for dispatching it.

"Yes," he says. My heart sinks slightly.

"Very well, we will ensure a clear path to the Alphur and restrain it for you to dispense the execution."

"Hopefully it is that easy."

"I sure hope so," I say quietly. If I lost Zaltas, I don't know what I'd do. Not just because I'd be alone in a strange world, but also... well, I love him. I need him in my life, now and forever. I wonder if he loves me. Sometimes his thought process is foreign to me and I can't really know what he thinks or feels. I know he cares for me. A tug in my very being draws my eyes to Zaltas'. That connection that's been there feels like a solid steel beam bridging the distance between us now. Unbending, indestructible, and unfailing. We stare at each other briefly and I feel indescribable warmth and love inside of me.

Commander Tarchond clears her throat and breaks us out of the spell we were under.

She retrieves a tablet from the back of her armor and it lights up as she taps on the screen. It's the same shape and size of a tablet on Earth, but it is completely transparent and doesn't look like it's anything more than beams of light. Yet, she holds it in her hand like it is a physical object. I tilt my head around trying to catch a reflection, but I don't see one. I can't even tell if there's glass on it.

"You seem to fear the Alphur greatly. Tell me what you know so I can inform my detachment," she says calmly.

"Seems like something we shouldn't have done last minute," I say.

"There has been little time to prepare for this excursion. We only received orders to go an hour ago and there is barely information on Alphur's aside from some old legends," the commander says to me curtly.

"What would you like to know?" Zaltas asks, voice hinted with irritation.

"Combat capabilities."

"Regeneration, claws, teeth, though I have not witnessed it using them in battle, and telepathy."

"All of which can be beaten. The telepathy could pose a problem," she says thoughtfully.

"All of it can pose a problem," Zaltas replies with frustration. "The regeneration is within moments. Its claws can tear through solid dradimantium, and its telepathy is much more powerful than you are understanding."

"Dradimantium is an outdated alloy, our armor is made of Tetrachlorium, it is far superior," the commander says; she thumps her chest for emphasis and it clangs loudly. "Regeneration is nothing new. Several species can regenerate rapidly. Do enough damage fast enough, it shall not recover."

"It can fully regrow a limb in seconds," Zaltas says sternly.

"Fully functional?"

"Like it was never removed."

Commander Tarchond's eyes actually grow a little wide but she still calmly says, "If there is nothing left to regenerate, it will not be an issue."

"I have personally fired an s-59 class plasma pistol into an Alphur's face multiple times. It completely disintegrated everything within its skull. The Alphur got back up like nothing happened less than a minute later."

Genuine concern flashes across the commander's face, ever so briefly, before she says, "S-59 class is an out..."

"Yes, it is a fucking outdated weapon. That does not make it any less effective at melting something's face." Zaltas draws the Melt Knife and places it on the table firmly. "This is the ONLY thing that can kill it. You can capture it, you can maim it, you can incapacitate it. All of that is temporary. Short of launching it into a star, this knife will be the only way to put it down completely."

"Any other weaknesses?" The commander asks, still appearing unconcerned.

Zaltas huffs and says, "Sunlight burns it and it is physically weaker during the day and its regeneration is slowed. Destroying the brain, albeit temporary, will diminish its telepathy but not remove it. Speaking of which, it will have no telling how many Skeldi with it."

"The Skeldi are of no concern. They go down like any other species. Their arms should not be able to penetrate our armor. Is ultraviolet light the thing that hinders it, or something else from starlight?"

"It is the ultraviolet light," Zaltas says calmly. He glances at me and a brief look of panic overtakes his face. He clearly meant to and forgot to mention that earlier. I hope that's not super important.

"Our armor is equipped with radiating circalia plates, ultraviolet is one of the spectrums it can project."

I don't know what that means, but Zaltas looks instantly relieved.

"Even weakened by sunlight, it is still imposing," he says. "When we first arrived, the planet we were on had three suns and while it moved slower, it was still powerful. Do not think that will be enough to protect you."

"Our armor will be more than enough."

"You are taking this too lightly," Zaltas says, clearly irritated.

The commander taps away on her tablet silently for several seconds, then tucks it back into her armor before standing up abruptly.

"I would like to use one of the relaxation rooms to prepare for the battle," she says stoically.

"Feel free," Zaltas replies, still irritated. "The armory is on the left. You can do any maintenance or get any equipment you need."

"I made sure my gear was in immaculate condition before we departed, thank you. I am well-equipped for the task at hand," she says, a little snootily for my taste.

I watch her saunter down the hallway and disappear into one of the relaxation rooms. She's tall, in shape, and honestly gorgeous. She just needs to drop the attitude.

"Before we departed, thank you," Zaltas says, imitating the commander.

"Be nice," I say with as stern a face as I can manage. It twists into a smile and a head shake.

"It seems like they are not taking the Alphur seriously enough. Besides, she is the one being combative," he says.

"They sent fifty-six Khuvex to help, though."

Zaltas shakes his head.

"I am concerned that will not be enough. The Khuvex are incredibly confident in their capabilities, but I can guarantee they have not faced a foe like this."

"I mean, you fought it off and it couldn't even kill a squishy little human."

"You... we got lucky. Diving through that wormhole after the Alphur alone was both the best and worst decision I have ever made."

"Why is that?" I ask, already knowing the answer.

"The best because I met you, my selkin. I would trade nothing for that. The worst because it was just a bad fucking idea," Zaltas says, grinning.

"But you've killed one before?"

"Yes, and we all almost died. It was no easy task, and it was already weakened. This one is not."

His grin slips away, and he becomes lost in

thought.

"I am going to see what the commander is doing," I say. Zaltas is busy staring into the abyss or something. I'll leave him with his thoughts. Besides, I'm curious what battle preparation looks like for a Khuvex.

I stand and start to move away, but Zaltas snags my hand and pulls me onto his lap. He stares longingly into my eyes before pressing his lips to mine. The kiss lasts an eternity, but not nearly long enough. The pit in my stomach retreats a little and I feel confidence. We're going to make it through this.

After our lips part, I relish in the taste of him. Something inside of me feels like it's a part of him. Something in my very being, and it radiates warmth and comfort through me in the most fantastic way. I never realized how much I was missing from my life before. This connection. It's everything I have ever needed.

The door to the relaxation room slides open, revealing a dense jungle. A burst of wet heat erupts from the room and makes me feel instantly sticky. The leaves look a lot like the jungles on Earth. Well, pictures I've seen. I've never been to a jungle. But they're huge, leafy, and green. Brown trunks stretch to the ceiling with thick vines hanging from them. The sound of rushing water comes from somewhere in the growth.

The ceiling is covered with leaves, mimicking a tree canopy almost perfectly. I see a few glimpses of the white metal peaking through, but the illusion is near perfect. There's even a sun somewhere up there as light beams through some leaves.

I push past the leaves in the doorway and take a few steps inside. There's a massive growth in front of me and I take a moment to press through. This is wild. I thought this room could make a few pieces of furniture and play some music. Not create an entire biome.

At the center of the room is a single large rock surrounded by flowing water. Commander Tarchond is sitting on the rock with her legs crossed and her eyes closed. This is something I had seen in movies before, a monk meditating in a river, a warrior preparing their mind for battle. What I had not witnessed, though, was a seven foot tall, blue, ripped, and completely nude warrior in the middle of a river.

Turning to make my way back out quickly, I bump into her suit of armor standing beside a tree. I let out a yelp of surprise and hear the commander's voice behind me.

"Do you enjoy meditation before battle, too?" She asks. "It helps me clear my mind and hone my instinct."

I turn around and find her standing, completely exposed to me, without a care in the world. Her blue and tattoo covered body would be goals for any bodybuilder on Earth, except maybe for the hefty bust. Not really thinking, I stammer out, "Yes."

"Please, join me. We can meditate together and then discuss plans," she says, patting the rock beside her. The rock stretches away from her, creating a perfectly sized spot for me to sit.

I hesitantly step into the river. My boots are waterproof, thankfully, and the water flows around and over them with a pleasant tinkle. I climb up onto the rock and stand next to the commander. Her figure is imposing this close. Somehow she's even more intimidating without her armor on.

"Let me assist you," she says comfortingly. A far departure from her demeanor previously. Maybe she just didn't like Zaltas.

"Assis..." I start. I was going to ask 'assist me with what,' but I got my answer immediately when she grabbed the corners of my jacket and pulled it off. Before I could even react, she had my tank top off and undid my bra in a quick flick of her fingers. She carefully piled my clothes on the rock behind me while I stood, mouth agape, not knowing what to do.

She looks me over and smiles reassuringly. I am still too shocked at what just happened to completely process the embarrassment I should be feeling. Her smile puts me at ease, though. This must be a normal thing for Khuvex. She seems so confident, bold, and unashamed that I can't help but feel a little of the same.

"Do you need assistance removing your pants?" She asks.

"Oh, no. I've got them," I reply quickly. After a few seconds of hesitation, I kick off my boots and slip my shorts off, setting them on top of the pile.

This feels so awkward. I shouldn't have even come in here. I was just curious how she prepared for battle. Now, I'm going to get firsthand experience of it. Not exactly what I was expecting.

Commander Tarchond sits back down and crosses her legs. She rests her hands in her lap and closes her eyes again. I feel a little less weird without her towering over me and staring at me. I gently seat myself beside her. The rock doesn't leave enough space for me to put any distance between us and our knees lightly touch as we sit side by side.

Her legs are almost completely flat on the

ground, ankle to knee, legs neatly tucked against each other. I wish I was that flexible. My knees hover a few inches above the ground. Okay, I've been staring at her for an awkwardly long amount of time. I've never meditated before. What do they always do in movies?

My eyes slide shut and the tinkling of the water as it passes through the rock fills my ears. The humid heat of the room feels less oppressive now that I'm nude. I open one of my eyes slightly and glance at the commander. She's still unmoving, with both eyes closed. I shut my eye again and focus on the sounds of the room.

A crystal clear image of the Alphur's face flashes in my mind and the terror of feeling its unseen tendrils snaking into my brain becomes all-consuming. A soft, sweet aroma cuts through my mind as the scents of the mock-jungle overtake me. I hadn't noticed the smell when I came in here, but it's incredibly soothing. The image of the Alphur melts away and is replaced by Aurelia sitting in a flat field. Zaltas is on her ramp waving me over, that goofy smile on his face. He looks happy to see me.

I rush towards him, ready to feel his embrace, but freeze and try to scream in horror as the Alphur appears from the darkness behind him. My voice is muted and I'm unable to make a single sound. Its claws extend over Zaltas' head as he continues to beckon me closer, unaware of the danger behind him.

The Alphur brings its claws down in one fluid motion and my eyes flutter open. The commander is crouching in front of me. Rainbow light dances across her blue skin as the water trickles around us. The rush of fear leaves me as the dream quickly fades from my mind.

"You fell asleep," the commander says with the slightest smile. "I struggle with that sometimes too. You get so relaxed, it feels natural."

I half-smile at her and say, "I guess I did, huh?"

"You had an unpleasant dream?"

"Yes, why do you ask?"

"You made distressed noises. I was going to wake you, but you woke yourself."

"Yeah, it wasn't a very good dream."

"What was it about?" She asks, settling beside me again. The kindness radiating from her is almost off-putting compared to her stern and stony demeanor from earlier.

"The Alphur. It was about to kill Zaltas."

"You both fear this creature greatly, do you not?" She tilts her head and stares at me with a concerned look on her face. Please, don't let her start showing fear. Zaltas is good at masking his, but I know he's worried. I don't need her to be too.

"It is as bad as Zaltas says," I say hesitantly. She needs to know everything. She needs to be prepared. My comfort isn't as important as others' safety. "It can control your mind. It snakes in and makes you feel like it means well. You genuinely believe it is good and there to help you. Some sense of reassurance comes from inside of you. It feels like it's your own instinct urging you to trust it. It's hard to resist..."

"Telepathic beings are nothing new for us. We have encountered them before," the commander says confidently.

"This one is supposed to be different. More powerful. Zaltas says that a single one has controlled entire armies before. Even over large distances."

"How large of an army?"

"Tens of thousands, as far as I know."

Commander Tarchond grunts thoughtfully and leans back on the rock. She stretches her legs out and hangs them over the edge, dipping her toes in the water.

"That is concerning."

"I think so too, commander."

"Call me Laurelyn," she says.

"Okay, Laurelyn. That's a pretty name."

"Thank you, so is Riley."

"Thanks."

We sit quietly for a bit before she breaks the silence again and asks abruptly, "Is your bond with Zaltas really that strong?"

"Bond?"

"You feel a connection with him, do you not? The Khuvex call it 'the bond.' Your true mate. Fated across the cosmos."

"Humans don't really have anything like that, I guess soulmates?"

"No, it is different. It is almost physical. Do you not feel it? Like a thread connecting you? I can sense it when you two are close."

The Baron had mentioned something about our connection being strong, but he was kind of a weird guy, so I thought it was just him being odd. I mean, I do feel something. I thought it was just my imagination, but being drawn to Zaltas is a very real sensation.

Closing my eyes, I search for that connection. It blazes to life in my mind's eye. The same connection I've felt, brought to life before me. Strong and unwavering. A solid beam of warmth, branching out from me into the unknown. Except, I know exactly where it goes. Straight to Zaltas. I can feel him on the other end, somehow. I just know he's there.

My eyes flicker open and I find Laurelyn looking at me with a warm smile.

"I do feel it, not a thread, a beam of solid metal."

Laurelyn's smile grows even wider, and she says, "To be able to sense it in another, it would have to be strong. I wish for my own to grow that strongly someday. Years from now, it will be powerful and unyielding, a complete connection. You and Zaltas must have been together for a long time."

"It's been like two weeks," I say sheepishly.

In an unnatural display, Laurelyn's jaw falls agape briefly.

"That is rare. You truly are a marvel."

I feel my face turn red and I look away from her, suddenly finding the rock under us very interesting.

"I'm just me," I say quietly.

"And you are a marvel. What I would not

give to have a body like yours and a connection that strong."

"What?" I say in shock. How could this gorgeous, powerful woman have any doubts about herself, let alone be jealous of my body? I think I've got some good curves. Nice tits, round ass. But she is unreal. She has to be at absolute peak fitness level and she's not hurting for curves either. Her armor hides it, but only slightly.

"Girl, no. You are perfection," I say to her, suddenly brimming with confidence. "You don't need to change a thing about yourself."

"That is kind of you to say."

"It's true. Don't doubt what you have." I feel strangely motivating right now. It feels weird that I'm trying to hype Commander Laurelyn Tarchond of Starclimb up, but here we are. She seemed so strong and in charge. I guess we all have doubts about ourselves. "You look like you could throw a tree across a river and still pull off a tight dress and heels in the sexiest way possible."

Laurelyn chuckles and says, "I suppose you are right."

"Of course I am. You are gorgeous and powerful. There shouldn't be a thing in the universe that can stop you from getting what you want."

"Except maybe an angry Glunther," she says with the shade of a smile.

"Maybe an angry Glunther... what are those, anyway?"

"They have long ears and are very furry, about this tall," she says, holding her hand about three feet from the ground. "Five arms, two long legs."

"Five arms? Aren't most things symmetrical with the number of limbs?" Everything I've seen so far has been.

"The fifth arm is the dangerous one. It has long, slender claws that are sharp and almost unbreakable. It can spin it at a rapid speed. Very disturbing to witness."

My face scrunches up at the thought of a large rabbit with a saw blade on its back rushing at me.

"That sounds terrifying."

"They are not fun to deal with."

A light breeze rolls through the jungle, er room, it's easy to forget I'm still in Aurelia hurtling through space. It carries Laurelyn's scent over to me and I get a slight hint of coconut. It's a little amusing that aliens use the same scented perfumes and soaps that humans do. They may have just gotten them from humans. Here at least, human goods are apparently popular.

I had to ask, Zaltas' need for gossip is apparently rubbing off on me, "So, your connection, it's with the Baron?"

"Yes," she says proudly. "He is a wonderful man, but we have to keep it quiet or I would have to give up my command on this planet. It is a conflict of interest, so they say. He gives me no special treatment. I have never understood the problem, but it is not my place to argue."

"What do you two have planned out then? Something has to give at some point."

"Two more years. His office will expire and he will not be running for re-election. As much as I love my position as commander, I long to journey the galaxy with my nuli. I will retire at that point and we will take to the stars." She sighs dreamily. The canopy above us fades away, revealing a starry night sky. The lights dim to match the mood and she sighs deeply again. "I cannot wait."

"That sounds wonderful," I say. Maybe me and Zaltas can do the same. I'd love to go see Earth and then travel the galaxy. As long as he is by my side, I will be happy no matter where we go.

"It will be the perfect life."

"Wait, so Baron is an elected position?"

"Yes?" Laurelyn looks confused by my question, then laughs quietly. "I forget you are not from here and politics vary greatly from planet to planet. Yes, the outer-worlds are elected positions. The Khuvex empire as a whole has a King by bloodline. He has final say on all matters, but most of the outer-worlds handle their own affairs."

"That is an interesting setup."

"It has worked for a millennium with few problems. There have been attempted coups and takeovers, but all have failed. Anvestea has stood the test of time and the royal line of Tychondranithulunexiandetrium lives on."

"What is Anvestea and Tchondra..." I give up trying to pronounce the rest.

"Tychondranithulunexiandetrium. That is the royal family name and Anvestea is the Khuvex capital planet. It is beautiful, vast blue oceans, vibrant green plantlife, and the capital city is a sight to behold."

"Maybe I'll get to visit someday," I say, still turning over the royal family's last name in my head. That's just as bad as the Baron's.

"I would recommend it. You know the queen is a human?"

"What? Really?"

"Yes."

"From Earth?"

"From Ethelox-12, but she was heading to Earth when the prince rescued her."

"That's amazing." A human queen on an alien planet. Maybe there is no limit to my possibilities.

"Thank you for talking with me," Laurelyn says. "I feel much better now. It is nice to have another woman to talk to sometimes."

I didn't even realize she hadn't felt well. She is so strong, I can only hope to be as resolute as she appears. I guess that's why she was being snippy earlier.

Laurelyn stands up and offers me a hand, helping me to my feet. She hoicks me into a bear hug, burying my face between her tits and almost smothering me.

"Anytime," I say muffled. I forgot we were naked until my face was smothered by bare blue boobs. At least she smells nice.

"I had a thought about the Skeldi attac..." Zaltas voice says from the doorway. I can just make out his face through the growth of plants, and he has that dopey grin on it. "It can wait, I'll leave you two to whatever you are doing."

"We just finished," Laurelyn announces loudly, failing to pick up on Zaltas' insinuation that we were up to more than talking and meditating.

"I hope you both did," Zaltas replies cheekily.

"Shut up, Zaltas," I shout.

"We are both finished," Laurelyn responds, still blissfully unaware.

Zaltas' laugh echoes through the room and he disappears from view. Fucking men, so immature. Can't two women just meditate and chat naked together on a rock in the middle of the river? Is that such a big deal? I giggle to myself and Laurelyn looks at me with confusion.

I put my clothes back on and Laurelyn crosses the river to retrieve her armor. She gets fully suited up before I do. She apparently has a lot of experience putting that armor on. Should I get some armor? That seems important, since we're about to go into a fight. Maybe I should just stay on the ship, but I've got some experience in sketchy situations. Being a paramedic, I was used to thinking on my toes. I could be of some help.

You can't help if you're dead. My old instructor's voice rang in my head. They drilled that into us. No matter how bad the situation looks, you need to wait until it's safe to help. Typically, that meant police clearing a scene for us. Here, I don't know if there will ever be a safe time to help. Hopefully, it won't come to that.

Laurelyn waits patiently for me by the door as I push my way through the overgrowth. Then it dawns on me that I can control the room, too. I imagine a clear path through the overgrowth and the plants melt away into a well-trodden dirt path. Much better.

"You know, I have thrown a tree across a river," Laurelyn says as the door slides open.

"I don't doubt that," I reply with a grin.

CHAPTER THIRTEEN
ZALTAS

Riley and Commander Tarchond both come into the kitchen and sit at the table. They both look suspiciously relaxed. I grin widely at Riley, and she just shoots me a dirty look.

"Aurelia, could I have some water, please?" Commander Tarchond asks the ceiling. I am glad I am not the only one that directs their voice to the ceiling.

"Of course," Aurelia responds. A small circle opens on the table and a cup rises out of it. The commander takes a long drink out of the cup, tilting it almost vertically. She sets the cup back on the circle and it disappears into the table.

"You can do that?" Riley asks, staring at the table. "Could I have some water too, please?"

"Absolutely," Aurelia replies."

Riley retrieves the cup that appears in front of her and sips it slowly.

"Important to rehydrate," I say. I cannot help it.

"Zaltas, I'll dump this on you," Riley says, grinning over her cup.

"Hydration is very important," Commander Tarchond says stoically. She seems in a better mood than earlier. They were in the relaxation room for a very long time. I suppose part of her battle preparation is chilling the fuck out.

I keep further comments to myself, though I have plenty. The commander is making this so easy. It's not that much fun.

"So, the Skeldi attack on the space station. I believe it was what Riley said. They were resistant to the Alphur's control, so it sent them to attack the station and die. However, there is more to it, I believe. Its telepathy is more powerful during moments of chaos. It takes control when the mind is weakened by fear. I think it used the attack to allow it a stronger connection with people on the station."

"Does it have the entire station under its control?" Commander Tarchond muses.

"Doubtful, but it would only need a handful to allow the Skeldi ships aboard. Once it is on the station, it will dig into every mind it can and use them to purge the ones it cannot penetrate."

"That is alarming."

"That's an understatement," Riley says. "How many people are on the station?"

"The most recent census states thirty-two thousand," Commander Tarchond says.

Shit, that is a lot of converts. If the Alphur even gets half of them, that could spell a disaster for this entire sector.

"Is its control permanent?" The commander asks.

"No, it fades with time. The longer and closer the proximity, the longer it takes to fade. The first Alphur we faced had an apparatus it rested on that amplified its abilities. How advanced are the Skeldi when it comes to technological development?" I ask. If they create something like that for the Alphur, it could be a big problem. I doubt they would have had time by this point, but if it takes over the station, it will surely have the resources.

The commander laughs. "Not much. Some Skeldi are intelligent and friendly. They have created some technology that is impressive. Most of them are not. Almost all of them are not. They pillage, rape, and loot. Most of their technology is stolen from other species."

"Small miracles," Riley says.

"Aurelia, how much time do we have before arrival?" I ask. Aurelia has been oddly quiet for the entire trip.

"Four minutes remaining," she replies hastily.

"Is everything okay?" Riley asks, also noticing the rushed tone in Aurelia's voice. "Wait, it's only four minutes away. How long was I asleep for?"

"Yes, I apologize. I have been speaking with the Starclimb ships. Palindria is quite amusing. I do not know how long you slept. I was locked out from the relaxation room," Aurelia says.

Commander Tarchond grins and says, "He is a funny one. Palindria is my ship." She leans over towards Riley and says, "You slept for several hours. I did not think to rouse you until your sleep became disturbed."

Who would have thought someone like her would have an A.I. that could be described as amusing? I would have imagined a stern monotone by the book personality on her ship.

"That's okay. Well, hopefully I'll get to meet him," Riley says.

"He is a fan of females. I am sure he would like that," the commander says.

A slight pang of jealousy strikes me, but I immediately feel foolish. Getting jealous of a spaceship? Even if it's an A.I., is Riley going to be a ship's mate? I shake my head at myself. I was slightly jealous when I saw her and the commander together, too. I assumed nothing unforward had happened between them, but it still dropped a stone in my stomach seeing her nude and embracing another. Had Riley not looked like she was being slowly suffocated, I might have been angry.

I feel for our connection and find it brighter and stronger than ever. Riley cuts her eyes to me and smiles widely. I have nothing to fear. We are unbreakable at this point. It is a little alarming how quickly it happened, but it is comforting nonetheless. What I have dreamt of so long is finally here, and it really is powerful.

"Dropping out of warp in thirty seconds, please secure yourselves," Aurelia says as restraints appear out of the chairs and secure us to the chairs.

"Why do you even ask us to secure ourselves if you're just going to do it yourself?" Riley asks.

"It is a courtesy," Aurelia replies. You

could hear a smile in her voice.

"If you had a face, I'm sure you'd be grinning as dopely as Zaltas does," says Riley.

"That is not very nice," I say with a stoney glare.

"Do it, I know you're going to."

"I will not do anything," I maintain my blank-face stare as best as I can. Riley is absolutely beaming at me, and I cannot help but grin at her.

"There it is," she says, clearly proud of herself.

"Warp exited. Two minutes from destination," Aurelia says. This time, she sounds more concerned.

"Why do you sound concerned?" I ask.

"I worry for your safety. I have heard your conversations about the Alphur. I would like to have you as my captain for more than a few weeks," Aurelia says.

"We're going to be okay," Riley says, her voice wavers slightly.

"Starclimb is unrelenting and skilled. We will crush the Alphur and the Skeldi with no issues. Do not fret," the commander says proudly.

The commander's promise rings hollow in my ears. She does not know what we are up against, none of Starclimb does. Hopefully, what she says will come to pass, but I have a feeling there will be bloodshed. The amount of Skeldi the Alphur has under its influence is also a variable we have not figured out.

"Destination reached. The other ships are hailing us. Should I connect us?" Aurelia asks.

"Yes," the commander says. I give her a dirty look and she does not notice.

A display appears in the center of the table suddenly, startling Riley, and eight Khuvex in full armor are shown. All of their armor is a deep emerald green and their eyes glow blue. The hologram displays only their torsos, but they fill the frames as imposingly as possible. I feel like they are showing off.

"Captain Zurandan, when was your last contact with the station?" The commander asks.

One of the Khuvex shifts slightly and his mechanical voice says, "Two minutes prior, they have reported that all is well, and they have had no issues."

"Good, are the Skeldi ships still present?"

"They docked at the space station thirty minutes ago."

"That is not good," I say. It is definitely not good. The Alphur is aboard the station, weaving its web.

"We inquired shortly after they docked and the station said there were no issues," Captain Zurandan says.

"That cannot be trusted any longer with the Alphur aboard," I say. The chances of it having control of station security are pretty high. It takes a while for it to gain full control, but the suggestions it can implant are still enough to sway most minds.

"Agreed," Commander Tarchond says to my surprise. She's finally not arguing. "We need to board immediately and assess the situation on foot."

The eight Khuvex salute on the screen simultaneously and in an overlap of robotic voices say, "Ready at your order, commander."

"Proceed to the station and dock immediately. We will meet in landing bay twelve," the commander says, and the transmission ends. The hologram flickers briefly, then vanishes.

"Take us in Aurelia," I say quickly, before the commander can. A little childish on my part, but she is my ship.

"En   route.   Estimated   arrival: ten

minutes."

Good, that is enough time to get prepared. Riley needs some protection. I had wanted to leave her on the ship, but the Alphur will hunt the both of us and I fear it will try to get into her mind again. Aurelia will no doubt have her defense systems disabled by docking protocol. It happened on Dexterion, I would assume that is common everywhere.

"Come with me, selkin," I say, standing and offering my hand to Riley. She takes it gingerly and the sensation of her touch sends warm relief flowing through me. I have been on edge this entire time and had not even noticed. Her essence dulls the sharpness of worry inside of me. We will be fine.

"Where are we going?" She asks, squeezing my hand tightly.

"To the armory, I need protection."

"Don't you have your vambrace forcefield?"

"Yes, the Crystashield is fully charged, but you will be wearing it."

"You're going to be fighting. You need it. As much as I want to come help you, I will probably get in the way and should stay on the ship," she says dejectedly.

"No, I cannot leave you alone. The Alphur may come for you."

"I'll be with Aurelia. I want to go. Staying behind will be tough enough. Don't make it harder."

"Aurelia cannot help aside from sealing you inside."

"Unfortunately, that is true," Aurelia says, backing me up. "I will be unable to shield you from a telepathic attack. My weapons systems will also be disabled due to docking protocol. I could only lock you inside and restrain you."

That would work, too. If she is restrained, she could not harm herself. Although, I do not know if the Alphur could cause permanent damage with no one around to ground her. They are very good at playing tricks.

"No, you need to come with us," I say. The risk of leaving her is almost as great as her coming along. At least out there I can protect her.

"Okay, but you need your Crystashield. Surely I can use something else."

The door to the armory slides open and reveals a full suit of Khuvex armor is a nice pastel purple. Large white polka dots are placed sporadically across the legs and the torso is sectioned off by a thick, wavy white line.

"Is that for me?" Riley asks, eyes wide. "It's way too big."

"It is for me," I say with a grin. "I will be protected, do not worry."

"Why is it purple?"

"What's wrong with purple? It's an intimidating color."

Riley giggles. For what, I do not know.

"Where did you get this from?"

"There's an armor-fitter in here," I say, motioning to the bulky armor-fitting machine in the corner. "I did it while the two of you were in the relaxation room."

"Oh."

I slide my vambrace off and push it onto her arm.

"This is too big, too," she says. She is impatient.

"There will be a small sting," I say, opening the lid on the vambrace and tapping through the menus. I tap on sync new biology.

"Ouch, you weren't kidding," she says, gripping her forearm through the vambrace. "Whoa..."

The vambrace shifts and moves as it resizes itself to her arm. It tightens drastically and Riley looks at me in a panic as her free hand grips the side of the vambrace and she tugs on it. Immediately, it loosens to fit perfectly.

"You could have warned me about the squeezing," she says, slapping me on the shoulder slightly.

"I should have, I apologize," I say with a smile. I actually forgot, I was not being mean. I have been wearing that vambrace for so long I forgot the entire process of first setting it up.

Riley leans back into me as I get in close behind her and bring my arms in front of her. I grip the vambrace lightly and pull her arm up so we can both see the screen. I bring up the neurolink and click activate on it.

"Wait, is this going to hurt?" Riley asks, but the process is already finished.

"It is already done," I say.

"What did that do?"

"You can control the vambrace with your mind. It is synced to your neural activity now."

"What all can it do?"

"Many things. Maybe one day we can get you your own. Although, Aurelia said the Crystashield was lost to time. The important thing is the armor. All you have to do is think about it being on."

"Do I have to think of anything in particular or just like 'star armor activate!' kind of thing?" A light blue light flashes across Riley's body and I feel her body repel me ever so slightly. The Crystashield is fully active.

Riley turns her hands over in front of her face as the light rushes quickly across her body, then disappears.

"Did it turn back off?" She asks.

"No, you cannot see it when it is activated."

"How will I know if it's on?"

"The armor activates easily with any near thought of turning it on. Removing the armor requires a deliberate thought and desire for it to be off. It is a safety feature."

"Armor off," she says. The light flashes and disperses rapidly.

"You do not have to speak it," I say.

"I know, but it's fun," she says, grinning at me widely, eyes glistening with joy.

My heart aches at the sight of her eyes. I wish we did not have to go through this. I want to keep her safe for eternity and put her through no pain or difficulties. That is not possible, as much as I desire it. There will always be strife to contend with. The best I can do is to stand resolutely beside her and always be there for her.

"I love you, selkin," I say abruptly. There has been no doubt in my mind that I love her, that she is my mate, that she is my destiny. But saying it aloud makes it feel much more real to me. That warmth I feel being in her presence burns like a fire inside of me now, a fire I wish to consume me.

Riley's smile grows large and her eyes start literally glistening as they fill with tears. They overflow and stream down her face that immediately buries itself in my chest. Arms wrapped around my waist, she squeezes me tightly and says something that is muffled by my body.

"I cannot hear you, selkin," I say gently.

She peels herself off of me and looks me in the eye through her tears. After a couple of sniffles, she says, "I love you. I've known it for a while now, but saying it feels so much better than thinking it. I know we're about to go into some crazy dangerous situation, but I'm so happy right now."

"Awwww," Aurelia offers her input.

Riley giggles and wipes the tears out of her eyes. "We will get through this, then we can do whatever we want."

"Yes, selkin, anything we desire. The universe will be ours to explore, anywhere you want to go, we will go."

Riley sniffles again and wipes her eyes. Her jacket squeaks quietly as it brushes her cheek and I cannot help but smile.

"We need to finish getting ready, go ahead and armor up," she says and gasps as the Crystashield forms around her. "It's going to take a while to get used to that."

"It does," I say. Light flickers across her as the armor dissipates. At least she's getting used to it. "Last thing, take this." I pull an e2532 plasma pistol from a holster at my back and offer it to her.

"Is this a gun?" She asks, taking it delicately.

"Yes, an e2532 plasma pistol," I say. I point at a red button flush with the top of the gun. "Press this to charge it, pull the trigger to fire. Plasma arcs but close range it will go straight." It is the only gun in the Khuvex aresenal that was small enough for her hands. Aurelia told me they are highly effective.

She turns it over in her hand carefully while I strap a holster around her waist. I guide her hand to slide the gun into the holster and a strange sense of arousal jolts through my body from the head of my cock. The motion, sound, and sensation of the gun sliding into the smooth holster while I felt her warm hand in mine felt heated and sexual. She looks up at me and I can see the desire in her eyes, too. If only there was time.

Riley leaves the room after a quick longing glance. I just want to stay here with her, in this metal and oil smelling room. The location does not matter, as long as she is by my side. She turns and walks out of the door, and I grab an eyeful of her round ass before it disappears from view. That is just a bonus.

The armor fits perfectly, as it did when it came out of the machine. I do a few stretches in it and sprint back and forth across the room as much as I can. It is form-fitting and flexible as far as metal armor can be. I would prefer the Crystashield, I am used to completely unimpeded movement, but this will do.

I grab myself a larger plasma pistol from the rack on the wall and holster it behind me. Before leaving the room, I pause and look towards the ceiling.

"The purple is good, isn't it?" I ask the ceiling.

"It looks highly intimidating," Aurelia replies.

"It does. I do not know why Riley found it amusing."

CHAPTER FOURTEEN
RILEY

"Docking initiated," Aurelia says. "Request to dock in landing bay twelve has been approved. The other ships are present in the same bay."

My stomach feels like a brick has been dropped into it. The weight of the imminent battle feels heavy on me and I can't help but feel fear and worry. I want to believe that everything will end up okay, I truly do, but there are so many things that can go wrong.

"Perfect," Laurelyn says. She places a hand on my shoulder, which startles me. "Be at ease, Riley. This will go smoothly. There is no need to fear. You may be smaller than me, but you are just as fierce. Besides, I will be with you the entire way. And Zaltas will too, I suppose. More importantly, you will have me, though."

Laurelyn smirks at me and I can't tell if

she's being serious or joking around. Neither one would surprise me.

She squeezes my shoulder gently, and I try to find comfort in her words. With Zaltas and Laurelyn by my side, how could anything bad happen?

Clanking footsteps signal Zaltas' arrival from the armory and I get a full view of him in his new outfit. He stands proudly in his lavender armor, hands planted firmly on his hips. I'm waiting for him to bend over and ask me how he looks through his legs, but sadly he does not.

"That is a very intimidating color choice," Laurelyn says, looking Zaltas up and down. I can't tell if she's being genuine or not. He's holding his helmet under one of his arms. I wonder what color the eyes will be. "It will strike fear into the hearts of all who see you, such as any suitable set of armor should."

She has to be joking. Zaltas picked the least intimidating color I can think of, it's just missing a floral print on the top half.

"I thought I should go all out," Zaltas says. He looks down at the armor and comes back up with a smirk.

"Are you two serious, or joking? I can't tell?" I ask finally.

"What do you mean?" Laurelyn asks, cementing the fact that they were serious.

"That color is not intimidating on Earth, like, at all."

"It is the color of the Vashwathian Moth. The terrible creature that plagued the galaxy tens of thousands of years ago. How could it not be intimidating?" Laurelyn asks, still confused.

"I have never heard of that, it's the color of flowers and Easter eggs on Earth."

"What is an easter? The name sounds like that of a dreadful creature. How could that not be intimidating?" She asks.

"Docking complete," Aurelia announces.

"We will continue this later, and you can tell me stories of easters," Laurelyn says as she slides her helmet on. It clicks loudly as clamps fall from the edges and connect with the armor. I slip my backpack over my shoulders and check to make sure my gun is in the holster and the vambrace is on my wrist. I don't think it could fall off, but it doesn't hurt to be cautious.

More clicks sound behind me and I turn to see Zaltas with his helmet on, his eyes light up in a vibrant yellow. Exactly like an Easter egg. I won't be able to think of anything else now.

My good spirits fade quickly as we descend the stairs into the cargo bay. The ramp is lowered and the bright artificial lighting of the landing bay infiltrates Aurelia. Laurelyn moves confidently in front of me while Zaltas follows closely at my rear. I feel safe between the two of them, at least, but that safety can easily be torn away.

"Be careful," Aurelia says as we walk down the ramp. "My systems are disabled due to docking restrictions and I will be unable to assist."

"We will," I say and pat her wall.

Please, let this turn out okay.

I knew they were going to be out there, but it was still startling to see the fifty-six Khuvex decked out in full armor. Massive spears in hand and a variety of weapons strapped to each of their waists. Some had swords, some hammers, some guns, and one even has an axe. Most of them wore silver, with eight standing up front in emerald green, several in blue were dotted amongst the others. I'm guessing it's a rank thing. All the captains in green, blue must be some kind of first mate. Silver is normal crew. Red for the commander. Laurelyn strides past me and stops in front of the group.

Zaltas stops beside me and looks down at me. I can feel that grin. I know it's in there. I shake my head at him and smile. And last, easter egg for Zaltas.

"Switch to private communications," Laurelyn instructs the group in a metallic voice. It's interesting how different their voices still sound, even with the distortion. It sounds more intimidating, but I can still hear Laurelyn's smooth voice in there.

Zaltas taps the side of his helmet and the group stands silently. All heads are turned towards Laurelyn as she motions like she's in deep conversation. Wow, just leave me out of it. Sorry, I don't have a fancy helmet.

Zaltas grabs my wrist gently and opens the vambrace. After tapping something I start to hear Laurelyn's normal voice in my head.

"So there has been no trouble so far from the Skeldi, that is good to know. Where did they dock at?"

Another voice echoes in my head. It makes me feel a little sick, it brings back memories of the Alphur in my brain. "Seven ships landed in bay five, three in bay seven, and three are here in bay twelve."

"Thirteen ships total... do we know how many were on board?"

"That is unknown at this time. Station control stated there were only three Skeldi ships currently docked, but our sensor picked up the thirteen signatures when we landed."

"The station control is compromised," Zaltas says in my head.

"It appears so," Laurelyn says.

"Skeldi normally travel in groups of twelve per ship, but there have been higher and lower counts before," someone says.

"So best case, there are one hundred and fifty-six Skeldi on board along with one Alphur," Zaltas says.

"Probably more," another voice offers.

This is just great. So each Khuvex will at minimum have to take on three or four Skeldi. Then the Alphur is lurking somewhere. The pit in my stomach grows deeper with each passing moment and I place my hand on Zaltas' cold armor for comfort. I wish I could feel his warmth.

"Captain Travalien, Captain Lirien, Captain Tarvan, Captain Yalurt, take your crews to bay five. Secure the landing bay. If the Skeldi are still in their ships, monitor them from a distance. Use your best judgement, but anticipate a fight," Laurelyn says. Four of the green Khuvex salute and immediately leave the group, followed by their crews.

"Captain Nuraland, Captain Bulrast. Take your crews to bay seven," Laurelyn orders. Two green Khuvex salute and leave with their crews.

"Captain Pelindrophin, Captain Zurandan. You will secure this bay."

Captain Pelindrophin and Captain Zurandan salute and disappear into the depths of the landing bay.

"That leaves us. We will be securing station control," Laurelyn finishes.

Laurelyn holds her hand out to her side and spreads her fingers wide. A metal tube extends from below her wrist rapidly and she grabs it out of the air. A blade springs from the tube and a crossguard forms around her hand. The blade ignites with a vibrant blue glow that greatly resembles a flame.

"That was awesome," I say quietly. It really was. Laurelyn is such a badass.

"Let us move. Ending private communication. Captain's maintain a link with me."

Dozens of voices echo in my head.

"Be safe."

"Watch your backs."

"Lunch after?"

"They stand no chance."

"Be careful."

"Keep your weapons sharp."

Abruptly, they all disappear.

"Why don't we just use that the whole time?" I ask. Maybe it has a limited range, but it seems like the surest way to stay in touch.

"It seemed unwise, did you not," Laurelyn begins, but the answer dawns on me before she finishes. Oh, right. The Alphur. "That the Alphur could produce voices in your head?"

"Yes, that makes sense."

"Speaking of which," Zaltas says as he taps on my vambrace screen again. "The neural-communication link is off. Anything you hear in your head that's not you, is not us."

I shiver. It's going to happen again, it seems impossible to avoid. The Alphur, in my head, tempting me, tormenting me, taunting me.

Zaltas puts a hand on my shoulder and squeezes gently. It helps, but not much. The cool metal against my skin isn't the most comforting thing. Then a burst of warmth blasts from inside me and radiates across my body. I feel Zaltas inside me, his love and protection, traveling across our connection and planting itself in my soul. It takes root and grows into a vibrant beacon of comfort and serenity.

I lean against his armored body and sigh deeply.

"Thank you," I say quietly.

"We will get through this, do not worry, selkin," Zaltas says in a robotic voice. I focus on his mannerisms and tone hidden under the machine and try to take his words to heart.

"Station control is through the fashion district and up one level. We are close, thankfully," Laurelyn says, plugging away at her tablet. "We must move. I wish to secure control before the fifth containment breaks loose."

Laurelyn tucks her tablet away and moves forward, confidence spewing out of her with every stride. I follow in behind her and Zaltas takes up the rear. Metal slides behind me and I glance over my shoulder to see Zaltas gripping a rather large gun, tubes run across the length of its body and glow a sickly green, it look like a bigger version of the one he gave me earlier; his other hand rests on the Melt Knife at his hip.

"What is the fifth containment?" I ask as we walk down the stairs of the landing bay.

"It is a place where the essence of evil

beings is stored," Laurelyn says.

"Like hell?"

"I do not know what that is."

"Yes, like hell," Zaltas chimes in.

"Did Scovein have a fifth containment?" I ask.

"It was the fourth containment in our time, but same idea," he says.

"The fourth containment was found to be outdated," Laurelyn adds.

"Yeah, yeah," Zaltas says with a head shake.

It was almost imperceptible, but Laurelyn had actually giggled quietly in her helmet. Look, she's amazing and super nice, to me at least, but I wasn't sure she had a sense of humor.

"Makes sense," I say, "On Earth we had heck, but it became outdated and they upgraded it to hell."

"Really?" Zaltas asks, then shakes his head at me too when he sees me smiling.

"You two are not as amusing as you believe," he says.

The exit to the landing bay slides open, revealing what looks like the street of a city. Shops line the bottom just like on the Khuvex world, but the buildings only go up around five stories before hitting a ceiling. The ceiling is green with pinpoints of light shining down onto the street, providing enough illumination to see clearly. All of the buildings are completely transparent on the first floor and change to a dark brown metallic shine going upwards. Lighted windows dot the sides all the way to the ceiling.

A myriad of aliens wander the streets. It's not as bustling as the Khuvex city was, but it's still plenty crowded. I recognize quite a few of the species from the planet, but see a few new faces too. One of them has two new faces itself, at the end of gangly yellow necks. They look sickly but grin from ear to ear as they chat with each other and browse the shops for something to wear on their shared body. The body just looks like a beach ball with two stubby legs and T-Rex arms. Not sure how much they can really do with that, but they look happy at least.

We get a wide berth as Laurelyn moves ahead. Even some aliens that are easily twice her height and size move quickly out of her way. One even muttered an apology. Maybe the Khuvex are as strong as they say. The other species seem to fear or at least greatly respect Laurelyn. Several of the aliens peer at us through windows up above and some of them look nervous. I guess I would feel that way too if I saw two people dressed like Laurelyn and Zaltas, and their size, moving by with weapons drawn.

Who am I kidding? I am that nervous. I peek into the shops as we pass, trying to distract my worries.

We get a clear view of the interiors of each shop, all manner of clothing is on display. In any size you can imagine and any shape. Every window contains an explosion of colors. Blues, purples, reds, greens, colors I can't even begin to describe. Material that shimmers and shifts to different shades. Even dresses that change length and cut depending on the angle you look at it from. One store has just one massive shirt on display that could fit fifty of Zaltas in it.

Laurelyn presses forward without so much as a glance at the shops but Zaltas seems even more mesmerized than I am. I keep checking behind me to make sure he's still there. He slows down occasionally to gawk a little longer at various things, probably mentally cataloguing what he wants to buy later, but he hurries back behind me after our distance grows more than two arm's lengths.

"We need to come back after this is over," Zaltas says behind me.

"I'd like that," I say.

Laurelyn turns into an alleyway and stops

in front of two large metal doors. They look well-fortified and heavy. Massive rivets line the solid metal frame and an even larger lock sits in the center with a small pad on it.

She taps on the pad and after a few seconds, a voice plays from the box.

"What?" The gruff voice asks impatiently.

"This is Commander Tarchond of the Khuvex. I require access to station command."

Several people murmur inaudibly over the speaker and the voice comes back. "What for?"

Laurelyn looks back at me and Zaltas with a slight head shake. Something's not right.

"Our communications transmitter was damaged and I need to signal Dexterion that we are returning from our expedition," Laurelyn replies coolly.

More murmurs from the speaker followed by a second voice. This one sounded like they ate gravel for breakfast. "Station command is undergoing maintenance and will be unavailable for the foreseeable future."

"I demand you let me in and allow me usage of your communications," Laurelyn says sternly. "Now." She slams her gloved fist on the door to accentuate the word 'now.' A metallic echo rumbles through the area and several people passing on the other end of the alley stop and stare for a second before scurrying off rapidly.

Silence from the speaker. Laurelyn gives them maybe ten seconds for a response before she jams her fingers between the doors and starts straining.

"I don't think you'll get through that," I say, concerned with her exertions. She's going to hurt herself.

Something loudly pops, then cracks in the door. To my utter shock, a small beam of light forms down the center of the doors as they spread slowly. The lock and speaker on the front shakes and another loud crack echoes down the alley.

"Okay, okay," the first voice says over the speaker. "You will be allowed to use our communications system. You may make your transmission, then you will depart the station immediately. Step away from the door."

"Remind me to never anger her," Zaltas says.

"I doubt you'll never anger her, it's not in your nature. She told me she threw an entire tree across a river. I believe it," I say with a grin at Zaltas.

The door clicks quietly and slides open with a groan, revealing a power lift. The three of us get on board and Laurelyn presses the button at the top of a long list of options. Another loud groan, and the doors clank shut. She places her sword beside her hip and the flames disappear from it as it jumps to her armor and sticks to the side. Zaltas follows her lead and holsters his gun.

Laurelyn taps something on her armor and a beam of green light explodes from her armor and envelopes the entire lift before disappearing as quickly as it appeared. She tilts her head and stares at a small box next to the buttons and slams her fist into it and rips out a handful of wiring and a small speaker.

"What are you doing?" I ask, puzzled.

"This is a microphone," she says. "We need privacy. Station command has been compromised."

"That is not unexpected," Zaltas says. "But, how are you sure?"

"They would have let me in without question. The Khuvex patrol and protect this sector. I have personally rescued this station from pirates twice."

"By yourself? That's impressive," Zaltas says.

Laurelyn turns toward him and opens her clenched fist. The wiring and speaker clatter to the ground. "We need to form a plan. There will be confrontation."

"Could there be anyone left unaffected?" I ask, fearing the answer.

Zaltas shakes his head and says, "No, they will have been disposed of. Anyone of weak mind will be under the Alphur's control and will have been used to remove the others."

Disposed and removed. I know what he means, they're dead. No telling how many bodies are waiting for us.

"We must be prepared for a fight, but we should allow them to escort us to the communications platform and stage our takeover from there," Laurelyn says confidently. She radiates confidence. I wish I could be so bold. Then again, she has the physical capabilities to back up any claim she has made.

"That will work," Zaltas says. "I am concerned the Alphur has sensed the two of us by now, but pretending that we are trying to leave will buy us some time."

"Once we have station command secured, we will have eyes on most of the station and will be able to locate the..." Laurelyn trails off and turns her head to the side, pressing a finger to her helmet. "Good. Stay in position and report any movements. Secure the entrances and prepare for a fight. We are nearing station command now. It has been compromised. I will report once we have taken it."

"Nothing bad has happened yet?" I ask hopefully. I know it's a pipedream but I'm hoping we can finish all of this without too much bloodshed.

"It does not appear the Skeldi have left their ships yet. All of Starclimb is in place and waiting for further orders. We will take station command and broadcast a signal to take shelter and lock the station down. The Alphur and Skeldi will have nowhere to run."

The power lift makes a very unpleasant and startling buzzing noise as it grinds to a halt and the doors open. I brace myself for the sight of blood and bodies but am relieved to find a clean hallway with several doors. Artwork of various galaxies and planets adorns the walls and there's even something that greatly resembles a watercooler next to a few chairs.

Each door has a placard above it: Command, Communications, Lead-Security Belrond, Security, and one with a blank placard.

The door labelled 'Command' slides open

quietly and a small pink man, well, small compared to Laurelyn and Zaltas, he still has a good foot over me, approaches us slowly.

"Communications is in here," it says with a rough voice. The fleshy tendrils in front of its face jiggle with each word. He has his arms outstretched, revealing stubby gray fingers at the end of lanky arms. His posture is unnatural and seems defensive. It sets me on edge.

Laurelyn nods at the man and motions towards the communications door. The man opens the door and steps out of the way for us to enter. Zaltas steps in first, cautiously, and sweeps the room. It is medium-sized and there's not anything for anyone to hide behind. A large, glowing circle is in the center of the room, and the walls are covered with screens and controls. A singular podium with more controls is situated next to the glowing circle.

He looks behind himself at me, and I join him in the room. Laurelyn scans the hallway and stares down at the pink man for a moment before coming inside.

I look around the room, taking in the mass amount of controls and wouldn't even know where to begin to start. My foot contacts the glowing circle and a pulse of light washes across the circle from where my foot met it. I wonder what thi... A sickening snapping noise interrupts my thoughts and a quiet groan causes me to turn around quickly.

Laurelyn is dragging the unmoving body of the pink man into a corner of the communications room. She drops him unceremoniously and digs through his thick clothing.

"Was that necessary?" I ask, horrified. They're being mind-controlled, it's not their fault.

"Everyone is a combatant. It is unfortunate, but I had no means of restraining him. We will ensure he has a proper burial in accordance with Zelustran customs," Laurelyn says, her voice tinged with emotion. I can tell she has genuine regret over killing him. She surprises me constantly. I didn't think she was just some robot, but she seemed so orderly and the-end-justifies-the-means-like. No regrets, no concerns for others.

"We can check the security office for non-lethal controls," Zaltas says, placing his hand gently on my shoulder. "I cannot guarantee we will be able to use them much, but we will try when we can."

"Okay," I say quietly. I can't help but wonder if that pink man had a family waiting for him.

"Selkin," Zaltas says. He removes his helmet with a click and I see those beautiful emerald eyes of his, locked onto mine. "Selkin," he says again gently. The smooth depths of his voice wash over me in a comforting wave. He takes my hand and crouches to be at eye level with me. "Please, do not hesitate. If you are in a situation and I am not around. Do not hesitate to use your gun. I cannot live if something happens to you." His eyes looked a little wetter than normal and it made me start to tear up.

"Okay," I say again, voice trembling as I try to fight back the tsunami of tears built up behind my eyes. Zaltas' undying love and need for me, paired with the stress and looming threat in front of us is almost too much for me to handle. "I promise."

Laurelyn expertly breaks the tension by striding towards the two of us and looking down. Her metallic voice confidently says, "I will be there to protect the both of you. Neither of your capabilities matter. You will get through this." She places a hand on each of our shoulders and squeezes them a little too tightly.

"Thanks," I say with a giggle. With the two of them, nothing will go wrong. I just have to keep reminding myself of that.

"I will be doing the protecting," Zaltas says, clicking his helmet back into place. His voice switches over to the modulated robot.

"Fear not, I am here." His hands clang loudly as he slams them against his hips and stands up straight, head tilted up like a superhero.

"My hero," I say with a grin. Laurelyn clears her throat, or so I assume. Some kind of grinding metal sound emanates from her helmet.

"I have the sensor for the doors," she says, holding up a small metal tube that is covered in a suspicious purple fluid. I start to ask where she got it, but I really don't think I want to know.

"What is the plan from here?" I ask, head turning back and forth between the two.

"We will take security and command. Then the Lead-Security office. The last door is relief facilities, but we must secure that too," Laurelyn says. She strides out into the hallway, sword blazing to life in blue flame as she draws it.

Zaltas draws his gun and places his free-hand on the hilt of the Melt Knife. The thought of just seeing the Alphur again stresses me out beyond all reasoning, but I'm intrigued to see what that knife actually does. It's been hyped up repeatedly.

The hallway is still and completely silent. Laurelyn and Zaltas take positions next to the security door and I slip beside Zaltas. I draw my gun and press the red button on top. It clicks quietly and the gun whirs pleasantly for a few moments before falling silent. The tubes pulse with a sickly green light and I squeeze the grip tightly. Armor on. Blue light flashes before my eyes and I feel a slight tingle as the Crystashield encases me.

Laurelyn and Zaltas exchange nods and she pushes the metal sensor against the door and it slides open quickly.

"Who are you, what are you doing here?" An angry voice shouts from inside.

The stomping of several sets of footsteps echoes in the hall, and I brace myself for the fight ahead.

Laurelyn enters the room in the blink of an eye and the sound of sizzling meat and cut-short screams meshes with the quiet 'whomp whomp' of Zaltas' gun as he fires into the room. I take a deep breath and start to go around him to help out, but I stop suddenly as one of his massive hands plants itself against my chest.

He fires into the room one more time and silence descends on us.

"I will be out in a moment," Laurelyn says from inside the room.

Zaltas turns back to me and says, "You do not need to enter every battle, just stay close to me."

I nod at him, thankful for the lack of lofty expectations from him on my combat prowess. I will help if I need to, but I hope it doesn't come to that.

"Will all of that noise not attract others here?" I ask. Zaltas and Laurelyn seem calm, but I'm sure not.

"The rooms are soundproof," Laurelyn says, returning from the room and passing me a fabric bag with a bunch of steel tubes in it. I look down at them and back up at her with a confused expression.

"Restraints. Place on the wrists and they will immobilize whatever you attach them to," she offers. "All of the ranged non-lethal weaponry is checked out. That is the best we will have."

Laurelyn glances into the room and sighs as the door slides shut. I'm guessing from the sounds that it wasn't pretty in there. I didn't want to know.

"A dispatch had been sent to the security forces. They were sent to various corners of the station and spread thin. No doubt to make a takeover easier. I sent another dispatch for them to converge at the landing bays."

"Good idea," Zaltas says.

"The relief facility is a smaller area and should not be compromised, let us take that before command," Laurelyn says, marching to the door with the blank placard.

She and Zaltas take their positions again and the door slides open. Thankfully, Laurelyn didn't rush in and there were no screaming or voices. Laurelyn quietly closes the door and turns towards the command room.

"All clear?" Zaltas asks.

"Yes," Laurelyn says grimly. "The ones that resisted are in there."

Zaltas takes his place opposite Laurelyn at the command door and I fall in behind him. The door slides open and Laurelyn strides into the room, sword raised high.

"Down, on your knees. Don't move," she shouts in her booming metallic voice.

"What is happening, what is this?" An airy voice demands from inside.

Zaltas moves into the room and waves me behind him.

The inside is much like the communication room, covered in monitors, switches, controls, and flashing lights. Several cushioned chairs are grouped in front of half a dozen consoles. Two of the chairs are spinning slowly behind two more of the pink men, currently down on their knees.

"Restrain them," Laurelyn directs me.

I slip one of the tubes out of the pouch and hesitantly approach the men. One of them side-eyes me and looks like he's about to try something. My body tenses, ready to move at a second's notice. His legs shift slightly and he manages to rise an inch off the ground when Laurelyn's sword swings through the air and stops just shy of his neck.

"I said, don't move," Laurelyn says eerily quietly. "Bend it in half and press it on his body."

I grip the metal rod in my hands. It feels sturdy and like solid iron. I don't know how I'm supposed to bend this. To my surprise, it bends with ease and illuminates in a pale blue glow. I push it against the pink man and the metal extends so fast I almost missed it. The metal wraps around the pink man thoroughly and completely, the blue glow dims and he falls to his side in the position he was in, completely immobile.

The same happens to the second pink man as I press another tube against him. Laurelyn grabs the metal wrapped around each of them and drags them to a corner before rifling through their clothing as best as she can between the metal.

A deep sigh of relief escapes my lips, at least two have been saved. Well, maybe saved, we still have a lot to finish.

A sudden burst of confidence and comfort swells inside of me and I feel for Zaltas' connection. The bridge between us pulses with warmth and serenity. My mind feels more at ease. I focus on the connection and try to send as much love and compassion back across as I can spare. Zaltas must have got it, because he grips my shoulder lightly and peers down at me. I can sense that grin of his hidden behind the helmet and beam up at him. It's incredible how he can put me at ease so effortlessly.

"I will put the station on lockdown and broadcast a shelter in place warning," Laurelyn says, gripping a card in her hand she retrieved from one of our captives. "The fifth containment is about to break loose."

She places a hand on the edge of her helmet and says, "A broadcast will be going out to warn the citizens to take shelter. The station will go on full lockdown. Brace yourselves for a fight."

Laurelyn slides the card into a slot on one of the consoles and a holographic display pops up above. It reads: 'Broadcast 'Take Shelter' informational message?' Laurelyn clicks a yes, followed by a confirmation yes, followed by yet another confirmation yes.

"Attention all denizens, visitors, and staff of Station Twenty-three Fivoran. A shelter in place mandate has been issued for everyone about the station. Please, take shelter in your homes or one of the secured facilities until further notice. This is not a test. Take shelter immediately."

The message repeats several times as Laurelyn pulls up another menu and confirms placing the station in lockdown. It warns that all bays will be sealed from the exterior and there will be no entry or exit until lockdown is lifted. She confirms the lockdown.

Red lights begin flashing from the corners of the control room and another message broadcasts overlapping the take shelter message. "Lockdown initiated. Lockdown initiated. Lockdown initiated."

The screen in front of Laurelyn informs her that three ships are currently mid-docking and for safety the lockdown will be delayed for ten seconds while the ships finish landing. She pulls up another screen and tabs through it quickly.

"Three more Skeldi ships just landed," she

says calmly.

"Where?" Zaltas asks.

"Bay twelve. We must return and assist the captains."

My heart starts to pound in my ears and I feel drenched in sweat. This is it, it's happening, and it's going to be so much worse than we thought. Three more ships, potentially thirty plus more enemies.

"What about command?" Zaltas asks.

"I placed an override lock on the console. They cannot disable it without this card now," she says, displaying the card she retrieved from the pink man.

Laurelyn leaves command and we follow her into the hallway. She stops in front of the 'Lead-Security Belrond' door and hesitates for a moment.

"We should check this one," Zaltas says, leaning against one side of the door.

"Yes," Laurelyn says hesitantly and leans on the other side. "Will you take the lead on this one?"

"Yes," Zaltas replies. Laurelyn opens the door and Zaltas slips into the room, gun raised. "Clear."

Laurelyn lets out a sigh that reverberates with the modulation.

"You okay?" I ask her, slipping up close to her.

"Belrond is a friend of mine. I was concerned at what we might find of her in here."

"Hopefully she's somewhere safe," I say, patting Laurelyn's shoulder gently. I felt like a small child reaching up for an adult's attention.

"Yes, she might be out on a mission," Laurelyn says.

"We are clear here," Zaltas says, walking towards the power lift. He stops a few steps away and looks back at me. I'm glad he's keeping track of me, makes me feel a little safer knowing that he is watching closely.

CHAPTER FIFTEEN
ZALTAS

Something had happened while I was in the office. Commander Tarchond is unnaturally quiet for the duration of the power lift ride and Riley keeps glancing at her with concern. I heard them talking in the hallway and could not make out what was said. I want to pry, but I decide to let it go.

The lift buzzes as it comes to a halt and the doors grind open. We are back in the original alley in the fashion district. The area is completely deserted and all the shops now have thick metal plates covering the windows. Several faces peep out of the windows above us and watch closely as we pass quickly. Riley has to jog to keep up with us.

Riley, my selkin, my mate. I desire her so deeply. Everything about her feels right. I want to make our mating official. I want to make her my lifelong mate. I have to just ask. Surely she feels the same. My stomach suddenly feels upset at the thought and I look at her as she jogs beside me, breathing heavily but determined to keep up, determined to help and be here with me. The feeling in my stomach grows stronger and I feel slightly ill. I feel that if I do not ask her, I will fall to the ground and not recover.

I pause, and Riley almost tumbles over as she does the same. I quickly grab her by the shoulders and steady her. She looks up at me and tilts her head, a look of concern plastered on her face.

"What are you doing?" Commander Tarchond asks me impatiently as I remove my helmet and set it on the ground. I crouch down to be at eye level with Riley and ignore the commander.

"We nee…" the commander starts, but I interrupt her.

"Riley, my selkin, this is perhaps the worst location and time to ask this, but I fear I will explode if I do not. Once this is over, and we are safe and secure." Riley's eyes start to tear up before I even ask my question, and I wonder if this is inappropriate, and she's not ready.

During my pause Riley quickly says, "Go on."

The commander has stopped a few steps away and is watching us intently with her hands clasped together. I had hoped she would busy herself with something else for a moment, but it appears she is dead set on observing us.

"Will you be my lifelong mate?" I ask quickly before I decide to back down.

"Aren't we lifelong mates? Is this just temporary?" She asks, confused.

"Yes we are, I mean. It is more of a title, an official statement to the universe."

"Like marriage?" She asks. "Are you proposing to me?"

I recall one of the other humans discussing this and I can't remember what it meant, but I believe it was good, so I say, "Yes?"

"Yes!" Riley responds, slamming herself into my armored body. The light of her Crystashield flashes as it makes contact and the clang rings in my ears. "Sorry," she says sheepishly. Blue light flashes around here and she kisses me deeply.

My heart feels like it's going to explode with how full it has gotten and Riley's eyes glisten in the pale light of the station. Her beauty is staggering, and I almost can't handle the feeling coursing through me.

Commander Tarchond makes an odd noise, almost like a snort, but distorted through the modulation in her helmet. She turns away from us quickly and says, "We can plan a mating ritual on Dexterion. There are beautiful locations for it. I am very happy for the two of..." she trails off.

The commander presses her hand against her helmet quickly and after a moment says, "We are heading to bay twelve now. Do not engage unless necessary." Her hand slides away from her helmet and she adds, "I hate to ruin this momentous occasion, but we have to get to bay twelve, now."

"Any word on the Skeldi?" I ask. If only I could whisk Riley away and we could just be with each other in peace. Soon, once this is finished, we will have free rein of our lives.

"The ramps on their ships have lowered but none have come out yet."

"Do you think they're making a plan of attack?" Riley asks, wiping tears from her eyes. The light of her Crystashield flickers into view as she turns it back on.

"The Skeldi are not brilliant tacticians, they usually just use brute force. It is alarming that I got word from all of my captains at once that the ramps were lowered, though."

"The Alphur may be helping them coordinate," I say.

"That will not be good," the commander says. Her usual confidence is still there but feels diminished.

We pick up the pace and, thanks to the deserted streets, we get to the bay quickly. The door to the landing bay rises up, and we are met by Captain Pelindrophin and Captain Zurandan. I assume, anyway; they are all but indistinguishable in their armor. One Khuvex in blue armor is watching a monitor showing a feed of the landing bay. Ships similar to the ones on the first planet are in view with ramps down. The eleven other Khuvex are facing the landing bay, spears raised and ready for a fight.

"No further movement has been detected," one captain says.

"Skeldi are leaving the ships," the blue Khuvex says a little too excitedly. I knew Scovein like him, eager to prove themselves in battle.

"The other captains are reporting the same, the battle is upon us, may our blades guide us to victory," Commander Tarchond says, gripping her sword tightly.

I check on Riley quickly. She looks nervous but is still holding strong. Her pistol is gripped firmly in her hand and is fully charged. I hope she does not have to use it, but I also hope she does not hesitate if it's necessary.

I take an opening in the line of Khuvex and level my gun into the landing bay. Riley moves up beside me, her gun pointed towards the incoming creatures. I start to reach out to her and push her behind me. I don't want her in the line of fire, but a shot blasts through the air and hits the frame of the door behind us. It sizzles loudly and molten metal drips onto the floor.

Fuck, here we go. I guide Riley behind me and feel her shift around my body, trying to get a view of what's happening. More shots connect with the wall behind us and I scan the area for where they're coming from. That's plasma, but the color is off, it's red instead of green. I don't know what that means, but it can't be good.

A red light flashes behind a nearby ship and I level my gun and fire off a shot. It connects with the chest of the Skeldi peeking around the landing gears and a bellowing roar echoes through the landing bay as the plasma eats away at the Skeldi.

"They are using Pelron spheres," one captain shouts. "Do not get hit. Touch nothing that comes off of the projectile."

A sea of green rushes from between the

ships and some of the most creative insults I've heard start flying through the air, audible over the fire of guns. The Khuvex level their spears and simultaneously fire blasts of blue light from the tips. The Skeldi that are hit instantly drop to the ground and convulse before going still. Their spears around me whir loudly as they charge back up and another round of shots is fired from them. Several more Skeldi go down, but the sea is almost upon us.

Most of the Skeldi are using melee weapons, which buys us some time, but several dotted amongst them have guns and fire them into our line. One of the red blasts connects with a Khuvex down the line and he drops his spear as he scrambles to remove his armor. The latches click loudly and he flings his breastplate into the landing bay. It melts in seconds, leaving a puddle of molten metal and a small red ball. The Khuvex grabs his spear and aims towards the horde again. Before he can fire, another burst of red connects with his helmeted face. The red bolt explodes on contacts like a water balloon filled with paint, splattering the armor of the two nearest Khuvex and eating away at their armor with loud sizzling.

The Khuvex that was hit tries to take his helmet off, but the fingers of his gauntlets melt as they touch the remnants of the Pelron sphere. He lets out a scream as his hands are pulled further into his melting helmet. His screams go silent and he falls to his knees, then collapses. The two Khuvex beside him quickly release the armor on their arms and it clatters to the ground. The metal of the armor drags towards the helmet of the fallen Khuvex, melting and sliding into the helmet. A small red ball sits in the middle of the puddle of metal.

"What the fuck is that?" I shout as I fire off another shot and take out one of the Skeldi snipers. I have never seen a weapon like that.

Riley falls to the ground behind me and I crouch down to check on her and make sure she wasn't hit. She's digging through her backpack and pulls out an h5 serum before she crawls towards the downed Khuvex.

I grab her quickly and say, "He's gone. Stay behind me."

Riley glances over at the Khuvex, then back at me. Her eyes are watering and she just nods and puts the serum back in her pack before tucking behind me again.

One captain steps to the front of the line and aims a very large tube towards the Skeldi. He presses a switch on the side and a deafening roar emanates from the end as a cloud of smoke fires out of the front. The smoke twists and bends in the air like a serpent before contacting the center column of the Skeldi. It blasts through the length and covers at least thirty of them. Roars of pain quickly turn to silence. The smoke disappears and reveals a straight line of ash where the Skeldi were.

"Just one shot," the captain says, dropping the tube to the ground and drawing a large, spiked hammer from his waist. It bursts into a blue flame like Commander Tarchond's and he takes a battle stance at the front of the line.

The Khuvex simultaneously drop their spears and draw their blades just before the Skeldi crash upon us and the sounds of battle drown out any other noise. Armor and blades collide, Khuvex and Skeldi roar at one another, and body after body thumps to the floor.

My focus now is on Riley and keeping her safe. I put a hand behind me and feel her there, then guide us backward toward the landing bay door. I fire off shot after shot, flooring several Skeldi as they lock blades with the Khuvex. I try to take stock of what's happening, but there is so much chaos I can't clearly tell who is winning.

A bright blue sword raises into the air and descends rapidly before appearing again. Commander Tarchond is okay, at least. I catch a glimpse of two more blue flames, what I assume is the other two captains. The number of Khuvex has dwindled greatly, silver-armored bodies are strewn around with one of the blue armored ones. The Skeldi pile up more numerous than the Khuvex and finally silence descends in the bay.

"Forty-two Skeldi down, plus however many the captain incinerated," the remaining blue-armored Khuvex says as he flips over a Skeldi corpse with his foot.

"And ten Khuvex lost," Commander Tarchond says stiffly. She turns to the four still standing Khuvex. Two green captains, one blue officer, and one silver-clad crewmate.

Riley drops to her knees nearby and places her feet on one of the downed Khuvex. She pulls on the shoulder of his armor and it pops off with a loud click. She instantly drives the end of an h5 serum into the Khuvex shoulder and buries her head into her hands.

I crouch down beside her and put my arm across her shoulder. She cries quietly for just a second before sniffing loudly and standing up. She throws her backpack on her shoulders and looks to me for direction. My little selkin, so brave and resolute. We will get through this.

The Khuvex on the ground gasps and sits upright before immediately collapsing onto his back again. Well, make that two silver-clad crewmates still alive.

"You saved him, selkin," I say gently to

Riley. Her face lights up and I can see the relief on her face. At least she can have a small victory for herself right now. I fear worse is to come.

"No one else is responding," Commander Tarchond announces. "We need to move to the other bays. Not enough of us to split up, so we will travel together. Bay seven is closest, bay five has the most Skeldi. We will stop at seven and hopefully bolster our ranks before moving to five."

With that, she marches out of the door and turns down a hallway connecting all the bays. The Alphur is here somewhere. I am concerned about it joining the battle.

Bay seven was a mess of bodies and burn marks, but thankfully, more than a few Khuvex survived the battle. Two more captains and seven silver crewmates joined our ranks, and we moved quickly towards bay five. The sound of battle from bay five could be heard from where we were, and the smell of burning bodies and death permeated the corridor. Shouts and gunfire grew louder as we passed bay six and closed in on bay five.

Flashes of red and blue light come into view further down the wide corridor, each burst of light reflecting down the length of the silvered walls. The sounds of battle become overpowering and I shout at Riley, "Stay close."

She says something inaudible and nods at me, drawing her pistol and holding it at the ready. Stay strong, selkin. I find our connection and push thoughts of comfort and confidence to her and hold it as long as I can. Her posture straightens and her face turns to stone as she steels herself for the coming fight. So fierce, so strong. We will get through this.

"Close the doors, seal them in!" A distressed voice shouts ahead. We round the curve of the hallway and see the chaos spread before us. The station security had arrived at bay five and was assisting the Khuvex in fighting off the Skeldi. They weren't faring well. The security's armor paled in comparison to the Khuvex. I wince as one of the Pelron spheres explodes across the uncovered face of a guard. He didn't even have time to scream.

"Bolster their ranks, move in!" Commander Tarchond shouts as the Khuvex break off into a sprint, weapons drawn. I take off towards them but move a little slower so Riley can keep up. She's sprinting with us with surprising speed.

Clashing metal rings through the area as the Khuvex collide with the Skeldi, who are almost out of the doors. Their spears pierce into green flesh and skewer the beasts where they stand. I get a view through the doors and the number of Skeldi is unbelievable. They must have crammed every spare inch in the ships with bodies. We thought there would be two hundred total. There are over two hundred just in this landing bay.

The Alphur is here somewhere. It would be present with the bulk of the forces and it's not going to let them lose.

Almost on cue, an otherworldly shriek fills the landing bay and all the Khuvex, Skeldi, and station guards falter at the noise. There it is.

"What in the blazes is that?" A guard shouts. His armor chipped and cracked, blood trickling down his cheek while one of his four arms hangs uselessly at his side.

"Can't be good," another guard replies. This one's much smaller and apparently faster. His armor is spotless. He ducks under a Skeldi blade and drives a stun rod into its throat. The impact was almost audible over the other sounds and a blue electric spark fired out of the rod and the Skeldi went down. The indention in its throat signalled a more permanent incapacitation.

"Seal the doors," the same voice shouts again from inside the landing bay. One of the Khuvex captains is standing next to the unmoving body of another. Her helmet has been ripped off, and she's swinging a flaming blue axe wildly at the Skeldi swarming her.

"Captain Lirien, retreat immediately," Commander Tarchond shouts, severing the arm of a Skeldi assailant mid-sentence.

"Seal the damned doors, Laurelyn," the captain replies in a frenzy. Fear and panic consume her voice, but the look on her face is pure determination.

The Khuvex surrounding her did not even look back. They never tore their eyes from the threat at hand and remained by their captain. Unwavering loyalty until the end of time.

"Seal the doors," Commander Tarchond shouts at a group of guards nearby. They scurry off to the door controls. The doors to the landing bay swing shut and a massive metal barrier descends slowly from the ceiling. Painfully slowly. "Seal the corridor and this section of the station."

The doors on either side of the hallway slide shut and shields drop quickly across them. Red lights flash and an announcement over the intercom says, "The Pranuvan District will be sealed off in thirty seconds. Vacate immediately. The Pranuvan District will be sealed off in twenty-five seconds. Vacate immediately."

The few Skeldi on this side of the door are put down quickly by the Khuvex and guards. The second the last Skeldi hit the ground, Riley took off to check on our downed allies. I placed myself between the door and her as she worked, peeling off armor and injecting h5 serum into as many people as she could. Bandaging others and trying not to weep over the rest.

Shouts and the sounds of combat, muffled by the doors, still rage on the other side. That screech penetrates the doors and echoes through the hallways, silencing the murmurs of the exhausted crew of people waiting for their next orders.

The shield over the landing bay doors is halfway down now. I fear it will not be fast enough.

"Can that fucking thing not go any fucking faster?" One guard at the control shouts panicked.

"Nope," another guard replies calmly. Her face is covered with fresh wounds and her armor is cracked and stained. The look on her face is blank and empty. She has been scarred deeper than the flesh wounds she's received. I fear Riley may experience the same. Deep emotional wounds that will take time to heal. I hope not, but if that comes to pass, I will be with her through the healing process. No matter what.

Riley finishes assisting as many people as she can before joining me at my side. I try to move in front of her, but she shifts and stays by my side. She looks ahead and has her pistol at the ready. The look of determination on her face is raw and unyielding.

CHAPTER SIXTEEN

RILEY

Fuck me, I'm terrified. I've patched up as many people as I can. Sadly, there are far too many that are gone already. This is awful. The wounds have been so devastating and grotesque. The ones that were hit with that red light are completely unsalvageable.

I sigh heavily and lean against Zaltas. I'm desperate to feel his skin against me, but the armor will have to do for now. My armor keeps me from even feeling anything except on my fingertips, so I guess it wouldn't matter, anyway.

Our bridge to one another glows brightly as I close my eyes and focus on feeling it. I still don't fully understand how this works, but damned if it doesn't help. It's like I can feel all of his emotions and draw strength from him. It works wonderfully for soothing my mind. I try to send good thoughts to him too, but I feel like

I'm half-assing it. Everything is so overwhelming.

The light of the bridge fizzles and fades. What was once solid steel, rusts and crumbles in the darkness and all thoughts of warmth and serenity vanish from my head.

Riley.

A cold chill climbs up my spine. It's here.

My eyes spring open and look at Zaltas. He pulls me in tightly and holds me in the midst of the carnage. My beacon of light in the pitch-black depths. I feel confidence swell inside of me again, but the comfort from the connection is muted and dim.

Riley.

"It's here, Zaltas. It's in my head," I say, panicked.

"Stay calm, selkin. It is resistible. Do not allow it to grab hold. Focus on our bond, focus on the connection."

My eyes close again. I'm not sure if that was voluntary.

Riley. There is no favorable outcome for your resistance. Give in to me. I can make you whole.

I try to ignore the voice and feel for Zaltas.

No hope. Stop the doors. Release us.

A small thread, that's all I feel, leading into the darkness.

The connection was never real. An illusion of trust. Deceitful. Fake. You have been used.

The thread grows thicker as I latch my thoughts onto it. I focus on where it leads and try to navigate to the end.

Riley. It is useless.

The thread bursts into a warm glow in my mind's eye and expands into the solid beam that I had felt before. Zaltas is there on the other end. The connection is true. The Alphur is trying to deceive me. I will have no doubts. You cannot control me.

An ear-piercing shriek sends my hands flying to my ears. I thought it was in my head, but it wasn't. Everyone else turns their attention to the door immediately. The shriek sounds once more, drowning out the frantic shouting on the other side of the door. The shield has ten feet to go.

It's too late. A massive green object bursts through the doorway and lands with a loud thud on the ground before sliding noisily to a stop. It was Captain Lirien. Her armor coated in the blood of no telling how many Skeldi, and long claw marks slashed down her torso. They went clean through the armor and revealed her torn flesh. Three holes were bored into the helmet, no doubt from the Alphur.

Skeldi poured through the doorway as the shield stopped moving once it touched the open doors. Through the throng of green bodies, I spotted the towering figure of the Alphur. It glided effortlessly through the crowd of Skeldi and ducked as it passed through the doorway. The Alphur crouches down amidst the Skeldi and disappears from sight. Several guards lift into the air, thick black claws impaling their bodies before they drop to the ground.

The Khuvex and guards clash with the Skeldi, trying desperately to keep them from spilling out into the station. Laurelyn swoops in and ruthlessly dispatches two Skeldi with a single swipe in front of me and Zaltas. She stays near us and fights off the swarm. Zaltas fires shot after shot into the Skeldi, but there doesn't seem to be much progress. There's way too fucking many of them.

A red blast hits a nearby guard and I turn my head away from the mess that's about to unfold where his face was. Those weapons are horrifying and whoever uses them is a piece of shit. I can't stand by anymore.

I whip around Zaltas and feel my blood boiling. So many lives lost because of this fucking Alphur and these fucking Skeldi. I fire a shot from the plasma pistol and overcompensate. I was expecting recoil, but the gun didn't even move when I fired. The shot connects with one of the Skeldi's legs and blows it off. It topples over and a Khuvex quickly thrusts a spear through its eye socket.

I'm not proud of myself, but he surely had it coming. I know they're being controlled by the Alphur and it's not completely fair, but Laurelyn said they were terrible creatures, anyway. Raping, pillaging, murdering. I remember all she told me to help steel myself for what I was doing.

Another green pulse erupts from my gun and slams into the chest of a Skeldi, it bowls over backward and twitches briefly on the floor before going still. Several guards and a couple of Khuvex go down to the blades of the Skeldi, and I have to restrain myself from rushing over. I will help when the fighting stops. I promise, hang in there.

Four Skeldi run at me and Zaltas. Laurelyn engages two and puts them down quickly, but the other two slip past her. Blades raised, they get within arm's reach. I fire off a shot and the arm of one of them rips off and falls to the ground, but it doesn't falter. It presses forward. Zaltas blocks the blow from the first Skeldi's blade with his gun. They cut one tube off, and the gun spews green steam.

"Fuck," Zaltas says, slamming the gun into the Skeldi's face and drawing his blade with his free hand. He drives the blade deep into the second Skeldi's throat and slams his gun into the other Skeldi's face again. Both collapse to the ground in pools of blood.

Zaltas tosses his gun through the landing bay doors, amidst the never-ending stream of Skeldi. A loud hiss drowns out the noise of battle and an emerald explosion coats the doorway with green goo. It eats into the metal and the roars and screams of Skeldi caught in the blast as their bodies melt away echo down the hallway.

Several dozen Skeldi slip past our group and disappear further into the station. Zaltas starts to follow them, but the Alphur shrieks again, drawing his attention. Several flashes of purple light amidst the bodies of Skeldi cause the Alphur to shriek with each burst. The UV light from the Khuvex armor must be working.

"Tarchond, Skeldi got into the station," Zaltas shouts at Laurelyn as he drives his blade into another Skeldi.

"Nuraland, Bulrast," Laurelyn shouts, pausing to skewer a Skeldi. "Into the station, protect the citizens."

Two of the captains rush into the station, followed by four silver Khuvex. Three guards take off after them. Our people are dwindling quickly, we have to figure something out soon.

The shield above the landing bay doors groans loudly and crashes to the ground, shaking the floor beneath us. The flow of Skeldi stops and the Khuvex and guards fight with renewed vigor. This might be winnable now. The shield over the landing bay doors rattles loudly as the Skeldi on the other side try to get through.

A shriek tears through the area and floors everyone and everything. The Alphur stands alone, wave after wave crashing across the room, keeping everyone pinned to the ground. It finally relents and before anyone can get to their feet, the Alphur tears through several Khuvex and guards. Easily ripping through their armor, streaks of blood flashing through the air as its claws tear through flesh and metal.

The battle resumes and the Skeldi go down one after another as we move our way towards the Alphur. Laurelyn follows close behind me and Zaltas clears a path in front. His freehand draws the Melt Knife from his belt and grips it at the ready. We're joined by the two remaining captains and thin down the herd of Skeldi as we move.

My plasma pistol 'whomps' quietly with every shot I fire. I've lost count of how many Skeldi I have downed at this point. All of those stress relief days at the gun range paid off, apparently. The bulk of the remaining Skeldi take off into the station, leaving just a handful alone with the Alphur. I'm not sure the Alphur needs anyone else. It seems to do just fine alone.

Three station guards drop at the hands of the Alphur as we approach cautiously. The rest of the station guards left in pursuit of the Skeldi, realizing they're clearly outmatched by the Alphur. Probably a smart decision, but not one we can make. Zaltas currently holds the only known method of putting it down. There's no going back now. The last four silver Khuvex with us fall to the hands of the Alphur and I focus on keeping a mental note on who I can help, there's few. The Alphur goes for the face and throat of everyone that draws near and the h5 serum can't bring back the dead. Likewise, the Skeldi go for dismemberment and the neck, there's hardly anyone I can save, if anyone.

The six remaining Skeldi turn their attention to us when the four Khuvex go down and lunge, blades raised high. Laurelyn swings at one. It tries to block her blow, but his blade shatters and hers slides through its neck. My plasma shot slams into the chest of one flanking us. Zaltas slashes across the face of one while he drives the end of the Melt Knife into the chest of another. The final two back-off quickly from our little deathball, but the two captains skewer them with their spears before they take two steps.

I swallow the lump forming in my throat and push the feelings of panic deep into my emotional safe and slam the door shut. I'll process all of that unhealthily at a later time. Preferably with a lot of candy and fried foods.

"Don't!" Zaltas shouts, and I follow his stare. Laurelyn has dove towards the Alphur, sword blazing in all of its glory, sliding through the air for the killing blow.

The blade connects with the Alphur and its flesh bursts into flames. Her armor glows purple as the UV light bathes the Alphur. The rest of its flesh sizzles and burns and another screech emanates from the depths of sharp teeth between its lips.

Yes, we've got this! Hope builds inside me that this is almost over. The body count is unimaginable, but we're going to win.

My hopes crash to the ground and evaporate as the Alphur drives a clawed hand deep into Laurelyn's abdomen. The claws pop out of the back of her armor. Her free hand grips the Alphur by the shoulder as it lifts her into the air and she slides her blade a little further into its torso. The Alphur's other hand rakes down the front of her armor and the purple light flickers then fades.

Her body collides with the nearby wall

with a loud crash and she falls to the ground, unmoving.

No, no, no, no. Rage builds to unbearable levels and my vision goes red as I fire shot after shot into the Alphur's torso. The plasma eats away at its skin, but its flesh regenerates faster than I can pull the trigger. Zaltas moves towards the Alphur, flanked by the two captains. The Alphur swipes at Zaltas, but he ducks under the blow and slices off the Alphur's hand. It screeches loudly and swings wildly with its remaining claws.

The two Khuvex and Zaltas explode into purple light and the Alphur shrieks as its skin sizzles. Its severed hand is already halfway reformed but slows down its regeneration in the light. I want to fire into the Alphur more, but I fear hitting Zaltas or the Khuvex and the urge to check on Laurelyn is overwhelming. I steel myself and stand at the ready with my gun raised. I don't know if it'll help, but I'll light it up if it escapes them.

The two captains drive their spears into both sides of the Alphur. Their spears slide through it and crisscross one another, each one poking out of the opposite shoulder. The Alphur latches onto one of the Khuvex with its newly formed hand and pulls her in close. UV slowed it down, but not enough. The other Khuvex pushes its spear as deep as it can and leaps onto the Alphur's other arm. He grips it tightly and pulls it behind the Alphur, bracing himself against its back and holding steady.

The Alphur's teeth bite into the Khuvex it has gripped and they sink easily into the metal. It rips off a chunk of the helmet, revealing her black hair. Luckily, it looks like there was a little gap on top of the helmets. She twists her body and grabs hold of the Alphur's arm. Swinging around to join the other captain at its rear. Zaltas takes this opportunity and dives towards the Alphur's chest, Melt Knife in hand, blade ready to drive deep into its torso.

One captain slips on the blood-soaked ground and loses his grip on the Alphur's arm. It quickly pulls free and knocks Zaltas away with a swipe. He falls onto his back, revealing a huge gash in his armor. It immediately slams its claws into the Khuvex woman's side. The other Khuvex snatches its arm quickly and pulls it back behind the Alphur, but the damage has been done.

My heart sinks and every emotion inside of me is replaced with burning, white hot, unyielding rage.

"Fuck you, you fucking asshole," I shout as I storm towards the Alphur, gun aimed at its face. I fire off a shot and it collides dead center in the Alphur's face. It screeches briefly before the plasma eats away at its face and muffles it. But it doesn't collapse. It stays standing and is still visibly struggling against the two Khuvex clenching it.

I start to pull the trigger again but stop as Zaltas rises to his feet and sprints at the Alphur. A mixture of relief, anger, fear, panic, joy, and I don't know what else coalesces inside of me into something indescribable and I feel completely overwhelmed. Everything moves in slow motion and my brain stops functioning past mere observation.

The tip of the Melt Knife drives deep into the sternum of the Alphur. It sinks up to the hilt and a dull light glows inside of it. The light gets brighter and brighter, eventually overtaking the purple light from Zaltas and the Khuvex's armor. A burbling shriek rises from the Alphur's partially regenerated mouth and goes silent. Its body becomes hard to look at; all of its features disappear into one mass of white.

Suddenly, the light disappears completely. My eyes burn from the intensity of the light and my vision feels fuzzy, but I can still make out the Alphur standing above the Khuvex and Zaltas. It didn't work? We're fucked. My eyes are greeted again by another flash of bright light that diminishes instantly; the Alphur's body melts away into a puddle of steaming sludge on the ground.

The Khuvex falls to the ground and laughs loudly as he lays back on the ground. Zaltas sits himself down and stares quietly at the sludge spreading in front of him. The female captain still stands, arms bent like they're holding onto the Alphur's arm.

"Pelindrophin?" The other captain asks, his laughter quickly replaced with concern. He gets off the ground and goes to check on her. I finally snap out of my daze and rush to check on Zaltas.

"Selkin, it is not life-threatening, it barely got through the armor," he says with an unconvincing wince, "check on the commander."

"Let me look," I demand.

"I will survive. Check on the commander."

I hurry to Laurelyn, she's face down on the ground and a pool of blood has formed under her. Oh, this isn't good. I do my best to not move her, no telling how much damage that impact did, and get her back piece off. The wounds are ragged around the edges and blood runs down her back, joining the rest on the ground. Sorrow overtakes me and I resume my crusade of fighting off tears, but then I notice her back shift, almost imperceptibly. I lean in and watch closely. It moves ever so slightly again. She's breathing!

Digging out an h5 serum from my pack quickly, I jam it into her shoulder and inject the contents. It only takes minutes to work. Hopefully the biggest damage will be healed up and I can patch up whatever remains. I've noticed the h5 serum seems to have a limit to what it can heal with one dose. It seems like it prioritizes life-threatening injuries and leaves smaller ones. I should have quizzed Aurelia on it more than I did. Bad medic, I know. The wounds on her back don't seem to be closing up at all, it's not instant, but you can see the progress.

I pull out another serum. I've only got four left. One for Zaltas, one for each captain, and one more for you, Laurelyn. I inject her one more time and see the holes in her back start to slowly close up. I sigh with relief. The dose limit is two in a four-day period, otherwise you risk neurogenic shock. Hopefully, that's all she'll need.

"Okay, she's healing up," I say as I approach Zaltas.

"Check the captains, selkin," he replies.

"I am fine," the male captain says as he seats himself in front of us. He sighs deeply and with a pained tone continues, "Captain Pelindrophin is dead."

Zaltas and I look towards the still standing captain.

"She's standing? I have more h5, I can help her," I say and move towards her.

"She locked her armor in place and deployed climbers. She bled out sometime during the fight. She is gone. There is no use. Her vitals monitor is flatlined," the captain replies solemnly. "It was my fault. I faltered and got her killed and you injured," he continues, motioning to Zaltas.

Zaltas winces as he moves, but pushes through and places a hand firmly on the captain's shoulder. "She died a hero, and you lived as one. It matters not that you faltered. The Alphur is an unimaginable monster. We would not have been able to destroy it without the two of you."

The captain rises to his feet and says, "Perhaps. We must go, the others are still hunting the Skeldi in the station."

Zaltas stands too, and I huff at him. "You need to let me treat you."

"How many serums do you have left?" He asks.

"Three, but the station surely has more somewhere."

"Surely it does, but we do not know where, and my injuries can wait. Save them for others that may need them. I will not die from my injuries."

The thought of Zaltas being in pain drives me crazy, but I give in and stand with the two of them. Zaltas sheaths his knife and draws his other blade, and the captain checks his weapon. I take my place next to Zaltas, gun in hand, and we head into the station.

"Oh, fuck me," a metallic voice says behind us.

All three of us turn simultaneously to see Laurelyn sitting upright. She tries to wipe the blood off her armor but gives up quickly, as she only smears it across a larger area.

"That fucking hurt, you were not jesting about its strength," Laurelyn says as she rises to her feet and strides towards us unimpeded.

I burst into laughter. The relief I feel for both Zaltas and Laurelyn pulling through paired with her sudden habit of cursing was too much.

Laurelyn holds out her hand and her sword flies towards it and ignites into blue flames on contact. "Where is the Alphur?"

"It's dead," I say between tears of joy.

Zaltas motions towards the steaming pile of sludge on the ground and says, "I would recommend containing its remains and interring them somewhere secure, just to be safe. Or launching it into a star."

"Launching it into a star sounds wise," Laurelyn says.

"Command Tarchond, I am glad to see you well," the captain says.

"Same to you Captain Zurandan," Laurelyn says, then her tone changes to a more somber sound. "Is there anyone still left?"

"No one is left here, still standing anyway. Riley likely managed to save several of our soldiers and some guards, but they are still unconscious. Nuraland and Bulrast went deeper into the station with four soldiers and a handful of guards to try to eliminate the Skeldi that breached our line. I have not heard from them."

I hope I saved some people.

"There are still Skeldi on the station? We must go to assist," Laurelyn says sternly and marches into the Pranuvan district.

Zaltas, Captain Zurandan, and I follow behind her quickly. Zaltas is moving slowly and I'm concerned his injuries are worse than he is letting on. If it dies because he is being stubborn, I will never forgive him or myself for not pushing the point.

"Are you three sure you are okay for another fight?" I ask the group.

"I have suffered worse," Laurelyn states.

"Minor injuries," Captain Zurandan says.

"I will be fine, selkin. I would not leave you," Zaltas says.

"You three better not be lying to me…" If I find out later they are worse off than they are letting on, I will berate them endlessly.

The Pranuvan district differs greatly from the fashion district. It's set up more like a flea market than anything. Small booths spread off into the distance, with a few buildings stretching to the ceiling. The pathways between the booths are mostly empty, save for a few aliens draped across their booths with vicious wounds on their bodies. Some of them still grip weapons, no doubt staying to defend their shops from whatever threat was on the station. This district didn't have the luxury of massive metal shutters to drop over their shops.

Many of the booths look like they've been rifled through and looted. By the Skeldi or opportunists, I don't know. It's sickening to me that someone might have taken advantage of this horrifying attack to steal from their neighbors.

A loud clattering comes from around the corner of one building and the four of us rush over, weapons at the ready. Relief washes over me as we are greeted by six Khuvex and a handful of station guards. At least a dozen Skeldi are currently restrained on the ground.

"Commander Laurelyn," one captain says. "The Pranuvan district is secure."

"Excellent work," Laurelyn says, removing her helmet. Her face was set in misery and she looked exhausted. "Was this all that made it through?"

"No, there are many more dead throughout the district. These surrendered suddenly and we put down the rest."

"This ain't right, we were not supposed to be 'ere," one of the Skeldi says as best as he can through the restraints covering most of his face.

"And yet, you were here," Laurelyn replies.

"Something was in my 'ead," another Skeldi says and the rest murmur in agreement. "We were scavengin' and got called 'ere. We gave up soon as the voice was gone."

Laurelyn makes a thoughtful noise and says, "We will take you to Dexterion and there will be a trial. The Alphur's ability to control the minds of others is known and will be taken into consideration."

"The fuck's an Alphur?" One of the Skeldi asks, but is ignored.

"Captain Bulrast, take some guards, load them up and secure them in Palindria," Laurelyn orders one of the captains.

"Yes ma'am," the captain salutes and starts stacking the bound Skeldi on a hovering cart that a guard retrieved from a nearby building.

Zaltas removes his helmet and sits on the ground beside me, motioning for me to join him. I take a seat and press myself up against him as he wraps an arm around my shoulder. Armor off. The blue light around me flashes and disappears, and I feel his arm pressed against me. I let out a quiet sigh and rest my head against his chest.

"Are you sure you're okay?" I ask.

"Nothing a healing bath won't fix," he says with a grin. "You can join me."

My body is too exhausted and my mind too frayed to even think about sex, but still… the thought of being in a warm, relaxing bath with my mate sounds tantalizing.

"Yes, please."

"What of the station?" One of the guards asks Laurelyn.

"Where is Lead-security Belrond?" She replies, more concern in her voice. I really hope her friend wasn't killed during all of this.

"She was dispatched to Darvon to consult for their new expansion."

Laurelyn sighs with relief and says, "I will contact her and get her back here. In the meantime Captain Nuraland will stay to assist with cleanup and reconstruction. I will contact Dexterion and have them dispatch assistance as well."

"Thank you," the guard says and returns to help load Skeldi.

"Captain Nuraland," Laurelyn says and places her hand on the captain's shoulder. "Get some rest, have a bath. You are now on leave for the next four hours. Then assist the station with command until Belrond arrives. Then you are to report home immediately."

The captain salutes and says, "As you order." He turns to leave, but Laurelyn grips his shoulder tighter.

"Take this," she says and passes the card from station command to him. "Remove the lockdown and shut off that damn broadcast before you rest."

The captain salutes again and heads deeper into the district.

I had drowned it out after hearing it a dozen times and just now realized the shelter in place broadcast was still playing over the intercoms.

"You two," Laurelyn directs her attention to me and Zaltas. Look, I'm happy to help with whatever they need and I'm sure Zaltas is, but we really need a minute. I wish I had Laurelyn's grit and determination to get the job done, but I can't keep moving forever like she apparently can.

"Return to Aurelia, head to Dexterion. Rest, heal," she says and looks between the two of us. "And work off whatever tension you have. We will meet tomorrow."

"I don't need to be told twice," Zaltas says, jumping to his feet and offering his hand to me.

"Thanks, Laurelyn," I say as we pass her and head towards the landing bays. She winks at me and wiggles her eyebrows at me. That lady is so confusing, I can't figure her out to save my life. I want to tell her she needs to take a break too and rest, but I know it will fall on deaf ears.

We began to head into the main corridor connecting the landing bays, but a guard waves us over to a smaller door inside the district.

"Where are you heading?" She asks. Her silky pink hair bounces gently as she tilts her head at us. Her armor is dented and cracked, but she looks uninjured. How she kept her hair so clean looking during all of that is beyond me.

Mine would be a tangled mess right now if I hadn't put it up.

"Bay twelve," I say.

"Here, go this way instead. Less... mess," she taps a console and the large metal plate beside her grinds loudly as it raises into the ceiling and reveals a small doorway.

"Thank you," I say as we pass through the doorway.

The path we follow hugs the wall of the landing bay hallway and has smaller doors dotted along it with signs above marking each bay.

As we pass bay eight, the broadcast stops and a final announcement plays. "Lockdown is lifted. The station has been compromised but is under control again. Please assist command with reconstruction if you are able."

The further we walk down the path, the more people we see milling about. They hesitantly come out of their shops and buildings. Most look relieved to see that their district is untouched. I feel bad for the people in the Pranuvan district. It sounds like there's a lot to clean up there.

Bay twelve finally appears, and we go into the doorway. The mass of bodies is almost too much to bear and I try to shield my eyes as best as I can. The adrenaline has faded from my body and now I just feel exhaustion and like I'm on the verge of a mental breakdown.

Some relief touches me, though. I see the Khuvex I injected with serum earlier had moved up against the wall by the door. He was still unconscious, but his head bobbed slightly as he breathed and a station guard was currently attending to him.

Luckily, once past the doorway, things in the landing bay looked mostly normal. It's funny how seeing a sprawling room full of massive spaceships was considered normal to me now.

Aurelia's ramp lowers as we approach, and she doesn't even wait until we're inside to greet us. Her voice booms loudly. "You are alive and appear intact. I am very relieved."

"Hi, Aurelia," I say.

"We are relieved we are alive, too," Zaltas says with a smirk.

"Did Laurelyn make it?" Aurelia asks, a little quieter now that we're climbing her ramp.

"Yes, she is alive and acting like she didn't almost die. Which she did," I say, shaking my head.

"That is a relief. You must tell me what happened once you have rested. I have only gotten bits of information from the other Khuvex ships in the station."

"We will fill you in, Aurelia, don't worry."

Aurelia makes a pleasant chiming noise and remains quiet.

The stairs to the main part of Aurelia loom above me, and I sigh deeply. Climbing stairs is the last thing I want to do right now.

"Carry me," I say to Zaltas with a smile. I'm just joking, but Zaltas tosses his helmet unceremoniously into an empty crate and scoops me up into his arms. He winces at the movement but smiles down at me. "I was kidding."

Zaltas carries me up the stairs and swings me carefully through the doorway before setting me delicately on my feet. His hand immediately goes to his abdomen, and he walks into the kitchen. I start to fuss at him for being injured and not letting me look, but I watch in awe as he drinks an entire pitcher of liquid and consumes several trays of food as he stands at the sink.

Eating over the sink is one of those things that I would have assumed is uniquely human. It seems like the mark of adulthood, standing over the sink and eating while staring out of the window. Such an odd crossover between humanity and aliens.

"Aurelia, take us to Dexterion," Zaltas says between mouthfuls.

"Initiating takeoff sequence," Aurelia says. "Departure confirmed. Exiting station."

The floor shifts gently as Aurelia lifts off and glides towards the exit. Zaltas pays the motion no mind and continues eating. I join him by the sink after retrieving a drink and a container of food from the fridge. We stand quietly, watching one another as we eat.

"Station exited, moving to warp clearance," Aurelia says.

A couple of minutes later she continues, "Warp clearance reached. Initiating warp in ten seconds, please restrain yourselves. Dampener failure chance at point zero five percent." I start to move towards one of the chairs but restraints come out of the floor and secure my legs in place, along with Zaltas'. He still pays no mind and keeps tearing through his food. More restraints come out of the nearby wall and cover our torsos and hold us steady. Zaltas winces when they constrict around him.

"Warp initiated successfully. Estimated arrival: five hours."

The restraints disappear from us, and we finish our meal.

Once he drops his last empty container into the sink, I break the silence.

"Armor off, now. Go to the relaxation room."

He's not fighting me on this any longer. Healing bath, dim lights, soothing sounds, a small waterfall, dark green walls. I send several directions for the relaxation room, shifting it into a quiet retreat for the two of us. Privacy mode.

"I like where this is going," Zaltas says with a smirk as he carefully removes his weapons from his belt and sets them on the counter. He drops the armor off his lower half first and removes the pants he's wearing under it. That big, blue cock of his pops into view, teasing me with a good time that I'm far too tired to take advantage of, sadly.

Zaltas saunters down the hallway towards the relaxation room, his juicy ass swaying with each step. He still has the top half of his armor on.

"Zaltas," I say sternly, trying to ignore the taunting display he's putting on for me. The view is delightful, but this is important.

He stops in the hallway and carefully removes the rest of his armor. It clatters to the ground noisily and he turns to face me, completely nude.

Three gnarly gashes slide from his collarbone down to his hips. The Alphur had gotten in much deeper than I thought initially. Trails of dried blood run down his body from the edges of each gash and the wounds glisten in the light.

"You said you were fine!" I shout. I'm trying not to be mad, he's injured and probably in immense pain, but he should have let me treat him earlier.

"I said it would not kill me. I did not say I was fine," Zaltas retorts.

I roll my eyes at him and huff, "Okay, you got me there. Get into the relaxation room and into the healing bath."

Zaltas grins at me and forces me to smile back at him. That man will be the death of me.

He vanishes into the relaxation room and I drop my backpack on the table and remove my holster and gun, setting them gently beside it. I can't believe we made it out. It's over and we're alive, safe in Aurelia, and heading to Dexterion.

My fears and worries diminish as the realization that it really is over and all I have to do is spend time with Zaltas now. A burst of warmth floods me from our connection and I sigh happily. My body is weary and I want nothing more than to pass it in bed now, but I make my way to the relaxation room.

The room looks just like I envisioned it would, with a few extra flourishes that I didn't actively think of but apparently desired. Large potted plants and bamboo lattice line the dark green walls and a large wooden tub is sunk into the floor. Steam drifts lazily from the hazy green water that my love is currently immersed in.

I can't help but smile through my weariness. He looks so relaxed and the healing bath is already working wonders; the dried blood has vanished from his chest and the wound looks smaller than before.

Zaltas raises his head up and motions for me to join him. I drop off my clothes and try to slide the vambrace off my wrist, but it is too snug.

"The button on the side, hold it," Zaltas says cheerfully. His eyes roam across my naked body as I fiddle with the vambrace. I love the attention he lavishes on me and can't wait for the feeling of his body against mine with nothing between us.

I place the vambrace gently on a table by the door and slowly sink into the hot bath. The temperature is perfect and the crisp herby smell of the bath invades my nose as I fully immerse. I made it deep for Zaltas, so it goes up to my shoulders, and it is wonderful. I can feel every negative emotion melting away and all the aches and soreness fade to nothing.

Zaltas raved about the healing bath before, and now I see why. The relief is almost instantaneous. My mental well-being even feels better and better with each breath I take of the steamy air. I sigh deeply and slide deeper into the tub until the water touches my chin.

With a relaxed sound, Zaltas sinks deeper too; the tops of his shoulders are all I can see in the hazy water. His body glides through the water towards me and I lean back, waiting to feel him against me. My desire is granted. Zaltas pushes himself snuggly against me and I lean my head against his shoulder. The feel of his skin against mine is more relieving than the bath, and that's saying a lot. He puts his arm around me, his fingers gliding effortlessly across my back before grasping my shoulder and pulling me close. I plant my cheek on the side of his chest and let out another sigh.

We sit next to each other silently for a little while, each processing our own thoughts over what had happened. It was easier to deal with the recent trauma while being buried in Zaltas' firm, thick arms.

"We're really done?" I ask, breaking the quiet.

"Yes, selkin."

I snuggle up to him again and listen to his heart thud loudly in his chest. Everything actually turned out okay. We really made it. My hand glides across his chest and the slipperiness sends a pang of desire through me. I run across his chest once more and feel nothing but the smoothness of his hard chest. His wound has completely healed. That's a relief. I knew these baths were supposed to be incredible, but that wound was rough and I was concerned it would take a while. I can't bear the thought of him being in pain anymore.

The touch of his smooth skin sends another ripple of heat through me and I rub a little firmer across him this time. Another slippery sensation runs up my side as his hand finds its way slowly up my side, stopping just under my arm before descending again slowly, sliding with ease. Our eyes lock and our expressions are the same.

Without a word, I climb onto his lap, the length of his cock pressing against my ass. I wrap my arms around his neck and slide my ass across his shaft slowly, up and down. He lets out a quiet groan, and I giggle into his chest. Such a big, powerful man, and I have complete control over him right now. I pull myself towards his face and our lips collide as he slides his hands down my back, across my hips and down my thighs. My body tingles at every point he touches me, ripples of pleasure radiating out across my body like the ripple from a stone cast into a pond. I start feeling insatiable.

To my surprise, Zaltas lifts me up out of the tub and plants me on the floor. He stays in the water, grabbing my legs and pulling them apart. My ass glides across the floor as he pulls me to his already waiting tongue.

His face approaches slowly, and I lean my head back. The anticipation of what's coming is almost unbearable. I feel his tongue rub along my clit, light pressure at first, barely enough, but he hones in on the perfect pressure as he grips one of my thighs. A moan slips out of me as my back arches, pushing me further into his face.

Zaltas, who I already knew was a professional at eating, was also a professional at eating. The gusto with which he licked my folds and clit was astounding, and his enthusiasm made it all the more satisfying.

Pressure builds inside of me and I feel my core start convulsing, sending electric shivers through my body. I'm about to come, and hard. The moans become uncontrollable and my body pushes itself further into his face; I can't help but grind myself on it. I briefly worry about suffocating the poor man, but he grips my thighs tightly and pulls me in even closer, his tongue keeping perfect track with my every movement.

I try to speak, try to tell him how good it feels, how amazing he is, how perfect. But I can't. My words are replaced with more moans and my mind blanks completely as I come on his face. He continues licking me, but I slip away from him; the sensations become too much to bear. My twitches helplessly on the floor by the bath as it bathes in euphoria from Zaltas' tongue. Just when I thought sex couldn't get better, this fucker blows my mind again.

I think I need a few seconds but Zaltas says, "You taste just as delicious as I thought you would." That sends me back into a frenzy of desire.

"Fuck me," I demand, spreading my legs for him. I really want to show him what I can do with my mouth, but my body can't wait. I'll get you next time, big guy, I promise. I wink at him as he positions himself between my legs and I try to say something else, but his cock slips inside of me and slides hilt deep.

"Mmm." Is all I get out. Zaltas' thick cock slides in and out of me, filling me completely and applying that delicious pressure inside of me. His finger finds its way back to my clit and dances along it as he thrusts deep inside of me.

Heat builds rapidly in me and explodes again in an ecstatic release from my core. Tingles of pleasure wrack my mind and brain, further amplified by Zaltas' cock pulsing deep inside of me as he unloads himself.

Zaltas pulls my arms up to him and I wrap them around his chest, as best as I can, and he sets us both back in the water, still inside of me. After a few moments of intense kissing, he slips himself out of me and nestles me in the water beside him. We lean against each other, bathing in the afterglow. This can be our life from now on, and there's nothing else I want more.

"Again, we need a shower after a bath," I say.

"It appears that way."

CHAPTER SEVENTEEN

RILEY

"Temporarily patching into the bedroom for important updates. Exiting warp in ten seconds," Aurelia announces, stirring me from my blissful slumber.

I turn over, feeling for the heat of Zaltas' body, but he's nowhere to be found. I stretch myself across the silky sheets and enjoy the feeling of being clean and relaxed after what feels an eternity.

"Warp successfully ended," Aurelia says. "Entering the atmosphere of Dexterion in five minutes, prepare to be restrained."

"Oh, so you're not asking anymore?" I say to the ceiling.

"After you pointed it out, I deliberated, and it seems unnecessary."

"It was still polite, that's always good."

"Fine. Please," Aurelia stressed the word please, "restrain yourselves."

"You've gotten sassy lately," I say, sitting up in the bed and leaning against the cushioned headboard.

"I learned it from you and Zaltas. You speak to each other this way and it seems amusing."

"Well, can't argue with that. I blame Zaltas mostly, though."

"That is an accurate assumption."

"What's an accurate assumption?" Zaltas asks, entering the room with my backpack. He sets it on the bed in front of me. It looks stuffed with fresh supplies. "I restocked your backpack for you."

"Thank you," I say with a smile.

"What is an accurate assumption?" Zaltas asks again.

"That you are a bad influence on Aurelia's personality."

"Oh, that is an accurate assumption."

We laugh together and Zaltas crawls into bed and situates himself beside me.

"I am restraining you now, do not resist," Aurelia says. Restraints pop out of the headboard and secure the two of us to the bed and headboard.

"The 'do not resist' also seems unnecessary," I say.

"You could at least say please," Zaltas

adds.

"*Please*, do not resist."

"Much better," I giggle.

"Entering atmosphere. Docking request approved."

Our restraints disappear back into the bed and Aurelia says, "Landing in two minutes."

"Thanks Aurelia," Zaltas says.

"I do not have a choice but to inform you of travel updates. Restoring bedroom privacy," Aurelia says.

"So sassy," I giggle.

I wish we could just stay on Aurelia and travel the galaxy. I could do with a two-week cruise through space with Zaltas. Laurelyn ordered us here, though, or maybe requested. It's hard to tell with her.

"We'll be back," I wave to Aurelia as her ramp closes behind her.

"Take your time," she says, a smile in her voice.

The landing pad is much more ornate than the one we landed on when we first visited the planet and the power lift empties us directly into the palace gardens. V.I.P. status, nice. Two Khuvex guards in glistening, ornate turquoise armor greet us and direct us to follow them into the palace.

We pass by Lukto multiple times and it

waves each time. Such an odd little creature. The guards take us straight to the throne room, where the Baron is on full display in dazzling golden armor. His helmet rests on a cushioned table by the throne, and he stomps down the stairs to greet us.

"Zaltas, Riley," he booms as he approaches us with heavy footfalls. I can't tell if he's angry or happy. Either way, he's loud.

"I received word from the soldiers at the station. It is both a celebratory moment and a somber one. We lost thirty-nine Khuvex soldiers, but the Alphur was slain and the Skeldi driven off. We have you two to thank for that."

Zaltas and I look at one another with a shrug and turn back to the Baron. It feels odd being so heavily praised when, in reality, the Khuvex did most of the heavy lifting. Although, Zaltas was the one that delivered the fatal blow to the Alphur.

"It seems the stories and legends of the Alphur paled in comparison to the real thing and I should have taken more caution in your words," the Baron continues. "I shall not make that mistake again. Plans are already in place for today and tomorrow."

"I should hope it is unnecessary for anyone to be concerned about an Alphur again. What plans?" Zaltas asks.

"We will have a day of remembrance for the heroes that gave their lives defending the system today. Their bodies are recovered and en route to Dexterion, proper burials will be given and we will mourn the fallen. You will not be requested nor expected to join the mourning ceremony. Tomorrow, we will celebrate the victory over the Alphur and we will honor the fallen and the survivors with an award ceremony. You will be requested to join that because the two of you will receive one of our highest awards."

"I didn't really do anything," I say shyly. Being on the spot is not my favorite thing, and I felt more than useless during the battle. I don't feel very deserving of an award.

"Nonsense," the Baron says with a hand wave. "Laure... Commander Tarchond informed me that your medical skills saved eleven of our soldiers, nine station guards, and Commander Tarchond herself. That deserves recognition if anything does."

I feel my face turn red as the Baron plants a hand on my shoulder and squeezes it gently. He leans close to me and quietly adds, "Thank you for saving Laurelyn."

The Baron draws himself back up and says, "I heard you two have decided to perform the mating ritual as well."

Only Laurelyn knows about that. She must keep in close contact with her man. Such a gossip.

Zaltas' face transforms into that dopey grin of his that I can't get enough of and he says, "Yes, we have."

I don't know what the mating ritual entails and I'm not sure if Zaltas does either, but we're both eager to do it. I can't wait to spend the rest of my life with him, and I want the universe to know that he's mine and I'm his.

"Excellent," the Baron says with a broad smile. "We will organize that for tomorrow, too. The commander has some suggestions she would like to run by you later."

"Of course she does," I say with a grin and head shake. Normally, I would want to plan and prepare for ages for what would be the equivalent of a wedding, but I'm ready. I want this to happen, and I want it now.

"She is very opinionated," the Baron says thoughtfully, the shade of a longing smile on his lips. "Now, you two have a full run of the palace. Lukto will show you to your quarters. They will be your permanent quarters, free to come and go as you please, for the rest of your lives you will always have a place here on Dexterion. Go. Rest and we will see you in the morning."

I feel like we should go to the mourning ceremony, but the Baron saying he will see us in the morning makes me feel like it could be a Khuvex only event. Maybe we shouldn't show up to it unannounced. I'll see what Zaltas thinks later.

"This way, please," Lukto says behind me, startling and causing me to jump. Zaltas laughs at me and I slap him gently on the shoulder. He thinks it's hysterical whenever I get startled.

We follow Lukto out of the throne room and into the sprawling hallway from our first stay. This time, it stops at the very first door in the hall. "This belongs to you now, by order of the Baron," it says as the door flings open.

The room is easily twice the size of the previous one. The walls are royal blue and trimmed with silver. Several couches that all look like the one someone died on in the other room sit in front of a fireplace crackling with a purple flame. Various silver-framed paintings of different sizes hang on the walls next to four doors leading off to other rooms. Tables and chairs for dining rest in one corner and the other has another thing that resembles a television.

"Bathing facilities, balcony, master bedroom, spare room," Lukto says, pointing at each door. "You may make whatever changes you desire to the room, and as always, call on me if you need anything." With that, it closes the door behind itself and Zaltas and I stand in awe of our new home.

"There's no gold," Zaltas says in absolute shock.

"It is very refreshing, isn't it?" I say with a giggle. "You don't think anyone died on these couches, do you?"

"I am not going to ask," he says and plops down on top of one.

"Me either," I say, following his lead and landing next to him. It's just as comfortable as I imagined. I snuggle up to Zaltas and breathe him in, fully relaxed and serene. I'm in heaven.

△△△

We decided not to go to the mourning ceremony. Zaltas agreed with my assumption that they meant it for the Khuvex only, and we lounged about the room for the night. Lounging is putting it lightly. We fucked each other silly, is a more accurate description.

Now, Zaltas is passed out in bed, but I'm feeling restless. I sit on the balcony, holding the control tablet in my hand and cycling through the various options for the view. Some of them are beautiful, with pink skies, lazy floating clouds, and rolling green hills.

Others, not so peaceful. One I clicked onto was a raging red sea that looked like blood. Red rain poured from the sky in an angry torrent and lightning flashed overhead. Two massive serpent-like beasts fought each other in the distance and roared with anger back and forth. It was cool looking after I calmed down. It nearly gave me a heart attack when the scene started.

I settle on the view of a white beach with gentle turquoise water washing upon the sands. It was as close as I could find to a scene from Earth and would do for now. Something that sounds like seagulls, but with a much lower tone, calls off in the distance.

I lean back in my chair and watch the gentle waves. The tablet says there are over six thousand different options for the balcony. I could easily spend hours out here flipping through them.

The door to the balcony slides open and I look over with a grin, expecting to see Zaltas, but instead I'm greeted by Laurelyn. She's shockingly not in her armor. I've only seen her in armor or naked, so it's very surprising to see her wearing a dress. It's long and flowy, reaching down to her knees. The pearl white fabric shimmers in the light of the fake sun and makes her blue skin really pop. She looks so pretty.

"Laurelyn, hi," I say.

"Hello," Laurelyn says. "May I join you?"

"Of course." I motion to the empty lounge chair beside me.

Laurelyn collapses into it, less than gracefully, and stretches her long legs before shifting to her side to look at me.

"I have some thoughts about your mating ritual tomorrow," she says with a smile. "Would you like to see?"

"That'd make me very happy," I say.

She pulls a tablet from somewhere. I didn't see her carrying anything and have no clue where it came from. While I puzzle over that, she taps on it noisily and sets it on the table between us. A hologram pops up centered in the air between the two of us and she slides her finger across it. The page on the screen moves with each top and she stops at a folder labelled 'Riley Mating Ritual Ideas pt.1.'

I grin at myself, she's so thoughtful. How did she even have the time to do this? I guess being a commander you can delegate a lot of the work, but she seems the more hands on type.

The folder opens up, revealing its contents to us. More folders. The number at the top says there are twenty-three separate folders and a total of seventeen hundred files. My head is already spinning at what she has contained here. It's sweet, though. Who would have thought I'd have an alien helping me plan my wedding? I didn't even think I'd have anyone at all to help me if I ever got married. No one I knew would have gone to any lengths remotely this far.

"Laurelyn?"

"Hmm?" She flicks through the folders, looking for the best place to start.

"Will you be my maid-of-honor?"

She tears her gaze from the screen and smiles softly at me, "I would be delighted."

After staring at me for a moment, she asks, "What is that?"

I giggle and say, "You would help me plan the wedding... mating ceremony, and during the ceremony you would get dressed up too and stand beside me on the... altar? Or whatever we stand at."

Her face lights up even further and she says, "I have never heard of this, maid-of-honor, before, but I will. I will be the ultimate maid-of-honor."

"I have no doubts about that," I say with another giggle.

"What is Zaltas' surname?"

"You know, he actually doesn't have one. Why?"

"The mating ritual, you will switch last names."

"Really? On Earth, one usually takes the name of the other. If he doesn't have a last name, will I just not have one anymore?"

"That is correct."

Dropping my last name that translates to 'butts' wouldn't be the worst thing. I will saddle poor Zaltas with it. I giggle at myself.

Laurelyn stayed for hours and discussed plans for the mating ritual with me. The massive amount of things she had collected looked exhausting at first, but her enthusiasm and company made the process go so smoothly and we came up with a plan for everything. Apparently, the Khuvex mating ritual is very, very brief, so most of what we planned was decor and an explosive finale. Less explosive than Laurelyn originally suggested, which was with literal explosions. Her and the Baron's mating ceremony will be intense, to say the least.

"Good night," I say to her as the door slides shut behind her. I yawn and stretch. We stayed on the balcony forever. Not a peep from Zaltas, he's probably worn out. I am too. He wore me out earlier and now I've stayed up far too late.

I slip quietly into the bedroom, strip my clothes off, and crawl into the massive bed. I hear Zaltas' steady breathing in the dark and carefully maneuver towards him. His warm skin contacts mine and I nestle down beside him. Groping in the dark, I find a couple of pillows and get comfortable. Sleep claims me quickly.

$$\triangle\triangle\triangle$$

The next morning, Zaltas and I awake and have plans to lie around for a while and enjoy one another, but the constant buzzing from Lukto at the door signals we won't get that luxury today. We bathe and dress quickly, have a small breakfast, and head out into the gardens.

The gardens of the palace are vibrant and full of life. They strung decorations across the golden walls and lined the pathways. Balloons, streamers, banners declaring victory, rows and rows of stands with all manner of food and drinks. Children run about, some of them in a clearly larval form, playing and laughing while an eclectic mix of aliens stand in crowds chatting and laughing. The amount of activity is staggering.

Triumphant music plays from a red wooden stage at the end of the garden with a crowd lounging in the surrounding grass. It sounds like an entire marching band is playing, but there is only one creature on stage. It has countless arms that deftly maneuver across the buttons of a massive instrument that I can't even begin to understand. The instrument twists and spirals twenty feet into the air, with tubes, horns, bells, and taut leather stretched across different sections. The creature's body is short and round and doesn't appear to have a face, but somehow it looks like it's having a wonderful time playing for the crowd.

I see it coming this time and brace myself, watching it approach. Lukto is bee-lining straight for us, and I won't be startled this time.

"Excuse me, Zaltas, Riley." A slight tug at the back of my dress causes me to jump and I spin around to find Lukto behind me.

"I thought you were coming the other way," I say, clutching my chest while Zaltas chuckles beside me. "You do that on purpose, don't you? A little conspiracy amongst the others."

"We are all one and the same," Lukto says, a hint of a smile on his face. "I would never purposefully startle you." It says with a wink. "The awards ceremony will begin in ten minutes," Lukto says, motioning towards the stage where the performer is wrapping up. I'm briefly mesmerized by the speed at which it dismantles its instrument. Tentacles whip through the air with blazing speed and pull pieces off and into a case at its... feet? Or whatever it has going on down there.

Before I can question it, it disappears into the throng of people. I see the other strange creatures zipping between the legs of the celebrants as they cater to the crowd.

"What did it mean by 'we are all one and the same'?" I ask Zaltas as we walk arm in arm to the stage.

I look him up and down. He looks very sharp today. I explained what a tuxedo was to Lukto, and it managed to find something close enough for Zaltas to wear during our marriage.... Mating ceremony. I want to feel like a bride and Zaltas said he would wear whatever pleased me. The outfit has the same jacket, tails, pants, and shoes as a stereotypical black tuxedo would, but the cut of the white vest trails almost to his belly-button. Under the vest, he has on a vibrant emerald green silky shirt that really brings out his eyes.

"One consciousness, multiple bodies," Zaltas replies with a gentle smile.

"So it's the same person inside everybody?"

"Yes."

"I knew it, he is fucking with me." This should feel weirder to me than it does, but at this point I'll believe about anything.

"Probably."

"I know you find it hilarious."

"Probably," he says again with that grin.

I lean my head against him, and we stop at the edge of the stage. Lukto waves us over and we follow it up a line of Khuvex, who all murmur there thanks to us as we pass. I'm happy to see so many standing and that so many pulled through. They're all wearing their normal colors, but they are dressed in much more formal looking armor. Lukto slides us in line behind one captain at the front.

The Baron is already front and center on top and begins bellowing to the audience while Laurelyn stands dutifully at his side. I told her to go wild with her bridesmaid dress and she sure did. She chose a bright green pinafore that stops just above her knee, with no shirt underneath, a huge golden belt around her waist, black and green striped tights and huge black boots. Golden bangles, that look like they weigh forty pounds, dangle on her wrists and bright green lipstick finishes her look.

She beams at me from the stage briefly before turning her attention back to the Baron. Her eyes soften when he glances back at her. I can't wait for them to be together. She already asked me to be her maid of honor, too. Of course I said yes. I can't imagine how much she has gathered for her own mating ceremony already. It'll take weeks to dig through, but I'm excited for her.

"We have put the Alphur down," the Baron says boisterously. The growing crowd around us cheers and quickly falls silent as the Baron continues. "It was not without loss. The thirty-nine Khuvex lost to us have been interred in the palace gardens and will forever remain. A heroic and valiant group…" He trails off for a moment before continuing. "But today is not the day to mourn, but to celebrate. And so today we bestow the Turlathian Medal upon the heroes that stand with us."

Wild cheering from the crowd erupts as the Baron opens a box, revealing one of the golden medals.

"Commander Laurelyn Tarchond, for bravery befitting the mightiest of warriors and leading your team into the unknown," the Baron says. The crowd erupts in cheers as he slips the medal over her head. She turns and salutes before dutifully marching off the stage.

"Captain Zurandan, for facing down one of the biggest threats to the galaxy and holding fast against it." More cheers from the crowd as the captain climbs the stage and receives his medal. A quick salute, and he moves on.

"Zaltas, the Scovein," murmurs roll through the crowd at the word Scovein. Apparently, that was still just a rumor to most of the citizens and they stare in quiet awe as Zaltas climbs the stage. "The hero who traveled through space and time to save us from catastrophe and purge the Alphur from this plane of existence." The crowd roars loudly with applause and cheering as the shock of a Scovein wears off and the joy for his accomplishment washes over them. It has grown to an overwhelming number of aliens.

Zaltas faces the crowd and waves to it, soaking up the spotlight. I swear if he had a microphone, he'd start telling jokes. I roll my eyes to myself and laugh quietly.

"Riley Butts," he announces.

"Bernardi," I whisper to myself as I climb the stage.

"For being there for our fallen soldiers and holding strong in the face of danger. For sacrificing your own safety for the wellbeing of others and making sure our wounded made it home."

The crowd cheers wildly and applauds. My face burns red as I turn to the crowd and give a small wave before hurrying off the stage. I join Zaltas and Laurelyn, who immediately fawns over me.

"You look wonderful," she says.

"So do you," I say with a grin.

"Not nearly as much as yourself."

Zaltas doesn't tear his eyes away from the entire time we stand by the stage. Each Khuvex that passes us after receiving their medals thanks us profusely, several of them focusing heavily on me with their gratitude. Being put on the spot is not my favorite thing and it keeps happening repeatedly, but I appreciate them and am happy I could rescue at least a few.

The Baron lists off a few more names still assisting at the space station and the crowd applauds with each name.

"We salute you all and thank you for your service," the Baron finishes and salutes our group.

The Khuvex all return their salutes in

unison and I feel awkward standing there unmoving, but would feel even more awkward trying to imitate them and failing. Zaltas draws me into him and squeezes me tightly with one of his arms.

"And now, one last announcement before we disperse for further festivities," the Baron continues.

My nerves are suddenly on edge and I glance up at Zaltas as he watches the Baron.

Suddenly, the entire area goes completely dark and the crowd of people gasps. I feel Zaltas pulling me closer in a protective gesture, ready to defend me against whatever attack is falling upon the palace.

A glowing white light appears as the only source of illumination and gradually gets brighter, before exploding into an array of colors and confetti that rains down on the crowd. Some confetti hangs in the air and twinkles merrily with a warm white light shining down on the stage and crowd. The palace walls behind and beside the stage are suddenly overgrown with leafy green plants and vines that stretch out and wrap around the stage.

The stage has transformed into a solid stone platform with a grassy patch in the center. A twisting vine arch sits behind it and the Baron's golden armor has become a light grey robe, with gold embellishments, of course. He stands under the arch and looks at us expectantly. White banners drop from the moss-covered roof of the stage and flap lazily in the breeze. Quiet music tinkles in the air merrily and the crowd grows completely still and watches intently.

I take a deep breath and break free of Zaltas' grip, slowly approaching the stone and moss covered ramp that replaced the wooden stairs.

"What's going on?" He asks, clearly confused.

"We're getting married, dummy," I say with a grin as Laurelyn locks arms with me and leads me up the ramp.

Laurelyn's arm releases mine at the top of the ramp and I feel a slight tug at the top of my pink dress. A heatless blue flame engulfs my body and explodes in a dazzling display of white light, completely obscuring my vision. I feel soft cloth coating my body as smoke envelopes me and slowly disperses. The scent of it reminds me of a fog machine.

As the smoke slowly dissolves, I am finally revealed to the world in my wedding/mating ceremony dress.

A bright and shiny white dress with lace made of a silver material that twinkles in the dim lights above. The cut isn't too deep, but leaves enough for someone towering directly over me to see some cleavage. A little treat for my husband-to-be. It's a mermaid silhouette but whatever fabric it's made bends and moves easily with me. I can't remember the name of it, but Laurelyn insisted it be made out of it. I'm glad I listened to her because this is one of the most comfortable things I've worn. It's apparently completely unstainable and won't wrinkle to boot. She also wanted me to have an obscenely long train, but I decided on a floor length. Topped off with a simple pair of comfortable emerald green flats to match Zaltas' shirt.

I fight the urge to look down at myself and admire the dress, and instead focus my eyes on the Baron. He, too, looks shocked. Besides Laurelyn, he was the only other that knew what was going to happen, but we didn't tell him about my dress reveal.

Laurelyn takes my arm again and leads me in front of the Baron. She releases me and wraps me up in a tight bear hug, lifting me off the ground and whispering, "I am so happy for you." She sets me down carefully and takes her place behind me. I glance back at her and smile as she grins down at me.

The Baron holds his arm out towards Zaltas, directing him to come and take his place. The look on Zaltas' face is new for me. Sheer panic mixed with an unending fount of happiness. He doesn't hesitate, though. He marches towards us with determination and takes his place opposite of me.

My eyes are unable to tear away from his handsome face as he peers down at me. I analyze every feature, committing it to memory forever. I never want to forget this moment. Our declaration of love. The familiar sting of tears hits me and I fight them back, closing my eyes briefly. When I open them, I notice Zaltas' gaze dart back up to meet mine. I knew he'd like the cleavage. I smile at him and that dopey grin of his that I fell in love with pops up on his face. Everything is unimaginably perfect.

"Greeting everyone. I am Baron Parinien Talintherineclanicalinethes the Twelfth. I will be the matemeister. This mating ritual shall commence now," the Baron bellows.

The surrounding crowd applauds loudly for a few seconds before the Baron raises his hands, calling for quiet. Silence descends upon the crowd, and they all stare at us in anticipation for our union.

My nerves are steady now that Zaltas is in front of me. The crowd watching us quietly isn't helping them, but I'm too happy to care anymore.

"Riley Butts, do you accept Zaltas as your mate for the rest of eternity?" The Baron booms.

The look on Zaltas' face contorts slightly with worry. He knows I'll say yes, but it's cute he's nervous too. He's just better at hiding it than I am. Usually, he's not doing a good job now.

"I do," I say. When the words leave my lips, Zaltas' eyes glisten gently in the light and it's too much for me. The tears finally win and start streaming down my face.

"Zaltas, do you accept Riley Butts as your mate for the rest of eternity?"

"Now and forever, with all of my being," Zaltas says, turning my trickle of tears into a full flood. It's all I can do to not sob.

"I now pronounce you Zaltas Butts and Riley. You may kiss."

"Bernardi…" I whisper before Zaltas scoops me up and buries his lips into mine as the crowd cheers wildly. An explosion of white light flashes behind my eyelids and Zaltas sets me down gently, still holding me tightly in his arms. I wrap my arms around his waist and lean into him as the moss covering the stage ceiling sparks and bursts into sparkling white light. A brilliant white flame consumes the ceiling before it fires off into the sky and it explodes in a rainbow of colors and sparkles. The crowd gasps loudly and a myriad of 'oohs' and 'aahs' fill my ears.

The embers of the explosion twinkle brilliantly in every color imaginable and as they reach the ground, everything they touch turns into the color of the ember, dotting the entire area in a beautiful and eclectic display.

"Go forth!" The Baron shouts, happily motioning us down the ramp. Another eruption of noise from the crowd cheers us along as we leave the stage.

Zaltas and I lock arms and walk down the ramp. He stops at the bottom and pulls me into him. I squeeze his waist tightly and he gently takes my chin and pulls my gaze to his. Those glistening emerald eyes of his go soft and he says quietly, "I love you, selkin. With every fiber of my being."

"I love you too, Zaltas. Everything in my

life has led me to be here with you and I wouldn't have it any other way."

Nothing could make my life any better. Everything is perfect and wonderful and I almost can't handle it.

We lock arms and head into the rest of the festival as the lighting returns to normal. The crowd behind us slowly fades into the distance and the smell of fried foods fills my nose.

"Let's eat," I say happily.

"You read my mind," he replies, squeezing my arm gently.

EPILOGUE: PART ONE

ZALTAS

Two weeks later

"Aurelia?" I ask the ceiling.

"Yes, Zaltas Butts?" The way she lingers on my last name feels like payback for making fun of Riley all that time ago.

"Are we stocked and ready for the trip?"

"Yes, I am fully stocked and have enough supplies to last two months."

"That is a little much."

"I like to be prepared."

"I like that she likes to be prepared," Riley says from the chair next to me.

I spin my seat and look at Riley. My lifelong mate, lounging in the co-pilot's chair in a short pink skirt and tight-fitting shirt. She meets my gaze and places a finger on the edge of her skirt and pulls it up her thigh slowly, teasing me.

"You are insatiable," I say with a wink.

"Don't act like you haven't been either," she replies, sitting upright in the chair.

She's right. Both of us haven't been able to keep our hands off the other since the mating ceremony. It's been several times a day. A few times, we both woke up in the middle of the night and immediately dove into the other. It's been blissful. Riley called it our honeymoon, relaxation and sex. It's been incredible and I look forward to many more honeymoons with her.

We discussed our plans going forward during the honeymoon and she said that she wished to see Earth. So, I am taking her there. They've apparently become a fully functioning planet again and I hope she gets what she finds what she desires when we arrive. While I'd rather roam the galaxy with her, if she wishes to stay on Earth, I will happily join her. Wherever she is, I will be. My place in the universe is beside her, no matter where that may be.

"Quit staring at me, weirdo," she says with a shy grin. Her hair spills into her face and she peers at me through it. I feel the familiar tingle from the tip of my cock and spin my chair back around before I delay this journey even longer.

"You are the weirdo," I say.

"You are both odd creatures," Aurelia chimes in.

Riley giggles behind me.

"Take us to Earth," I say.

"I'm sorry Zaltas, I'm afraid I can't do

that."

"What, why?" Slight concern fills me. Aurelia has never declined to do anything I've asked before. Is something wrong with the ship?

Riley giggles again.

"I am just joking," Aurelia says. "Riley instructed me to tell you that occasionally. Charting course for Earth. Total travel distance: two hundred and sixty-eight point eight light-years. Calculating arrival. Arrival time: six hundred and seventy-two hours."

"So, right around four weeks," Riley says behind me. "Guess our honeymoon is getting an extension."

"I have an extension for you," I say.

"I bet you do," she says. I can hear the smile in her voice.

"Please, do not resist," Aurelia says as restraints slide out of the seat and secure me in place. Riley is teaching her too many things from Earth.

After a couple of minutes, the restraints release, and Aurelia announces we are in warp and en route to Earth. Riley has already left her seat and is strolling casually towards the hallway. She pauses and looks over her shoulder at me, her eyes close slowly, then reopen as her hand slides up to the strap of her shirt and slides it down slightly. She disappears slowly into the hallway.

I know what that means. I trip over my

seat as I try to hurry around it and almost tumble to the ground. My cock is doing all the thinking now and my body does not have the resources to power my brain as much.

Aurelia makes a mocking noise that sounds a lot like laughter, but I pay her no mind. Riley is expecting me and I will not keep her waiting.

EPILOGUE: PART TWO

RILEY

Four years later

"Two of them?" Zaltas asks, hovering over me and splitting his stare between my stomach, my face, and the towering Khuvex midwife. She was so delicate while tending to me. It was incredible that those massive hands could be so gentle. Then again, the things Zaltas can do with his hands are impressive, I guess I shouldn't be surprised.

"Yes, two," I say with a giggle. It surprised me to find out, too. Twins are on the way. I never thought I would have kids, let alone two. I also never thought I'd get married, travel to an alien planet, and fly in a spaceship. Here we are, though.

Apparently, with the Scovein at least, cross-species pregnancies are rare. Clearly, though, they are not impossible. Either way, I'm excited. Nervous, too, of course. But I couldn't think of a better father than Zaltas, and I look forward to raising our children with him.

We spent almost a year on Earth and were met with joy by the other humans. They were fascinated by me being from the original Earth and I became a celebrity there. I was quizzed and paraded around the sprawling city they had constructed.

Most of humanity stuck to a single area, but they were slowly spreading to further corners of the planet. Earth was mostly flooded, but the waters were receding at a steady pace. They showed me a map, and I told them where they are now was called South America. Geography wasn't my strongest subject in school and the map they had looked much different compared to the ones in my time, but I was pretty sure it was Ecuador. They didn't mind my doubts and promptly renamed the city from 'Zx-231' to Ecuador, which was definitely an improvement.

I toured the city and hosted lectures and Q and A's. Zaltas proved to be quite popular, too. They were almost as fascinated by him and wanted to know what the galaxy was like back then.

Some people had been diving in the ocean and searching for artifacts from the original humans and had a large museum set up. They were thrilled when I came and helped them identify objects they found. It was funny how many mundane things they found interesting and did not know what they were. My favorite was the 'thermal exhaust coupling for a submersible vehicle.' It was a power strip. How they concluded that it was part of a submarine was beyond me.

To the human's great disappointment, Zaltas and I both began to long for travel and some alone time, so we left the planet and wandered the galaxy. We ate, shopped, visited insane planets and saw some incredible sights. We also had gratuitous amounts of sex, which led to our current situation. I started feeling sick frequently and knew it was the telltale signs of pregnancy. Once my stomach started to expand, I knew for sure.

We headed back to Dexterion for some stability during the birth and were welcomed back with open arms. The Baron, who took over the position of the old Baron, was thrilled to have us return and got us the best medical care available to the Khuvex.

We were planning to come back soon, anyway. Laurelyn and the Baron, er Parinien, still can't get used to not calling him the Baron, were finally able to be together and were having their mating ceremony in a couple of months. I was her maid-of-honor, and we had a lot of planning to do.

Zaltas' hand gently touches my now enormous stomach, and the warmth of his fingertips is soothing to my achy body. Most of the time I'm uncomfortable, but his touch always makes things a little better.

"Two," he says quietly, still stroking my belly.

"Yes," I say. "Two."

"A boy and a girl," the midwife adds. "I

will give you two some privacy. Call me if you need anything at all." She finishes packing up her equipment and leaves our quarters.

I shift myself and pull my legs up on the couch to lie down. Zaltas hurriedly grabs my legs and helps lift them onto the couch; he strokes my forehead gently.

"Are you going to be fretting over me constantly?" I ask with a grin. He already has been. I'm not going to lie and say I don't enjoy it, but I don't want him to always be on his toes. He needs to relax occasionally, too. Especially since Scovein pregnancies usually last twelve months. With human pregnancies at nine, the midwife expects it to meet in the middle at ten and a half.

"Yes," he says quietly, still caressing me.

"You don't have to. I am fine. I can still mostly take care of myself at the moment. Now, I can't promise I won't be more demanding in a few months."

"You can demand whatever you like from me, selkin. I will be here for you no matter what you need," he says with that dopey grin.

I feel myself swoon slightly. How he always manages to be so sweet, even when he's being infuriating, makes my heart melt.

"Sit down," I demand, and lift my head up from the couch as best as I can. After some maneuvering, Zaltas slides his thighs under my head and I snuggle up to him. He caresses my head again and stares absently at the blue fire burning in the fireplace.

"Well, any thoughts? Besides taking care of me and two?" I ask.

"I am just overwhelmed with happiness," he says flatly.

"You sure sound like it," I say with a giggle.

"I am sorry, selkin," he says, a little more cheerful. "This is a lot to process, but I am happy. This is what I have always desired."

"Me too." I never knew it, but I did desire this. Our perfect alien family is growing soon. Maybe we should get a dog before the babies come. Do they have dogs here? They had them on Earth. I should have got one while I was there.

We cuddle on the couch quietly, both grinning and staring into space. Our future is looming on the horizon and the anticipation is killing us both. Life couldn't be better.

END

Printed in Great Britain
by Amazon

84826123R00228